EARTH LOST

EARTH LOST

EARTHRISE, BOOK II

DANIEL ARENSON

CHAPTER ONE

There is something in the darkness. There is something after me.

Kara walked down the streets of Corpus City as the sky
bled. The sky was always bleeding here. The sky always reeked of
death. Corpus, this desolate moon, orbited a gas giant that
blocked the stars, that consumed the firmaments, that swirled,
gurgled, belched. It was a painting all in red and dripping black
and globs of yellow. It seemed to crush her. Whenever Kara gazed
above between the iron towers, the refinery domes, and the
pumping chimneys, she seemed to gaze upon the festering,
ulcerous stomach lining of some beast that had consumed her.

"Mommy," her son whispered. "Mommy, I hear it. Behind
us. In the shadows." The boy pointed. "I see it."

Kara looked to the alley. Shadows loomed between the
pipes and sooty walls of the refineries—elongated, watching,
twisting.

"Only the shadows, darling," Kara said. "Only your
imagination."

But she felt it. She heard it too. A clattering. Clicking.
Hissing of low breath. Only old banging pipes, she knew. Only
steam from the bowels of the city, of the mines that delved deep

into this world, the engines that forever rumbled there, the drills that always dug deeper.

Kara kept walking, holding her children's hands. To her right, her son, seven years old, brave and somber. To her left, her daughter, only three, barely old enough to keep up. And in her belly, her third child, still so small, a child that filled her with nausea, with guilt. How could Kara bring another child into this world, into Corpus, this wretched mining colony so many light-years from Earth? How could she bring life into a world where the sky bled, where shadows always loomed, where you never saw the stars or the sun?

Kara had not wanted to move here. She missed Earth. She could barely remember trees or waves or blue sky, but she missed them. Her husband had brought them here, a miner by trade. He was a hard man, a man burdened with memories of poverty, a man who believed that his greed served only his family, never himself. He believed that if only he dug deep enough, mined enough of the azoth—this precious material found here in the darkness—they could find enough wealth to return home. To retire on Earth. To be eternally happy. But Kara didn't care for wealth. She would live in a cave if only she could look outside and see the stars, breathe air that didn't stink of fumes, hold a husband who wasn't covered in grime and cinder.

And yet I came here with him, Kara thought, walking through the labyrinthine mining colony. *I came here to keep our family together, but I'm falling apart.*

"Mommy," said her daughter. "Mommy, it's getting closer."

"There is nothing there!" Kara said, speaking too loudly, too harshly.

The girl started to cry. But Kara dared not pause to comfort her. She kept walking, faster now, gripping her children's hands, pulling them deeper through the city. The lights flickered around her, then went dark. Streetlamps, windows, neon signs—all died. The world plunged into blackness. The gas giant above turned a deeper red, spilling its bloody glow across the colony. The city seemed to shrink, the crimson canopy to swallow it.

"Mommy," her son whimpered.

"Just another power outage," she said, walking onward. "Like last week."

It seemed like every week now, the power flickered and died across Corpus. Kara had mentioned to her husband the irony of it, that miners of azoth, the most precious energy source in the cosmos, should suffer so many blackouts. He had laughed and said that the cobbler's children were always last to get shoes. He would not laugh when she saw him next. She would demand they leave, fly home to Earth, forget about this moon, this rock, this hell where lights died, where the sky bled, where things scurried in shadows.

"Mommy, it's behind us!" Her daughter gripped her hand tighter. "Mommy, it's looking at me."

"There is no—" Kara began, turning around, and fell silent.

In the shadows on the road behind her. Two eyes. White. Watching her. Then vanishing into shadows.

A creature in the dark.

Kara shook her head wildly, banishing those stories, those tales the miners told their wives in the night.

Watching us. Following us. Studying us.

And in the shadows—a hissing. A patter. *Tap. Tap. Tap.*

Kara turned away. She walked stiffly, holding her children. They walked silently with her, and they quickened their steps, and behind them that tapping. Scraping. The sound of many feet scratching against stone, and a hiss, and Kara dared not look around, dared not run, dared not let the creature know she saw it.

It's stalking us.

No. Nonsense! No such thing. Legends. Ghost stories.

But Kara could smell it. God, the stink of it. This wasn't the stink of soot or ash or smoke. It was organic, rancid, worms after rain and dripping pus.

"I want to go home," her daughter whispered. "Please."

But where was home? Kara was lost here. She had been on this distant world for three years now, but still she didn't know the maze of alleys, and in the darkness she was lost. She walked faster. She sought a familiar path, a landmark, but the buildings were all jagged black blades, all the same, and she saw nobody. A city of twenty thousand souls, but they were only shadows in the distance, wrapped in cloaks, hiding indoors, waiting for the power, the heat, the light to come back. For their music. Their electronic distractions. The colors and sounds that held back the terror.

Kara began to run. The clattering was louder behind her, and she saw the eyes—above her, watching from a rooftop, vanishing again, and pattering closer. She couldn't breathe. She pounded at a door, begging whoever hid within the black house to let her in, but there was no answer. She ran onward, but she was in the neighborhood of the migrant workers, those who had come here with no families, and they were all underground now, digging for the azoth, digging too deep, awakening whatever lurked there.

She ran and it followed. It leaped from building to building. A strand of blackness in the crimson night. Claws digging into metal and stone, scraping, scuttling, its eyes white, gazing, hissing, dripping saliva, calling to her.

Come to me, Kara.

Come to me like you came to him.

Be with us.

Be us.

Give us.

Kara ran, tears in her eyes, pulling her children with her, and she knew that this dark god wanted them, wanted a sacrifice as the god of Earth had wanted Isaac upon the mountain. But she would not appease this older god, this deity of the mines. She would resist him. She would flee him. She pounded on another door, begging entrance, hearing no reply. She ran toward a man in the shadows, but he fled. All was darkness. All was the labyrinth, the twisting alleyways, pipes above her, dripping water, dripping blood, and the sky kept roiling, vast, drowning her, a sanguine maelstrom above her, and the creature laughed like rusty drills grinding through stone.

Grinding. Stone. Darkness.

They were all underground. Her husband. The men of this place. The few other women who had been foolish enough to come here. All in the deep darkness far from this sky, seeking the material, the dirt, the dust, the precious blue crystals with a thousand names, the treasure that had let humanity venture to the stars. Yet there were no stars here. They should never have come to this place, this hive of iron and reek and things that hunted in the night.

Underground.

Hissing.

Scraping.

Kara . . .

"Mommy!"

"Underground," she whispered.

She saw an archway ahead, leading to a tunnel, leading to the mines, leading to the miners, leading deep into this rocky planet under a blood-red giant. Kara ran, holding her children, and plunged into the darkness. She heard the shadow behind, the many legs pattering, the claws scraping across stone, the hissing growing louder, the stench growing stronger. Only a few scattered lights flickered in the tunnel, running on backup generators, blinking and buzzing like clouds of insects. Pipes coiled overhead, and tracks ran below. Kara ran with her children, and here too she found a labyrinth, narrower, darker, so cold. It was so cold underground.

"Hello!" she cried, and her voice echoed through the tunnels, bounced back toward her, mocking her, laughing, and a thousand hissing voices answered. They were everywhere. They were everywhere here.

Kara spun around, and she saw it. Moving closer in the tunnel. The creature. Elongated. Rising up like a cobra about to strike. Lined with claws. Speaking in her mind.

Kara. Kara . . . Give them to us . . . Praise us . . . Sacrifice them to our glory . . .

She turned and ran onward, seeking her husband. The tunnel branched, and she chose one path at random, then another, and the corridors all twisted, becoming so narrow she could barely move. She clung to her children's hands, and both were weeping as they ran with her. Lost. Lost in darkness. Trapped. These were no paths for miners. She had made a wrong turn. She had made a mistake. She should never have come here—to this mine, to this moon, to this nightmare, and tears burned down her cheeks. She cried out again, for help, for mercy, but her echo only mocked her with deep laughter, and Kara fell to her knees.

Her children clung to her.

Pipes, machines, and engines rose all around her. She had entered an engine room, a city underground, its towers coiling and rising toward stone, great stalagmites of metal, belching steam and sulfur, and cauldrons bubbled, casting out sickly golden light.

Here was a towering, cluttered hall like the tomb of some ancient king in the bowels of a mountain. Her own tomb.

Through the shadows it advanced, claws—so many claws, rows and rows of them—reaching out, and Kara pushed herself backward, clutching her weeping children.

"Kara?"

A shadow and light approached.

Kara blinked, gasped, exhaled in relief.

"Tom!"

Her husband stepped toward her, frowning, light shining from a flashlight strapped to his helmet. Soot covered his wide face and rough hands. He hurried toward her, his light casting back the shadows.

Kara looked back to the creature.

It was gone.

She exhaled in relief.

"Just a dream," she mumbled. "Just my imagination."

Her husband stared at her, brow furrowed. "Kara, are you all right? What's wrong?"

As she rose to her feet, her son pulled free from her grip. The little boy ran toward his father.

"Daddy!" The boy leaped onto the miner. "There was a monster."

Tom smiled and held his son in his powerful arms. "Your dad's here now. Your dad banished the monster. Your—"

The claw tore through Tom's chest with a sickening *crack*.

Kara screamed.

The boy fell from his father's grip, and the claws reached out, grabbed the tiny child, and ripped him apart, pulled meat off the bones, cracked the chest open, dragged father and son into the darkness to devour them, and the engines burst into life as the power returned, clanging, ringing, belching fumes, churning metal and crushing stone.

"Daddy!" their daughter screamed, reaching out, and Kara grabbed the girl, muffled her cries in her palm, and ran.

They're dead. She wept. *They're dead. They're dead. But my daughter is alive. The child in my belly is alive. I am alive. We must live. We must live.*

As the creature fed, Kara pulled her daughter past pipes and behind an engine, and there she pressed herself against a wall, shivering, weeping, her son gone, such coldness in her, her son ripped away, torn apart, her husband gone, shattered, consumed. She could still hear it—ripping flesh, cracking bones, slurping. She could still smell it. She could still see it again and again before her. Her husband. Her son. Gone. Gone. Shattered. Taken from her. And this couldn't be real. This had to be a nightmare, just one of those nightmares where she was lost in a labyrinth, lost in her life, seeking a way out. Soon she would wake up in her bed, her sheets soaked with sweat, feeling so hot even though the room was so cold, desperate for air. Soon she would roll over, find her husband at her side, and her son would leap into their bed.

The claws scraped again.

She heard it approach. Dripping. Snorting. Licking. Clacking. Shadows danced.

"Ka . . . ra . . ."

She wasn't sure if it spoke in her mind, spoke at all, or if her imagination was playing tricks on her. She pressed herself against the wall, hiding behind the pipes and pumping engines. Still she heard its breath. Heard it sniff. Smell for her.

"Ka . . . ra . . ."

Getting closer. Closer. Dripping blood. And she could see its legs beneath the pipes, pair after pair of legs, moving in unison, a great centipede, an alien, a god, and she knew him. The one they called *scolopendra titania*. The one they called the scum. One of a swarm, those who had devastated the earth fifty years ago, those who lurked in shadows, who demanded the flesh of humanity to consume, who had taken her husband. Who had taken her son.

"Momm—" her daughter began, and the creature spun toward them, and Kara slammed her palm over her daughter's mouth, silencing the words, holding her close, nearly crushing her.

The creature moved closer. Sniffing. Leaning low. Feelers like wires stretched under pipes, touching, smelling. She could hear it. She could hear it in her mind.

Where are you, Kara? Where are you, my sweet meat?

She cowered. Her daughter wriggled, then writhed, screaming into Kara's palm, but Kara held the girl firmly, keeping her mouth shut, stifling her, smothering her, keeping her silent. *Don't scream. Don't scream. Don't breathe. Don't make a sound. Don't cry. Don't whimper. Don't even breathe. Don't scream.*

The creature began moving away, exploring another
engine, and Kara shuddered, but still she held her daughter close,
held her palm over the girl's mouth.

Be silent. Don't scream. Don't whimper. Don't make a sound.

It moved away, leaving a trail of her son's blood.

Her daughter kicked wildly, struggling to free herself.

Don't scream.

Don't make a sound.

Don't even breathe.

Slowly her daughter's kicks weakened. Slowly the girl
ceased struggling, grew limp, and still Kara held her so closely,
covering her mouth, keeping her silent.

The creature left.

The darkness breathed around them.

The power vanished again, and the light faded, and the
engines stilled. Only a single flicker of light in the dark chasm—
her husband's discarded flashlight, a single star in the night.

Kara laid her daughter down. Still. Silent. Sacrificed.

"Daughter?" she whispered. She shook her. The girl would
not move, only stared, eyes wide, betrayed, gazing into darkness.

And Kara howled.

It was a howl that filled the chasm with her grief. A howl
that echoed through the mine, that all could hear in the darkness,
that would never end.

The creature spun around at once, raced toward her on its
clawed legs, leaped forward. It reared ahead of her, twice her
height, a massive black centipede, thirty-six legs tipped with claws,

dripping venom. A god. It lashed down, so fast she barely saw it move. It grabbed her daughter, sucked the body into its gullet, gorging itself, its body shivering with delight.

Sacrificed.

Silenced.

Howl. Howl. Don't scream. Don't even breathe.

Kara cowered against the wall, ready to join them, to fill the belly of the beast as a child filled her own belly. She placed her hands on her stomach, felt the boy kicking inside her. Tears flowed down her cheeks.

The alien approached and leaned its head toward that swollen belly. Its feelers poked her like needles seeking amniotic fluid. Its mandibles opened and closed. It seemed to smell, to inhale deeply, its head larger than hers, tilted, eyeless, thinking. Always thinking.

It looked up at her.

Ka . . . ra . . . you . . . will . . . be . . . us . . .

It slithered around her, circling, coiling, wrapping around her like a python. Its claws did not stab her. It was gentle. It took her into its embrace, carrying her away from this place of reeking death, deeper into the labyrinth, deeper into its domain. It carried her into darkness. It carried her home.

CHAPTER TWO

Earth was a blue sphere behind them, barely larger than a marble, when the clunky rocket turned toward the slick, silvery starship ahead.

"Now that," Addy said, "is a starship." She nodded and thumped her boots against the floor. "Not like this bucket of bolts."

"Well, this isn't a starship at all," Marco said. "We're sitting in a Y67-class solar transport rocket, used for traveling within our solar system. It'll take you to the moon, even Mars, not much farther. A starship is a far more sophisticated vehicle, equipped with an azoth-powered warp engine, capable of traveling the vast interstellar distances between star systems." He pointed out the window at the other vessel. "Like that."

"Nerd," Addy said.

Fifty soldiers sat here in the rocket, a single platoon. The fuselage was tall and narrow, and tiers of seats formed rings around a central ladder. It felt like sitting in a very narrow, very tall Colosseum. They all wore olive drab combat uniforms, their T57 assault rifles propped up between their knees. Marco didn't know most of them. Here was a newly formed platoon, its soldiers handpicked for a mission into deep space. They had named themselves the Ravens—an appropriate bird, they had thought, for a mission into the blackness of space. Marco saw lots of hard faces, some soft, most scared. None of them had flown beyond Earth's orbit before. All of them would now face the scum, the aliens that had ravaged the earth, in the depths of space. On the front line.

But some faces were familiar to Marco, and that comforted him. Addy was here, his oldest and best friend, her long legs stretched out, her boots dangling over the shaft, her blond hair spilling out from under her helmet. Beast sat across from them, massive and brutish, swallowing his seat, his arms like tree trunks. Much smaller and thinner, Elvis sat by the burly Russian, softly crooning a tune by his namesake. Corporal Diaz was here too, handsome and scarred, as was Sergeant Singh, bearded and wearing a military-green turban. Marco had survived basic training with these soldiers, had fought with them in the deserts of Africa. They were his brothers and sisters in arms. They were soldiers he trusted with his life.

And one that he loved.

Marco turned to look at Lailani. She sat at his side, the smallest in the platoon. Even with her legs stretched out to their full length, they were barely longer than Marco's thighs. At four-foot-ten, her head shaved down to stubble, Lailani looked like a little boy in a man's uniform, and her rifle dwarfed her. Her small stature might have disqualified her from military service if not for her viciousness. Her almond eyes were narrowed, simmering, ready for battle, her lips tight. She was the daughter of a teenage prostitute, had grown up rummaging for food in the slums of Manila. She had been fighting hunger and disease all her life. Now she fought the scum. In Marco's eyes, she was the best soldier in the platoon.

And it's not just because I love her, he thought.

Marco placed a hand on her arm. "You all right, de la Rosa?"

She nodded. "Can't wait to kick scum ass, Emery."

Marco thought about last night, how she had sneaked into his bunk, how they had made love in the darkness, in secret—a secret that most of their friends already knew. During the day, they were comrades. Fellow warriors. Alien killers. At night, they were lovers. Marco much preferred the nights.

As the rocket flew closer toward the starship, the soldiers all craned their necks, staring out the viewports. The starship outside dwarfed their own vessel. A ring of solar panels lazily spun around its silvery hull like a Ferris wheel. On closer inspection, Marco noticed that the hull itself was spinning, perhaps to create centrifugal force and generate the illusion of gravity. Several gun turrets rose along the hull, thrusting out cannons. At the back of the ship, engine vents glowed pale blue, the hallmark of azoth engines capable of interstellar travel. Marco saw no wings, no landing gear. Here was a ship that never landed, that spent its life in space. As the hull spun, it revealed golden letters: HDFS *Miyari*.

Addy pointed at a golden plaque bolted onto the *Miyari*'s hull. "Ooh, party ship!"

A few soldiers in the platoon snickered and elbowed one another. The plaque featured a man and woman, larger than life and stark naked. The man had his hand raised in greeting.

"Love me tender," Elvis whispered in awe, staring out the viewport.

"I not taking my clothes off," Beast grumbled. "In Russia we fight with uniform."

Marco sighed. "Guys, don't you recognize the Pioneer Plaque?" When they only blinked at him, he groaned. "In 1972, one of humanity's first spacecraft was launched. The Pioneer featured a smaller version of this plaque. It was an introduction to aliens, showing what humans look like."

"Look like naked," Addy said.

"Yes, Addy, naked," Marco said. "The way Darwin made us. It's now the symbol of the STC. That's Space Territorial Command, for you ignoramuses."

"Ignore what now?" Elvis said, then returned to crooning.

Addy peered at the plaque on the starship's hull. "Rich bastards. Is that real gold?" She narrowed her eyes, scrutinizing the *Miyari*. "Where's all the rust and dents? I'm so confused."

Marco smiled wanly and patted her knee. "No rust. No dents. This isn't Earth Territorial Command anymore. STC is one percent our size and has a hundred times our budget."

"Fuckers," Addy said.

Marco nodded. "We're about to join them, remember?"

"I *love* them," Addy said.

A hatch above opened, and the fifty soldiers of the platoon fell silent. Near the hatch, Sergeant Singh stood up in his seat and saluted.

"Platoon—attention!" the bearded sergeant bellowed.

Fifty soldiers, all around the cylindrical fuselage, rose in their seats, held their guns to their sides, and squared their shoulders. All stood perfectly still, expressions blank. Marco dared glance toward the hatch above, and he struggled to stifle the smile that threatened to bloom.

Lieutenant Einav Ben-Ari came climbing down the ladder that ran down the center of the fuselage. The young officer had a sensible blond ponytail, solemn green eyes, and the weight of generations on her shoulders. Unlike his fellow privates, Marco had grown close to Lieutenant Ben-Ari. She had shown him the medals of her ancestor, a survivor who had fled a Nazi concentration camp to fight as a partisan. Since then, every generation of Ben-Ari's family had fought in a war. Her great grandparents had fought the devastating wars in the Middle East. Her grandfather had fought the scum when the aliens had first destroyed the world. Her father had been a colonel in the HDF. And now she, Einav Ben-Ari—a young officer, barely into her twenties—led a platoon deep into space.

Many in the platoon, Marco knew, referred to Ben-Ari as an ice queen, as a robot, as the pampered daughter of a colonel. But Marco had spoken to her in private several times, perhaps the only soldier here who had, aside from Sergeant Singh. He had seen her fear. Her sadness. And her kindness. She was his commanding officer, but she was also his friend.

"At ease," said Ben-Ari, climbing halfway down the shaft. The platoon returned to their seats, and the lieutenant continued speaking, voice filling the fuselage. "Some of you have been soldiers for years. Others for only months. One thing you have in common—you all wear the green. You're all soldiers of Earth Territorial Command."

"The poor ninety-nine percent," Addy whispered, leaning toward Marco. He hushed her.

"I've handpicked you," said Lieutenant Ben-Ari, "to join me in space, to join the STC. This is an honor. Only the best, the brightest, the toughest warriors serve in space. You all distinguished yourselves on Earth. Some of you fought at Fort Djemila. Others in the Battle of Rome. Some in the Siege of Yokohama. But here, in space, you are all green recruits—literally and figuratively. You've never faced horror until you've faced the scum in the darkness of space, on the front line."

Marco gulped and looked around him. He had fought only one battle, had slain only a handful of scum. Corporal Diaz, who sat across from him, had been fighting for over a year, had killed many enemies along the Appalachian Trail. And Sergeant Singh was even more experienced, a veteran with several years of combat under his belt. Here were strong men, armed with grenades and assault rifles. It was hard to imagine that up here the platoon was helpless.

Marco thought back to the battle at Fort Djemila. To the thousands of scum swarming. To the soldiers dying in the dust. To his friends screaming, then falling silent. Those memories still haunted him. Yet that had been only a small battle at a forgotten military training base. Now they were flying toward the very front line. Marco didn't want to imagine what awaited them there.

"On the HDFS *Miyari*," Ben-Ari continued, "our platoon will serve alongside the Latona Company, a unit of the Erebus Brigade. I don't need to tell you, I think, anything about Erebus."

Marco inhaled sharply. The Erebus Brigade? Across the fuselage, soldiers gasped and mumbled amongst themselves.

"But Erebus is barely human!" somebody said. "Aren't they genetically engineered? I heard they're genetically engineered."

"They're super warriors," Beast said. "Almost strong like Russians."

"Ma'am, are you sure we're worthy of this?" Elvis said, cringing.

"I am!" Addy interjected.

"Me too!" said Lailani.

Marco felt less confident than the girls. Like everyone, he had heard of Erebus Brigade, a legendary fighting force. They had fought in almost every legendary battle over the past fifty years. Since the Cataclysm, humanity's greatest heroes had served under those banners. Erebus alumni became generals, CEOs, prime ministers. Perhaps Sergeant Singh was worthy of this honor, but Marco? The rest of them?

"The *Miyari* will take you to Nightwall Outpost, a space station on the very front line," Ben-Ari said. "At Nightwall, you will be given new uniforms and new training, and you will become Space Territorial Command warriors. For the duration of our journey, you will be on your best behavior. While aboard the *Miyari*, you will serve right alongside Erebus warriors, and you will make me proud. You will make them respect you. You will prove that I was right to choose you for this honor. Understood?"

"Yes, ma'am!" they all cried out, but Marco wasn't so sure. He began to regret accepting this mission. He could have, perhaps, convinced his lieutenant to let him stay on Earth, to find a cushy job in the archives. Space was terrifying enough. But to fight alongside heroes? To take the most dangerous missions deep into enemy territory?

I'm not a warrior, he thought. *I'm just a librarian's son.*

He forced himself to inhale deeply. No. That librarian's son had been another boy, another life. Marco had trained for this. He had fought in a battle, proven himself at war. He could do this.

When he looked out the viewport, he saw a jet bridge expanding out from the silvery starship toward the rocket. With a thump and click, the two vessels connected.

"All right, soldiers!" said Sergeant Singh, emerging from his seat and floating toward the ladder. "Follow your officer. Single file. Be silent, be respectful, and Elvis—cut out that humming."

The sergeant climbed down to the bottom of the rocket, where he pulled open the door, revealing the jet bridge. Lieutenant Ben-Ari floated through the doorway first, followed by Singh. The platoon's forty-eight other soldiers descended the ladder and followed along the connector bridge.

Marco floated behind Addy, using handles on the wall to propel himself forward in zero gravity. He had never actually floated through zero gravity before. Until now, he had never left his seat aboard a rocket. It felt like swimming. His assault rifle floated above him, secured by only its strap. Other soldiers were losing coins, pens, photographs, and Marco even saw a dirty magazine float free. He sighed as he advanced along the bridge. If anyone from STC saw them now, this miserable platoon of earthlings would make a poor impression.

As they passed by a viewport, Marco gazed outside, and he could see Earth—a pale blue marble in the distance. He had been to space before, but only in low orbit. It was hard to imagine that the entire world he had known, all of history, his family, his life— all was contained within that distant sphere. And soon, once he stepped onto the *Miyari*, once they blasted toward another star system, even that blue marble would be gone in the darkness, and the sun would be just one star in a billion.

Someone bumped into him from behind.

"Marco, go on, you're stalling!" Lailani whispered.

Marco nodded and pulled himself onward. The bridge led him through another doorway, and Marco floated into the HDFS *Miyari*, starship of Space Territorial Command.

Gravity grabbed him at once, and Marco bit down on a curse, nearly falling and making a fool of himself. He avoided tumbling over but did have to kneel and briefly touch the floor before standing again. Others were even less graceful. Some soldiers fell down flat and quickly leaped up, faces red. Marco joined the rest of his platoon in formation, and Lailani—the last soldier—came to stand behind him.

Once his head stopped spinning, Marco looked around him, and it took all his training not to gasp.

Well, goddamn, he thought.

The Human Defense Force, he knew, was divided into two main corps. Ninety-nine percent of its soldiers served in Earth Territorial Command, defending the planet. They guarded Earth's land, air, and water. They flew planes, drove tanks, fired guns, patrolled the seas. They swept floors, analyzed data, developed new weapons, cooked meals, built roads, died in battles. They had emerged from the ashes of the Cataclysm to reclaim the world. And a few of them, just a handful, went on to join Space Territorial Command. Only one percent of the HDF served here, guzzling over ninety percent of the HDF's budget. And looking around him, Marco saw every penny spent.

Back on Earth, everything was rusty, third or fourth-hand, falling apart. Uniforms were passed down from soldier to soldier. Guns were old and prone to jamming. Tanks creaked and spilled out bolts. Even the war jets patrolling the skies were cobbled together. Here in space, though, no expense had been spared. The walls were silvery and polished, not coated with flaking paint. The floor was woven with a rich carpet, not cracked tiles. Touchscreen monitors gleamed on walls rather than antique radios.

This must be what the world looked like before the Cataclysm, Marco thought. *Before the scum wiped out most of humanity and destroyed everything we had built.*

As the platoon was still finding its gravity legs, a door swished open at the back of the room.

"Attention!" shouted Sergeant Singh.

Three soldiers stepped in from the depths of the *Miyari*. These were the first STC soldiers Marco had ever seen. Though both Earth and Space troops operated under the Human Defense Force umbrella, these soldiers seemed to belong to an entirely different military. They didn't even bear assault rifles. Instead of heavy T57 submachine guns, they carried graceful plasma rifles. They reminded Marco of seamen from the Golden Age of Sail before steamboats replaced the glorious sailing ships of old. Instead of worn out, olive drab fatigues, they wore fine navy blue uniforms, the sleeves sporting brass cuff links. Instead of berets, they wore peaked caps, complete with golden badges above the visors. The fabrics were rich, the color deep. And these uniforms were obviously *new*. Back on Earth, soldiers—even officers— wore threadbare, used uniforms. Since the Cataclysm, even fabric was expensive. Marco began to realize where his family's taxes had been going all these years.

Marco was suddenly ashamed of his own platoon. Their drab fatigues were tattered. Their boots were cracked. Their guns were old and creaky. Addy's back pockets were torn, revealing the dirty playing cards she kept there. Lailani's helmet still bore the words she had drawn onto it with a marker: *Life is a bag of dicks with syphilis.*

Marco sighed. *We look like filthy mutts by purebred show dogs,* he thought.

Two of the STC soldiers were staff sergeants, displaying three chevrons and a semicircle on their sleeves—one rank above Singh. They seemed to be twins, tall and dark and dour. The third soldier was much smaller and far higher ranking. On each shoulder she wore three golden bars. She was a captain—one rank above Lieutenant Ben-Ari. Marco thought back to his training. While lieutenants could command platoons of fifty soldiers, captains could command companies of four platoons. On her breast, the captain wore a laurel pin, denoting her a graduate of the prestigious Julius Military Academy, the same institution where Kemi was now a cadet. Marco realized that Lieutenant Ben-Ari wore no such pin; she must have gone to a humbler school to receive her commission.

"Well, look at what we have here," said the captain, narrowing her eyes. A smirk played on her lips. She looked to be about thirty years old, with olive skin, black hair pulled into a severe ponytail, and a sharp, angular face. She wasn't unusually short but extremely thin, bordering on anorexic. Her eyes seemed to bug out from her gaunt face, practically dripping scorn. She reminded Marco of some neurotic Chihuahua in a uniform. He had to struggle to suppress a smile at the ridiculous thought.

Lieutenant Ben-Ari saluted the higher-ranking officer. "Ravens Platoon, reporting for duty, ma'am!" the lieutenant said.

The captain stared at the platoon of earthling warriors—their fatigues old and green, their berets limp, their guns outdated and chipped. Her lip curled in disgust. Marco felt like a homeless beggar who had wandered into a rich man's banquet. He suddenly wanted to smooth his uniform but forced himself to remain standing at attention.

The captain turned toward one of her staff sergeants. "Is this the type of rabble they're now sending into the STC?" She scoffed. "I've seen Meruvian asteroid worms who are better dressed."

One of the twins nodded. "Indeed, ma'am."

The captain turned back toward the platoon, smirking. She raised her voice and spoke slowly, as if explaining something to a slow child. "My name is Captain Coleen Petty! I command the Latona Company, the finest company in the Erebus Brigade. For the next few days, unfortunately, I will be babysitting you lot until I drop you off at the integration unit of Nightwall. Then you're somebody else's problem. Maybe at Integration, they can wash Earth's stench off you, burn those rancid rags you're wearing, and turn you into proper soldiers. But I doubt it. If the STC has any sense, they'll stuff you with rat poison and feed you to the scum."

Addy leaned an inch closer to Marco. "Hey, is there a Chihuahua yapping in here?" she whispered.

Captain Petty fell silent. Her head whipped around so fast Marco half expected it to fall off. Sneering, the company commander marched forward, shoved a few soldiers aside, and came to stand before Marco and Addy.

"What did you say, soldier?" Captain Petty demanded, staring at Addy.

Marco cringed. Insulting Sergeant Singh or Corporal Diaz was one thing. Infuriating an STC officer was quite another.

"I said I can't wait to give scum food poisoning, ma'am!" said Addy.

Eyes narrowed, the captain stared up at the taller Addy. She turned to stare at Marco, and her buggy eyes drove into him.

"Is that true, soldier?" Petty said. "Is that what she said?"

"Yes, ma'am!" Marco said, silently cursing Addy.

Captain Petty sneered. "This isn't Earth anymore, soldiers. I don't know what kind of lax discipline you learned on the planet, but if you *ever* speak out of turn again here in space, I will have you court-martialed." She pointed at the floor. "Now drop down. Both of you. Give me thirty."

Marco and Addy glanced at each other. Drop and do push-ups like a recruit? Soldiers past basic training were never given this punishment. Ranked soldiers could be given extra guard duty, sent to the brig, denied leave, even discharged, but push-ups were punishment given to recruits, not warriors with confirmed kills. It was like a boss sending her employee to stand in the corner.

Lieutenant Ben-Ari was obviously thinking the same thing. She stepped forward and addressed her captain. "Ma'am, I will discipline them later." She turned to glare at Marco and Addy. "Harshly."

Captain Petty scowled at the lieutenant. "Are you contradicting my orders, Lieutenant? Do you want to drop and give me thirty too?"

Marco couldn't help but gasp. To publicly discipline privates was bad enough, but to chastise an actual commissioned officer—in front of her troops, no less? Marco hadn't been in the military very long, but this seemed unthinkable. And he could see the red splotches of rage blooming across Ben-Ari's face.

"Now drop!" said Petty, turning back toward Marco and Addy.

Dutifully, Marco and Addy dropped and gave a push-up.

"Count them," said Petty.

"One, ma'am! Two, ma'am!" They counted until thirty, then rose, red-faced.

Captain Petty nodded, a thin smile on her lips. "Good. No chow for the rest of today. Next mealtime, you two take empty trays, empty plates, empty mugs. If anyone asks you why, you tell them that you don't deserve to eat. Then you clean every other soldier's dish, all two hundred of them."

"Captain Petty!" said Lieutenant Ben-Ari, those red splotches growing. "These are battle-hardened soldiers. They fought at Fort Djemila. They have many kills between them. They—"

"Lieutenant, this is your final warning," said Captain Petty. "If you ever contradict me in public again, you will be court-martialed here on the *Miyari* and, if you're lucky, emerge with a dishonorable discharge. We do things differently here in space." Petty raised her voice for the entire platoon to hear. "Some of you killed scum on Earth. Some of you might even consider yourselves heroes. You are no heroes here! You are worms. Your salad days in the sun are over. You belong to the STC now. You will obey. You will fight like machines. Or by God, I will blast you out of the airlock." She turned toward the twins. "Sergeants, show them all to the showers. I want them disinfected before we blast into warp drive."

The sergeants saluted. Captain Petty left the chamber, not bothering to return the salute.

Marco glanced toward Addy. She made a silly face and gave a tiny yap. Marco sighed. He already missed Earth.

CHAPTER THREE

"She really is a Chihuahua," Addy said, staring glumly at her empty plate. "You thought so too! Admit it."

Marco glared at her. "Shh! Do you want to end up scum food?" He glanced around him. "Keep your voice low."

"So no yapping?" Addy said.

Marco looked around him, hoping nobody was listening. He and Addy sat in the *Miyari*'s mess hall, both with empty plates and mugs. The soldiers of their platoon sat around them, still in their olive fatigues, tucking into their meals. Marco glanced at their plates with envy. The chow here certainly smelled and looked better than the glop and Spam from Fort Djemila. There was canned fruit here, bread and butter, synthetic chicken, and mac and cheese. The delicious aromas spun Marco's head, but thanks to Addy, he wouldn't be enjoying any of it until tomorrow. Already his stomach was growling.

He looked around him. Three other platoons filled the mess, all in the navy blue uniforms of Space Territorial Command. The two forces did not mingle. The blues kept glancing toward the greens, snorting, and muttering under their breath.

"Land-leggers," one of them mumbled.

"Fucking earthlings," another said.

"I'd rather serve with scum," said a woman across the hall, loud enough for her voice to carry everywhere, and her friends laughed.

Addy rose to her feet. "Oh yeah?" She wielded a fork like a knife. "I actually fought scum face to face, not just sat on a ship and pressed buttons while—"

"Addy!" Marco grabbed her and pulled her down. "Shut up!"

Wincing, he glanced toward the officers' table. Lieutenant Ben-Ari was there, along with several officers in navy blue. Thankfully, Captain Petty wasn't here, perhaps preferring to dine privately in her quarters. Everyone at the officers' table turned to look at Marco and Addy. Lieutenant Ben-Ari leaped in to the rescue, touching one officer's shoulder and continued a story she had been telling. As the officers turned back toward her, the lieutenant shot Addy a glare.

"Addy, you really do need to learn how to keep your big mouth shut," Marco said.

Addy snorted, fork still clutched in her hand. "Nonsense. Back in the hockey rink, we talked smack all the time, and I still kicked ass."

"You're not a hockey player anymore. You're a soldier. A soldier who's heading toward a space station light-years away from any hockey rink, where you'll be integrated into the STC."

Addy gasped. "They don't have hockey rinks?"

Marco glanced toward a screen on the wall which showed the countdown: "2:59 to hyperspace." In just under three hours, the warp engines would be ready, and the HDFS *Miyari* would leave the solar system, blasting off toward distant stars. Then Earth wouldn't even be a blue marble out the viewport; it would be lost in darkness.

"Hey, Poet." Elvis reached across the table and tapped Marco's arm. "You're a librarian, right?"

"I was," Marco said.

Elvis nodded. "Good enough. That means you're smart, right?"

Marco shrugged. "Compared to who?"

"Oh, he's smart!" Addy wrapped her arms around him and kissed his cheek. "He's writing a book, you know. *Jarhead*!"

Marco sighed. "*Loggerhead*, Addy. I told you that a thousand times."

"Enough, you two lovebirds." Elvis pointed at the clock on the wall. "What's this hyperspace thing?"

Addy guffawed. "You don't know what hyperspace is?"

Elvis shrugged and popped an entire boiled egg into his mouth. He chewed and swallowed. "I'm a musician, babe, not a genius like Poet here. Do *you* even know what hyperspace is?"

Addy bristled. "Of course I do! Everyone knows what hyperspace is."

"Well, what is it then?" Elvis asked. He placed his elbows on the table, leaned forward, and stared at Addy.

"Well . . ." Addy shifted in her seat. "It's space. That's hyper. It's all hypered-up." She elbowed Marco hard beneath the ribs. "Tell him, Poet. You have to dumb it down for him."

Marco rubbed his side. "Ow, stop that." He looked at Elvis's plate, where two other hardboiled eggs had been carefully peeled. "Slip those under the table to us, and I'll tell you."

Elvis widened his eyes. "My precious eggs!"

Addy kicked him under the table. "Hand them over, or I'll kick your other pair of precious eggs."

Once Marco and Addy had secretly eaten the eggs, Marco spoke. "See, Elvis, my boy, right now the HDFS *Miyari* is floating through regular spacetime."

"Space-what-now?" Elvis said.

"Spacetime." Marco patted the table. "Spacetime is sort of like this tablecloth."

"You mean it's covered with crumbs and Addy is chewing on it?" Elvis said.

"I'm still hungry!" Addy said through a mouthful of linen.

"Addy, stop!" Marco tugged the tablecloth out of her mouth, ignoring her cries of protest, and smoothed it across the table. "Look. Spacetime is a flat surface, that's what I mean. Well, no, it's not actually flat at all, but for our purposes, pretend it's flat. And pretend you want to fly between my plate and the saltshaker. Well, you just have to travel straight from A to B." He moved his finger across the tablecloth. "But across regular space, we can't travel very fast. Theoretically, the fastest you can go is the speed of light, though realistically, no starship can travel anywhere *near* that fast. Flying through regular spacetime is fine to reach planets within our solar system. It's pretty easy to fly through regular spacetime from Earth to Mars, say. That only takes a few weeks with a good nuclear engine. But to travel through interstellar space, to reach other stars? The distances are *vast*. Regular spaceflight would require thousands of years to reach even the nearest star."

Elvis shuddered. "Thousands of years with Captain Chihuahua? No thanks."

Addy grinned. "See, Poet? *See?* She *is* a Chihuahua, and everyone knows it."

Marco scowled. "Stop calling her that. She probably has ears growing under the tabletop. Anyway." He pulled the tablecloth up, bunching several folds of fabric together, pulling the saltshaker close to his plate. "Hyperspace sort of works like this. We bend spacetime. Now the distance between the two points is smaller. Spacetime itself, the fabric of the universe, is bunched up. Well . . . it's not really like this at all. The math is beyond me. But it's the best analogy I have unless somebody wants to bring me a bedsheet."

Elvis nodded. "Ah, I see. So the giant hand of a celestial librarian comes down from the firmaments and bends space."

"Sort of," Marco said. "Only it's an azoth engine that does it."

"A sloth?" Elvis said.

"Ooh, I like sloths!" said Addy, licking her lips. "I could go for one now."

"Azoth." Marco rolled his eyes. "How can you know the word *firmaments* but not *azoth*? You know, only the most precious material in the universe, mined in the colonies?"

"You can buy me an azoth ring someday," Addy said. "I'll bend spacetime whenever I punch my enemies."

Marco brushed a few crumbs of yolk off her shirt. "I wouldn't even buy you an onion ring. In any case, azoth engines take a while to warm up. That's why there's still some time left on the clock, counting down. Once they're primed, get ready for craziness. The universe itself will bend all around us, and we'll zip toward the frontier. We won't be moving faster than normal. But we'll bend spacetime into a far smaller distance. It doesn't break any law of physics. In a sense, we're just taking a shortcut."

For a long moment, the entire table—their squad of fifteen soldiers—was silent, even Addy. Marco knew what they were all thinking. The frontier. The front line. What awaited them there? Back on Earth, soldiers heard little of the battles in space where humanity's finest clashed against the scum. And they said there were other alien civilizations out there too, some benevolent, others demonic. Almost every bit of information from the frontier was classified. Marco knew they were heading toward a colony called Nightwall, but he knew nothing more about it. Would he undergo more training there? Or would they simply dump him straight into a battlefield on some desolate planet in no-man's-land?

He glanced at the clock. Two and a half hours until hyperspace. Two and a half hours until he left not only Earth but his entire solar system behind.

Marco rose from his seat, walked between the mess tables—careful to avoid the ones where the STC soldiers sat—and approached a viewport. He stared out into space. In the distance, he could just make out the earth, that blue dot among countless distant stars. The rocket that had brought him here was already returning home, a silver cylinder growing smaller, smaller, soon vanishing.

Earth. His father was back there. Kemi was back there—the woman he had loved, who had broken his heart. All his life, memories, dreams, ambitions—all on that pale blue dot which would soon vanish in the darkness. Marco didn't know much about the STC, but he knew this: Most STC soldiers never came home. He pressed his hand against the viewport, saying goodbye.

"Goodbye, Father," he whispered. "Goodbye, Kemi."

Yes—goodbye to Kemi too. They had parted ways, had "broken up" as they called it. She had joined Julius Military Academy. He was an enlisted private. Her service would be a decade long, if not longer. His might be cut short on the frontier. And Marco had found new love in the army, had found Lailani—new joy in his life.

But he still thought about Kemi. A lot. Her bright smile. Her kind, intelligent eyes. The years they had spent together, boyfriend and girlfriend in a city crumbling under war—but also a city of light, laughter, love. Marco had spent too many years loving her to simply forget her here, even with Lailani in his life. Back on Earth, he had run into Kemi briefly during his service, had hoped for more such encounters. But now, he knew, he was truly leaving her behind. Forever. He moved his hand on the viewport, shielding Earth behind his palm. This was farewell.

Marco frowned.

He peered into the distance.

A vessel was flying toward the *Miyari*.

It was smaller than the rocket that had taken the Ravens Platoon here. It seemed barely larger than a car. As it flew closer, he saw the logo painted onto it—a golden laurel. Symbol of Julius Military Academy. The vehicle came to hover alongside the *Miyari* just outside the window where Marco stood. A jet bridge stretched out from the *Miyari*, like the one Marco had floated through, and connected with the small spacecraft. In the craft's window, Marco glimpsed a mane of black curls and dark eyes that looked up, that met his gaze.

Marco lost his gravity legs. He nearly collapsed.

Oh God.

He turned and ran.

He ran between the tables of the mess hall, heading toward the door.

"Bad egg, Poet?" Addy called after him.

"Private Emery!" said Sergeant Singh.

But Marco kept running, leaving the mess hall to the sound of laughter and jokes about his digestion.

He barged into the entrance room, the place where he had first met Captain Petty, in time to see the door open, to see her enter the *Miyari*.

She wore the white uniform of a cadet, a golden laurel pinned to her lapel. Her black curls spilled out from under her cap. She still wore the pi pendant he had given her. She looked at Marco, and her eyes dampened, and she gave him her old crooked smile.

"Hi, Marco."

"Kemi," he whispered.

CHAPTER FOUR

"Marco." Kemi took a hesitant step toward him, then hugged him. "Hello again." She pulled back, still holding his shoulders, and gave him a huge, goofy grin. "You just can't get rid of me, can you?"

"Kemi!" He laughed and shook his head in bewilderment. "How? How is this possible? Did you graduate already from the academy so quickly, or . . ."

He let his voice trail away, and icy guilt filled him.

Lailani. Lailani is here. Kemi and Lailani don't know about each other.

"No, silly." Kemi laughed and held his hand. "I've only been a cadet for a couple of months. But sometimes, even in the first year, they let us cadets go on missions, to shadow officers in the field. Or in space, in this case." Her smile widened. "My parents pulled some strings. They found out that you're here, serving under Lieutenant Ben-Ari, and I requested to shadow her for my field assignment."

"Kemi." He held her hands, serious now. "We're heading to the front lines. It's dangerous."

She gave the slightest pout. "You don't want me here? You seem almost . . . worried? I wanted us to be together again.

To be close. Even in the army." She lowered her head. "When we parted—before your enlistment—it broke my heart. I thought our relationship was ruined. That we wouldn't see each other for a decade. And it broke my heart, Marco. It broke it." She wiped away tears. "But I'm here now. You see? We're together again, even if it's not for long. We're together."

Marco's head spun. Suddenly anger filled him.

Your heart was broken? Your heart? You dumped me! I wanted us to stay together even at a distance. You told me no. Now you come to me here, just as I found another woman, just as—

"Ma'am!" Kemi suddenly pulled back from him, stiffened, and saluted. "Cadet Kemi Abasi, reporting for my assignment, ma'am!"

Marco turned to see Lieutenant Ben-Ari enter the room.

Ben-Ari looked at Kemi, then at Marco, letting her gaze linger, and Marco wondered how much the lieutenant had heard, how much she knew. Then she turned toward Kemi.

"Welcome to the HDFS *Miyari*, Cadet Abasi," Ben-Ari said. "Have you eaten? There are still a few minutes of chow time left. Come, we'll get acquainted."

Kemi nodded, eyes filling with awe. "Thank you, ma'am. And may I just say right away: I've heard many tales of your family. Your father was legendary! We studied about him at Julius. And your own courage in battle is inspiring. I'm honored to shadow you on this mission. I look forward to assisting you and learning from you."

There were classes about Ben-Ari's family? Marco knew they were famous, but he hadn't known they were *that* famous. What had her father achieved to make him a legend? Suddenly Marco felt woefully ignorant about his commanding officer, a woman Kemi seemed to know far more about. As the two women walked back toward the mess hall, Ben-Ari looked over her shoulder at him.

"Emery, get back to your seat."

He nodded. "Yes, ma'am." He followed them back into the mess hall and sat back down with his squad. Kemi, meanwhile, joined the officers at their own table. When Marco gazed toward her, Kemi smiled at him, gave a little wave, then turned her attention back toward Ben-Ari and the STC officers.

Addy was still sitting here among the enlisted. She gaped at Kemi across the mess hall, then at Marco who sat beside her, then at Kemi again. She rubbed her eyes.

"Is that . . ." Addy frowned, gaped at the officers' table, then spun toward Marco. "Is that Kemi Fucking Abasi? From school?"

Marco nodded. "It is. She's shadowing Ben-Ari."

Addy's jaw nearly hit the tabletop. "Fuck me."

Marco glanced toward Lailani. She sat across the table, busy arguing with Beast—something about whether Russia manufactured better starships than the *Miyari*, a position Beast was vehemently defending. Lailani glanced toward Marco only once, met his eyes for a split second, then turned her attention back to Beast.

"This is just cheap American material." Beast pounded his boot against the floor. "Looks pretty, yes, but weak. In Russia, we build *real* spaceships. You know, we put first satellite in orbit. First man in space. First dog in space too."

"That was two hundred years ago!" Lailani said. "That's like saying Greece makes the best tanks because once they had the best chariots."

"Greece makes best tanks?!" Beast's face twisted with fury. "You obviously never saw Medvedov tank in action. Now *that* is tank. Smashes Greece like grape."

Lailani did not glance at Marco again, but that one look had been enough. Lailani understood, and Marco's heart sank. He didn't want to deal with this now. He was blasting toward the fringe of the galaxy to face bloodthirsty aliens in battle. Didn't he have enough to worry about?

"Hey, Poet." Elvis moved to sit beside him and elbowed him in the ribs.

"Why does everyone keep doing that?" Marco grimaced and rubbed his side.

Elvis ignored him and gestured with a jerk of his head. "Psst. Look. That table beside ours." He whistled softly. "Check out the ice queen. Hot as hell!"

Marco looked. Nearby was a table of STC officers, all in navy blue uniforms, golden insignias sewn onto their sleeves. At the end of the table sat a tall woman that Marco had to admit was indeed beautiful—achingly so. She had alabaster skin, a platinum bob cut, and features that could convince Marco that God existed and was a sculptor. Yet there was something indeed icy about her too. Something eerie. She wore no insignia, and she ate nothing, didn't even sit in front of a plate.

The woman seemed to feel them staring. She turned her head, and she stared right at Marco. Her eyes were lavender, the color of scum miasma, and seemed to penetrate Marco.

He and Elvis quickly looked away.

"Oh shit," Elvis whispered under his breath. "Why did you stare? Just glance, never stare." He gulped. "She's coming over. Oh God, she's coming over." He passed his hand through his hair. "How do I look? I stand a chance with her, right, Poet? I—"

The woman came to stand by their table. She leaned down. She stared at Marco, then at Elvis. Her skin was perfectly smooth, almost waxy, deathlike. Her eyes were almost luminous, almost inhuman.

"You stink of scum," she said, voice emotionless.

Elvis cleared his throat and rose to his feet. "Um, it's actually Hammer body spray. Do you like it? The commercials promised me that women would chase me, and—"

The woman's hand lashed out. She grabbed Elvis by the throat and squeezed.

"Section Three, article four, *Enlisted Soldier's Handbook*," the woman said, voice monotone. "Soldiers of the HDF may not wear perfumes, and all soaps and aftershaves must be odorless."

"Whoa, hold on!" Addy said, leaping to her feet, and tried to pull the woman back. Elvis was gasping for breath, trying to pull the woman's hand off his throat, but seemed powerless to stop her. When Marco grabbed the woman, she lashed her free hand against him. She was amazingly strong, knocking Marco onto the table. Plastic plates clattered to the floor. When Addy attempted to pull Elvis free, she too was knocked down. Soon their entire squad was on their feet, then the entire mess.

One voice, louder than the others, tore across the hall.

"Osiris! Release him!"

Instantly the tall woman with platinum hair opened her hand. Elvis fell to the floor, gasping for air.

"So," Elvis managed to croak, "does that mean you'll date me?"

They all turned toward the doorway; the voice had come from there. Across the mess hall, the soldiers rose and stood at attention.

Captain Petty walked through the hall, approaching Marco's table.

"Who antagonized Osiris?" Petty said, then turned toward Marco. "Was it you?"

Marco shook his head. "No, ma'am. She just grabbed him. She—"

"I didn't ask you what happened, soldier." Petty looked across their squad's table. "You're all assigned to kitchen duty for the duration of our flight. If you *ever* misuse STC equipment again, you'll be dropped off at the nearest penal asteroid. Is that understood?"

Marco glanced toward Osiris. STC equipment? The tall, platinum-haired woman gazed at him, and now there was no mistaking the glow in her purple eyes. The eyes weren't just reflecting the overhead lights. They emitted their own glow.

My God, Marco thought. *She's an android.*

He had heard of androids before—in old books from before the Cataclysm, mostly. Such high technology was largely gone from Earth now. Some on Earth claimed that they still existed, but Marco had never seen one until now.

"Listen up, soldiers!" Captain Petty said, marching toward the back of the mess hall. "In less than two hours, we activate our warp drives. The journey to the frontier will take twenty days. STC soldiers may spend their time in the entertainment lounge, the commissary, the mess, and the gym." She looked at Marco's table. "Earth Territorial Command soldiers will spend the journey confined to their bunks, except for chow time and morning inspections in the corridor." She glanced toward the officers' table. "That includes officers and cadets too. Once we reach Nightwall, they'll decide what to do with you. Until then you are cargo, nothing more. Perhaps a few of you will end up wearing the blue. If the rest of you are ejected into space, try to be eaten quickly. I like keeping space clean." She pointed toward her staff sergeants. "The twins will show you to your bunks."

With that, the captain turned and left the mess.

Addy leaned toward Marco. "I told you," she whispered. "Chihuahua."

He nodded. "I just heard lots of yapping."

The officers left the mess first—and with them walked Kemi. She wasn't an officer yet, wouldn't be one for a couple years, but even as a cadet, she apparently would eat and sleep separately from the enlisted troops. As she walked out the door, Kemi turned toward Marco, smiled, and waved. Then she quickly hurried after the officers.

The STC soldiers left next. As they passed by Marco's platoon, they snorted and muttered under their breath about the "land-leggers" and "dirty earthlings." Addy growled and seemed ready to leap up and fight, and Marco and Elvis had to hold her back. Finally the Ravens Platoon left their tables, still in their dusty green fatigues from Earth, their heavy guns clattering across their backs. They followed an STC sergeant through a narrow corridor, passing by viewports showing the stars. Marco saw Saturn in the distance, the ring just vaguely visible. It seemed almost like a toy from here, as if he could reach out and grab it like a Christmas ornament.

"Will you buy me that ring?" Addy said.

"I'm not buying you a ring."

The sergeant led them to a corridor lined with small rooms. Each room included three bunk beds. Marco found himself bunking with his closest friends: Addy, Lailani, Beast, and Elvis. They all quickly claimed beds. Marco was too slow and missed the chance at a top one. He resigned himself to a low bunk by the door, but at least he could see the room's single viewport from here. He looked forward to seeing the starlight bend once the warp engine kicked in.

"Hey, six beds, five soldiers!" Addy said. "Sweet, room for my stuff." She dumped her duffel bag onto the free bed, and the others followed. They piled up their weapons by the duffel bags.

"So, do you think I still stand a chance with Blondie?" Elvis said.

Lailani groaned. "Elvis, she's an android."

Elvis's eyes widened. "Fuck me! Really?" He frowned. "So, do you think I stand a chance?"

Beast muttered something about how robots in Russia were built big, metallic, and intimidating, not these weak, girly American robots.

"Maybe you should date Captain Chihuahua, Elvis," Addy said, then gave her best impression of a yapping Chihuahua.

"It sounds more like this," Lailani said, adding her own yapping to the chorus.

"What about that cadet who showed up last moment?" Elvis said. "She was pretty. God, all those black curls, those big eyes. Maybe—"

"No." Addy stopped barking and shook her head. "That's Kemi. Kemi Abasi. She's from Toronto too. She's Marco's—" She hesitated, glanced at Lailani, then back at Elvis. "His friend."

Elvis tilted his head for a moment, and then his eyes widened. "Hang on!" He gasped. "No way. No way!" He spun toward Marco. "Hey, Poet, show me that photo again. The one you always carry in your pocket."

"I don't carry a photo in my pocket," Marco said.

"Sure you do." Elvis leaped forward, and before Marco could stop him, he grabbed the book from Marco's pocket and pulled out the photo. "Yes! It's her. The famous Kemi! The one you kept talking about at boot camp. Your girlfriend from back home. Fuck me, how did she end up here?"

Marco was silent for a moment, not sure what to say, not sure how to avoid hurting Lailani.

But it was Lailani who answered. "She came here to be close to him. To be with him again." She nodded. "She's a lucky girl." With that, Lailani climbed onto her bunk, lay down, and rolled toward the wall.

Awkward silence filled the bunk. Elvis blinked and stared around, mouth wide, looking utterly confused.

The silence died as the door banged open.

"Speak of the devil," Addy said as Kemi raced into the room, curls bouncing.

"Marco!" She hugged him, then turned toward Addy. "Addy!" She looked around, beaming. "Lieutenant Ben-Ari said I can live with the enlisted soldiers." She tapped her cheek, smile faltering. "To be honest, I don't think the officers want a cadet in their bunk anyway. I won't be one of them for a while, not until I graduate and earn my commission." Her smile returned. "But that means we can be together! For twenty days!"

Elvis sketched an elaborate bow. "Your highness, you are most welcome to sleep here in the hut of the peasants. You'll find us rude, crude, a bit stinky in Beast's case, but far more pleasant company than Captain Chihuahua."

Kemi gasped and covered her mouth. "You thought she looks like a Chihuahua too?"

"I told you, Marco!" Addy said. "It's obvious." Soon she was yapping again.

Beast grumbled. "Chihuahuas are useless dogs. In Russia we have *real* dogs. Big like wolf. Bite your head off."

A monotone voice emerged from hidden speakers, interrupting the conversation. "One minute to warp jump. All troops, remain in your bunks. Less than one minute to warp jump."

Marco walked toward the viewport and stared outside, his mundane troubles momentarily forgotten as he gazed at the stars and floating Saturn. The others crowded around him, gazing out the small window. All but Lailani. She remained in her bed, facing the wall, sending another pang of guilt through Marco.

"Three," spoke the voice from the speakers. "Two. One. Azoth engines engaging."

At first nothing happened. Saturn still floated outside. The stars still shone as usual. The only difference was blue light glistening against the solar panels circling the starship, perhaps emitted from the engines. Marco didn't remember the solar panels being that close to the viewport. They seemed to be shifting, moving faster, widening, pulling backward. He blinked as the viewport stretched before him, growing more and more distant, and he reached out, trying to touch the silica pane, unable to grasp it. It felt like trying to perform surgery in a mirror. And suddenly Saturn was floating right by the ship, closer than the ring of solar panels, and then it floated inside the ship, right beside Marco, hovering like a lantern. He was outside. He was actually outside— in space, unable to breathe, but finally he touched the viewport, felt the cold surface, and the walls stretched out. The stars moved. The stars bent. All the fabric of the cosmos, rippling, coiling, forming fold after fold like flowing linen. The stars formed waves of light, and they were beautiful. They were so beautiful that tears filled Marco's eyes. Everything was light. Everything was emptiness. And then Saturn was gone, Earth was gone, the sun was gone, and they hovered through a sea of starlight, rising and falling on the waves until the surface smoothed out, and they sailed over a shimmering ocean of silver and blue.

Marco stepped back from the viewport, blinking, and it was a moment before his head stopped spinning.

"So, just like a folded tablecloth, see?" he said.

"That was amazing!" Kemi breathed, eyes alight.

"I think I'm going to throw up," Addy said, turning green.

Beast shrugged. "That nothing. In Russia we—" He groaned as Elvis punched him.

The robotic voice emerged again from the speakers. "Jump to hyperspace complete. Time to frontier: twenty Earth days. Lights out in thirty minutes. Morning inspection at 6:00 a.m. standard HDF time."

Last year, Marco would have cringed to wake up that early. But after ten weeks of 4:30 a.m. freezing boot camp mornings, it seemed a luxury. He had walls and a roof around him here, not just a tent. Pinky was millions of kilometers away. His friends were with him. This wasn't too bad. It really wasn't.

Yet that night, when Marco lay in the dark bunk, the memories resurfaced. He saw the scum again, swarming over the sides of his armored vehicle. He saw the giant centipedes stabbing Caveman, ripping the legs off Pinky, tearing Corporal Webb apart. Those memories morphed in the darkness of the ship, becoming visions of a distant, rocky world, the scum emerging from canyons and caves, thousands of them drawing nearer, killing his friends, reaching toward him.

CHAPTER FIVE

Lieutenant Einav Ben-Ari tried to steel herself as she walked down the corridor of the *Miyari*.

I faced scum in battle, she thought. *I'm descended of a long dynasty of warriors. I can certainly face her.*

And yet, as Ben-Ari walked toward her commanding officer's cabin, the fear wouldn't leave her. It felt like walking toward Abaddon itself, homeworld of the scum.

Ben-Ari paused for a moment in the hallway and turned toward a viewport. The lights in the corridor cast her reflection back at her. She wore her drab uniform from Earth, its hems threadbare, its pockets frayed, the knees torn. If not for the insignia on her shoulders, denoting her an officer, she would look like any other private crawling out of basic training. Here in this fine, expensive starship, she felt out of place like a donkey among prized racehorses. She placed her fingertips on the viewport, touching her reflection's fingers. She was young, barely into her twenties, and could still pass for a teenager. She had the curse of the baby face, her cheeks too round, too soft. But her eyes were old. From those eyes gazed the souls of the generations, of all those in her family who had fought, who had died.

She let her eyes focus past her reflection, to gaze into the vastness beyond, the streaming lights of stars stretched across warped spacetime. Despite her father's illustrious career in space, Ben-Ari had never left Earth's orbit before. To her soldiers, to her dear platoon, she tried to appear wise, experienced, an officer who had fought many battles, who had been to the edge of the galaxy and back. In truth, she was scared. In truth, she had never fought before Fort Djemila. Sergeant Singh, her own soldier, a man she commanded, was older, stronger, had killed far more scum. Only a year ago Ben-Ari had been a mere cadet, and not even at a fancy academy like Julius. She had attended a simple Officer Candidate School. Her family, despite their long history of service, was too poor, too unconnected, too *ethnic* to afford an education at Julius.

But I have to be strong for my soldiers, Ben-Ari thought. *For Marco. For Addy. For all the rest of them. They are my soldiers. They are my children. They will never know how much I love them. I will fight for them—against the scum and against her.*

She turned away from the window and walked onward.

She reached the door of Captain Petty's quarters. Again Ben-Ari hesitated. Her own family was esteemed in the military, for their ranks if not their wealth and connections. Her father had been a colonel, her grandfather too, and for two hundred years the Ben-Aris had commanded troops. But Captain Petty's own father was a general in Space Territorial Command, outranking anyone even in the Ben-Ari military dynasty.

And Ben-Ari knew what the dynastic military families, especially those in the STC, thought about her people. Oh, they all pretended that religion and ethnicity didn't matter in the HDF, that humanity had moved beyond that. But Ben-Ari saw the looks, heard the murmurs, the jokes. She saw others receive scholarships to Julius while she was passed over. Fifty years ago, Israel—a tiny country, barely larger than a city—had been obliterated in the Cataclysm, completely lost in the scum assault. The surviving soldiers of that nation, with no more land to call their own, had integrated into the fledgling Human Defense Force. Many had risen high in the ranks, had distinguished themselves in battles . . . and yet were still considered nomads. Still looked down upon by the great American and European military families, those who owned land and manors and wealth, who exuded influence even in civilian life.

To somebody like Petty, Ben-Ari thought, *my family is just a group of vagabond commoners.* She shuddered. *And if I know people like Petty, she cares deeply about dynastic lines, even more than rank, certainly more than character. I might be an officer, but to her I'm a peasant.*

But there was no use stalling. Captain Petty was her commanding officer aboard this ship, and without Petty's help, the Ravens Platoon would not thrive. Ben-Ari knocked on the door.

A long pause.

Finally from inside: "Enter!"

Ben-Ari opened the door and stepped into a large chamber, more like a command center than an officer's quarters. Captain Petty sat behind a heavy oak desk. It looked like real wood. A handful of other soldiers stood with her. Ben-Ari recognized Major Sefu Mwarabu, the tall and stern commander of HDFS *Miyari*, as well as a pair of young helmsmen. The twin staff sergeants were here too, along with a navigator. They were busy at a handful of terminals on the walls, but they all turned toward Ben-Ari as she entered.

Ben-Ari took a deep breath. She had hoped to speak to Captain Petty alone, but it seemed she would have an audience—including Major Mwarabu, who outranked them both, yet who had little authority over the infantry company he was transporting.

Ben-Ari stood at attention halfway toward the desk and saluted.

"Ma'am, Lieutenant Ben-Ari reporting," she said, not sure about protocol on the *Miyari*. Back on Fort Djemila, she had been on a first-name basis with her company's commander, at least when away from the recruits. She had a feeling that Petty was a stickler for protocol.

Captain Petty stood up. She stared at Ben-Ari for a long time, silent. Ben-Ari remained at attention, still saluting, until finally—by God, it seemed like ages—Petty returned the salute.

"At ease," the captain said. "What do you want, Ben-Ari?"

Ben-Ari, she called me. Not lieutenant. She doesn't want to acknowledge my commission, only my family—which she certainly looks down upon.

She took another deep breath. "Captain, I wanted to—"

"Call me ma'am," Captain Petty interjected. "We all know my rank."

Ben-Ari blinked, cursing herself for her accidental breach of protocol. She nodded. "Yes, ma'am," she said, feeling a little like a recruit on her first day at RASCOM. "I wanted to properly thank you for this opportunity, ma'am. You too, Major Mwarabu, sir. It's truly an honor to serve here aboard the *Miyari*, part of an Erebus company, and—"

"You do not serve here, Ben-Ari," said Captain Petty, returning to her seat. "You and your platoon are merely hitchhikers on the *Miyari*." She narrowed her eyes and leaned forward. "Did you come here to truly thank me or to kiss my ass?"

Ben-Ari curbed the instinct to take a step back. Across the room, she noticed the others glancing around uncomfortably, but they did not interject.

"Ma'am, I—" she began.

"Why is your uniform so frayed?" Petty said. "Your pocket has a hole in it. Your trousers are torn. Your boots are old. Is this how soldiers present themselves to superior officers on Earth?"

Ben-Ari stiffened. The initial shock gave way to anger. "On Earth, we don't have the same budget as the STC. If you have any spare uniforms aboard the *Miyari*, I—"

"You will not wear our uniforms! You are not an STC soldier, Ben-Ari." Petty rose to her feet again, face flushed. "If you survive Integration—and that is unlikely without a recommendation from me—perhaps they'll scrub the filth off you, disinfect you from fleas, and let you wear the navy blue. Until then, you are not one of us. You are nothing but cargo. Do you understand?"

Ben-Ari winced. *Well, this is going well.*

"Ma'am, I came here today because I felt we started on the wrong page," Ben-Ari said. "I came here to mend bridges, not to offend you."

"Offend me?" Petty laughed, a mirthless sound. "Ben-Ari, I know your type. You fought a scuffle or two on Earth. You stomped on a centipede in some desert. And now you think you can come here, into a venerable institution, into a state of the art starship that cost more than everything on your planet, and instantly act like you're one of us." Petty walked around her desk to face her. "You have no idea what is out there. You haven't yet drunk of the darkness. You faced the simplest, smallest breed of scum, the fodder they send to backwaters like Earth. The bug grunts." She snorted. "You have no idea what awaits you, do you?"

Ben-Ari met her commanding officer's gaze. She stared steadily into those buggy eyes. "I am an officer in the Human Defense Force. I fought for this force. I killed for this force. This force is my home. Whatever waits in the darkness, I will face it."

"It will kill you," said Petty.

"Then I will die," said Ben-Ari, "for my species, for my planet."

Petty narrowed her eyes and tilted her head. "I see. So you have dreams of glory. Perhaps of being a heroine. You're so certain that you'll survive Integration? But first you must earn your recommendation from me. And to do that, you will show your subservience." A strange light filled Petty's eyes. "You can start now. I want you to repeat after me: I, Lieutenant Ben-Ari . . ."

Ben-Ari frowned. "What?"

"Repeat!" Petty shouted, spraying saliva, so loud that a few of the others in the room jumped.

Ben-Ari squared her shoulders. She forced a breath in, out, in again.

In twenty days I'll be rid of her, she thought.

"I, Lieutenant Ben-Ari," she repeated.

"Am nobody," said Petty.

Ben-Ari ground her teeth. "Am nobody."

"I am worthless," said Petty. "Say it."

Finally one of the others in the room spoke. Major Mwarabu, the stern commander of the *Miyari*, took a step closer to Petty. "Coleen, maybe—"

"She's my concern, sir, and I will deal with her," Petty said to the major, but she kept staring at Ben-Ari. "Repeat it. I am worthless."

Ben-Ari forced another breath, trying to swallow her fury, her pride. *Twenty days.*

"I am worthless," she repeated.

"My only purpose is to serve my commanding officer," Petty said.

"My only purpose is to serve my commanding officer," Ben-Ari repeated, voice strained.

For my soldiers. Twenty days.

Petty's smile stretched into a cruel grin. "My family are traitors."

Ben-Ari gasped. "What—"

"Say it!" Petty said. "I know who they are. I know how your father lost the Battle of Cape Town. I know of his cowardice. Say it! My family are traitors. Say it!"

Ben-Ari could not curb her rage now. Her fists trembled at her sides. She spoke in a strained whisper. "You may humiliate me, but you will not bad-mouth my family."

"Are you disobeying an order?" said Petty, then whipped her head toward the other officers. "Sit down! All of you, sit down! This is between her and me." She looked back at Ben-Ari. "Say it, or by God you will never be part of the STC. I will see to that myself. I—"

Red lights suddenly ignited across the monitors on the walls. Beeps filled the chamber. Petty spun toward one monitor. The others—the commander, the helmsmen, and the twin sergeants—stared at other monitors. Ben-Ari narrowed her eyes, staring with them.

"It's a distress call," Ben-Ari said.

Captain Petty hit a few buttons on a monitor, and the lights vanished and the sounds died.

"Coleen," said Major Mwarabu, turning toward her. "We should chart a new course."

Petty shook her head. "No. Ignore it, Major. My father, a *brigadier-general*, wants us at Nightwall as soon as possible." She raised her chin and gave a smug smile when reporting her father's rank, making it clear that while Mwarabu outranked her personally, he did not outrank her father. "We continue on our present course."

Ben-Ari inhaled sharply. "Ignore it? Ma'am, that was a Priority One distress call from Corpus Mining Colony. They need immediate military assistance, and we're the only HDF ship within light-years."

Petty spun toward her, livid. "That information was classified."

"Not to me," said Ben-Ari. "I have security clearance. Yes, even me, a lowly ETC lieutenant. Ma'am, we cannot ignore a Priority One distress call. Corpus is an important azoth producer. The same material this very ship uses. They need help. It might be the scum. We're nearby, we have two hundred armed soldiers aboard this vessel, and—"

"Silence!" Petty barked. She turned toward the twins. "Sergeants, escort Lieutenant Ben-Ari to the brig. She will remain locked up until we arrive at Nightwall, and there I will personally court-martial her for disobedience. I—"

"When you court-martial me," said Ben-Ari, "you will need a higher-ranking officer in attendance. And what will that officer say, I wonder, when they hear why I disobeyed you?" Ben-Ari was in too deep now. It was too late to back down. She would fight this battle. "What will they say at Nightwall when they hear you abandoned an azoth mine, that you ignored a distress call from a human colony? What will they do when they hear—and I have witnesses here in this chamber, including the commander of this starship!—that I demanded we obey proper military protocol, and you chose to ignore it?" Ben-Ari leaned closer. "I know who your father is, Petty. That doesn't scare me."

Petty stared at her, silent, eyes bugging out and face red. Behind the captain's back, Ben-Ari swore that she could see Major Mwarabu stifle a smile. Ben-Ari was willing to bet that Mwarabu had bitten his tongue many times in the presence of this company commander he had been transporting.

"You miserable worm," Petty whispered.

Ben-Ari smiled, staring into Petty's eyes. "On this ship, ma'am, you are my commanding officer. But don't think that I will bow down to you. I will fight you. My family has been fighting for generations, and we fought enemies far worse than you. I will not back down. If you antagonize me, I will make your life a living hell. You will miss the scum once I'm done with you." She bowed her head. "Ma'am."

I came here to make amends, Ben-Ari thought. *I just made an enemy for life.*

Captain Petty turned back toward one of the monitors. From where she stood, Ben-Ari could make out some of the words.

Mayday. Mayday. Power failing. Hundreds dead. Poison in the tunnels. Requesting military assistance.

Petty hit a few more buttons, and the last monitor died. She nodded.

"Major Mwarabu," she said, "return to the bridge. We're taking a detour. Set a course to Corpus. We'll provide our assistance." She turned to look at Ben-Ari. "And since our dear lieutenant is so eager to prove her worth, she will take the vanguard. Let our earthling friends be our canaries in the mines."

I won't die so easily, Petty, Ben-Ari thought, *no matter how much you crave it.* But she only said, "We will prove our worth, ma'am."

She saluted.

Petty stared at her like one stared at a rotting scum carcass. "Dismissed."

Ben-Ari left the room, shoulders squared. Once outside in the hallway, she leaned against the wall, closed her eyes, and breathed heavily.

Scum on Corpus. War. Blood. Death.

"War, blood, death," she whispered. "My life. My job. My destiny."

She took another deep breath, clutched her gun for comfort, and walked down the hall toward her bunk.

CHAPTER SIX

For the first time in three months, Marco sat down to work on his novel.

The *Miyari* was not a large ship. Aside from the mess and gym, it was all narrow corridors, cramped bunks, ladders and narrow stairwells and crawlspaces. This was not one of the massive cruisers that could transport entire brigades across the galaxy. There were only a couple hundred people on board—the ship's small crew, along with the infantry company they were transporting—and the ship was crammed to capacity.

But Marco had found this little nook near the engines with walls that rattled and hummed, smaller than his bedroom back home. There was a dusty old coffee machine emblazoned with the words *Colonel Coffee* and a drawing of a smiling, mustached man sipping from a mug. There were a few drawers with plastic spoons and packets of jam, a small table, and three armchairs. The sign outside read *Officer's Lounge*, but given the state of the room—he found cobwebs inside—Marco doubted any officers ever used it, and so he decided to risk an hour of privacy.

There was a lot more time here on the *Miyari* than back at Fort Djemila. It would be almost three weeks to the frontier, even traveling through hyperspace, and there would be morning inspections, training, propaganda videos, and all the rigors of military life. But also long hours of just waiting. Just idling away the time until they reached Nightwall Outpost, the military base at the edge of humanity's sphere of influence, where he'd be integrated into the STC and sent to fight the scum in space.

But Marco hadn't been born to fight. He wasn't a warrior by nature. This had all been thrust upon him. His true calling, he had always thought, was with words. To read. To write. To tend to books, consuming, preserving, contributing to knowledge.

And so he sat with his notebook open, a pen in hand. He looked at the first page.

Loggerhead, by Marco Emery.

He had been working on the novel for two years now, had written many chapters, tossed them out, written them over again. He had never written anything longer than short stories before, and even now, after quite a lot of effort, he was only six chapters into *Loggerhead*. The rest was all in his mind, the entire story living inside him.

"I just need to get you out onto the page," he mumbled.

He stared at the page. A story of loss. A story of remembering. A story that linked him to who he had been, to a boy in a library, not this soldier. Not this weary, haunted man. He looked at the gun that hung at his side, looked at his hands—hands that had killed, that had held dying friends. Once these hands had tended to books, scribbled by candlelight. Once he had dreamed of being a writer. He flipped through the pages he had written, but they had been written by another person. A softer, kinder person.

I lost something here, he thought. *I grew too hard. I built a shell around me, like an exoskeleton of the scum. I have to find who I was.*

He didn't want to be a soldier. He was stronger now, perhaps wiser too. He had learned about loss and memory firsthand in the army, more than he ever had back home. But he didn't want to be this man with a gun. He didn't want to be a soldier on a warship, staring at a blank page, drifting away from the writer he had been.

Loggerhead. The story of a man who had lost his memory. Who had woken up on a beach, a strange world, his mind broken, able to communicate only with letters to a loggerhead turtle in the deep ocean. Once a successful doctor. Hurt. Tossed aside. Now lost on a beach, his family gone, his past life a haze. Marco wrote the first sentence he had in three months.

I don't know who I am.

He stared at the words.

He lowered his pen again, but before he could write more, the door to the lounge burst open, and two soldiers spilled in.

"I told you there's a coffee machine in here," Elvis was saying. "This ship's a whorehouse. Chicken. Good beds. Coffee too."

"Who cares?" Beast said. "Who wants to drink *coffee?*" He pronounced that last word as if it were mud.

"I do!" Elvis said. "Coffee is wonderful, and you're trying some, and—Oh hi, Poet. Have you seen the coffee machine?"

Marco put down his pen. He pointed at the old coffee machine behind the paper cups and tins of rations. "Colonel Coffee. I think I saw a few spiders inside."

Elvis pushed his way past boxes and spent a few moments pounding on the machine. Colonel Coffee finally spurted out brown flecks followed by a blast of black liquid and a few bubbles. Elvis took a sip, and his face wrinkled up. He spat.

"Ugh, spider juice!"

Beast took the cup, sipped, and nodded. "Not bad, actually." The beefy, bald soldier looked at Marco. "You writing your book, Poet?"

Marco nodded. "Well, sort of. I only wrote one sentence today."

"Can I read a little?" Beast reached for the notebook, flipped to the first page, and nodded while reading silently. "Not bad. Not bad. Good story." He placed down the notebook. "Of course, nobody can write as well as the Russian masters. See, it's impossible. No matter how good you write, you cannot beat them."

"I loved *Crime and Punishment* by Dostoyevsky," Marco said. "I read it two years ago. The full, unabridged version too, not the short version they have you read at school."

Beast gave him a pat on the back so powerful Marco nearly fell from his chair. "Good man! Of course, there's no beating the original Russian. You Americans always mess up the translation."

"We're Canadian, you doofus," Elvis said, wrestling with the coffee machine. "You stupid, goddamn—argh!" Elvis kicked the machine. "Fuck you, Colonel!"

"Ah, American, Canadian, same thing," said Beast.

Elvis managed to pull out a bundle of cobwebs from the machine. "That's like me saying Russians and Ukrainians are the same."

"What?" Beast fumed. "You say Russia is same as Ukraine? Ukraine is weak!"

"Calm down, big boy!" Elvis attempted to shove the giant Russian, who was easily twice his size, into a chair. "You're about to explode and crack the hull of the ship."

They sat down at the table with Marco. With a sigh, Marco closed his notebook. Writing would have to wait for another day.

"Russia must be beautiful," he said to Beast. "You must miss it."

"Miss it?" Beast shook his head. "Never been there."

"What?" Elvis gaped. "What are you talking about? Your accent! Your constant talk of the motherland!"

"Of course!" Beast said. "Russia still the motherland. My mother born there! I was born and raised in Queens, New York."

Marco rubbed his eyes. "I don't believe this. And don't tell me, the neighborhood bully was Ukrainian."

"*He* was the neighborhood bully," Elvis said, poking Beast's massive arm. "Look at the size of him. Hell, he was the neighborhood period."

"So why are you always on about Russia, Beast?" Marco said.

"Well, because Russia is great!" Beast said. "Russia is best country in world, and—" Beast bit down on his words, stared into his cup of dark liquid, and was silent for a long moment. Finally he sighed. "I was not happy in Queens."

Elvis and Marco glanced at each other, then back at Beast.

"Why not?" Elvis said. "Not enough Dostoyevsky in the libraries?"

Beast swirled the drink in his cup. "My mother raised me alone. Father left back to Russia when I was baby. I only spoke Russian until I went to school, and other kids picked on me."

"Picked on you?" Elvis said. "You're the size of a starship."

"That's why they picked on me," Beast said. "Called me Bear. I prefer Beast, actually. I was too ashamed of my size, so I never fought back, just let them bully me. Growing up with no friends, with a drunk mother, no father, no brothers . . . Well, I always dreamed that Russia was a better place. That I could have a better life there. That somewhere in the world, I belonged. But I've never been there, only heard stories."

Marco nodded thoughtfully. "Next we'll learn that Elvis is actually a fan of polka music."

"Not a chance of that, buddy," Elvis said. "I give up on coffee. Here. How about we drink some of this?" He pulled out a silver flask from his pocket. "Good Canadian whiskey. And don't say anything about Russian vodka, Beast!"

Marco's eyes widened. "How did you smuggle that on board?"

"I told you, I have sources." Elvis took a swig, then passed the flask to Marco. "For Earth, for space, and for kicking alien ass."

"I'll drink to that," Marco said, took a sip, and passed it to Beast.

They all turned to look out the small viewport, at the stars that streamed outside through the darkness.

"They're out there somewhere," Elvis said. "The scum. Those bastards who killed our friends back home. Fuck. You know the average STC soldier only has a fifty percent chance of making it home? I'm scared, guys."

"Me too," said Marco.

"I'm terrified," said Beast.

Elvis gave a weak snort. "Some soldiers we are. A poet. A farm boy. A New Yorker—and yes, that's what you are, Beast, so shut up. Are we really the best warriors humanity has to offer?"

"I think that mostly we're fodder," Marco said.

"Lovely." Elvis sighed. "You sure know how to cheer a man up."

They all stared outside in silence for a long moment, and Marco thought back to his dream, standing on a dark planet, thousands of scum racing toward them. He could have, perhaps, resisted Lieutenant Ben-Ari and remained back on Earth. Yet he had followed his commander here—had, in fact, insisted on bringing his friends with him.

Did I doom us all to death in darkness?

"Ah, to hell with sightseeing," Elvis said. He pulled a pack of cards out from his pocket. "Let's stop staring at space and play. Poker, anyone?"

The door slammed open again. Addy's head thrust into the room. "Did I hear poker? And I wasn't invited?"

Elvis sighed. "If Maple is ever kidnapped by the scum, we just need to shout out 'Poker!' and she'll magically materialize near us."

"Damn right." Addy pulled up a chair. "Now deal."

Elvis dealt the cards, and they played, and they laughed, and they drank again from the flask. But every once in a while, they still looked outside, at those stars, at what awaited them in the shadows.

Fodder, Marco thought. *Fodder for scum. But if we die, we die fighting. For Earth.*

"Marco, your turn to deal," Addy said, lighting a cigarette.

He took the cards and dealt. They played as *Miyari* streamed through space, moving ever closer to the frontier.

* * * * *

"It's so beautiful in hyperspace." Kemi stood by the viewport in their bunk, staring out the window at the streams of bending light. She turned toward Marco, smiling. "So . . . you wanted to be alone with me?"

Their bunkmates were all in the *Miyari*'s mess. Marco had skipped the meal, had convinced Kemi to skip it too. Elvis had promised to smuggle them back some food. Marco needed this— to speak to Kemi alone.

"I did," Marco said. "We haven't been alone since you came aboard, and—"

Kemi practically leaped onto him, kissing his lips with desperation, clutching his hair. "Oh, I missed you. I missed your lips." She touched his cheek. "My beautiful boy."

As she kissed him, her lips full and soft, Marco closed his eyes. He couldn't help it. He wrapped his arms around her, and God, he wanted this. God, he had missed her. God, this felt right. This felt like home. Suddenly, as her lips kissed him, as her curls brushed his cheek, the past few months seemed to vanish. Suddenly it was the old days, him and her, and all the pain—of the war, of the memories—all melted away.

"I love you, Marco," she whispered, tears in her eyes. "I'm so sorry about how we parted. I missed you."

Marco wanted to forget everything, wanted to kiss her, to make love to her, to pretend that none of the past few months had happened. Reluctantly, he pulled away from her, and it was as painful as pulling off a part of his body. Kemi looked at him, confusion in her eyes.

"What's wrong?" she said.

What's wrong? Marco thought, incredulous. *Whenever I close my eyes, I see the scum. Whenever I sleep, I dream of my friends dying. We're heading to war, to face the aliens in the depths of space, and I'm terrified, and I don't know if I'll live to be nineteen.*

But he couldn't say all those things. And this was not why he had asked to speak to her alone.

"Kemi." He held her hands. "When we said goodbye, on Earth, before I was drafted . . . I thought it was over between us. And I missed you. For weeks in basic training, I couldn't stop thinking about you, showing your photo to friends, hoping that maybe someday we could get back together."

"It was the same with me," Kemi said and tried to kiss him again. He held her back.

"Kemi, wait. Hear me out. I missed you so much. But as time went by, I began to realize that we wouldn't see each other for a decade. Maybe never again. And I remembered what you told me. How our relationship had to end. And . . ." He sighed. "You'll hear it eventually. If not from me, then from somebody else in our platoon." He looked away, unable to look her in the eyes. "I slept with Lailani. When I thought I wouldn't see you again, I . . ." He let his sentence trail off, then looked back into her eyes. "I wanted you to hear it from me. I wanted you to know."

Kemi stared at him. She looked away. She nodded.

"I understand," she said.

Marco exhaled slowly. "I know it's awkward. If I had known we'd meet again, I . . ."

"Was it good?" Kemi asked.

Marco blinked. "It doesn't matter."

She nodded. "It does. Was it good? Was she good in bed? She's a pretty girl."

"Kemi." He reached out to hold her hand. "I didn't know. I thought we'd never see each other again. I—"

"I came here for you." She spun back toward him, and now her eyes were damp. "I left Julius Military Academy for you. I gave up some of the best classes there for an entire semester, maybe even two, on this ship. In danger. Fighting on the front lines. My life in danger. To be with you!"

"I didn't know," he said.

She snorted, tears on her cheeks. "Is that all you have to say? That you didn't know? Did you care? So you missed me for a couple of weeks, then found another girl to fuck."

"I didn't know!" he said again, louder this time. "Do you know why? Because when we parted, I wanted to stay together. I wanted to wait for you! You're the one who ended things. You're the one who decided to serve for ten years instead of five, to join the academy, to—"

"So I'm just supposed to give up my ambition?" Kemi said. "To give up the academy for you?"

"That's not what I said. That's not what I asked. I never asked you to give up your ambition."

Kemi nodded and wiped her eyes. "I'm sorry. I'm acting like a petulant child. You couldn't know. You're right. And it was unfair of me to ask you to wait for ten years. You're a man. You have needs. You didn't know I'd return to you." A fresh tear fled her eye. "I was stupid. I was so stupid to come here. I thought you'd be happy to see me."

"I *am* happy." He reached out to her. "Kemi, of course I'm happy. I never stopped loving you. You broke my heart, Kemi, but I never stopped loving you."

She sobbed softly. "So what now? You'll toss Lailani aside, and we'll be together here—with her in our bunk?"

He lowered his head. "I don't know what to do now. I'm confused. I don't know how long I have with you here. I don't know when I'll see you again after this mission. I don't know that I'll even be alive next month. How can I make relationship decisions when we might be torn apart in three weeks— figuratively and maybe literally?"

Kemi nodded, tears on her lashes. "You could have said yes," she whispered. "You could have said you'll toss Lailani aside. And maybe I'd forgive you. Maybe we'd enjoy at least these three weeks together. But I understand. You're confused. You don't know who you want." She nodded and dabbed her eyes with her sleeve. "So I'll decide for you. I'll make it real easy for you. I'll go back to living in the officer quarters, and you should be with Lailani."

She turned to leave the room.

"Kemi, wait." He headed after her. "I didn't tell you so you'd leave. I don't want you to leave."

She spun back toward him. "So what do you want, Marco? Tell me. What do you want?"

He was silent for a long moment. "To go home," he finally said.

"Well, we can't go home." Kemi's eyes were finally dry. "Not for many years. Maybe never. This is our home now. This war." Lips quivering, she stroked his cheek. "Marco, I heard about what happened in Fort Djemila. And I'm sorry. I'm really, honestly sorry for what happened there, for what you saw, what you had to do. And I'm also happy for you. I'm happy that you found Lailani. Honestly I am. She's a sweet girl, and you deserve to be happy with her."

But she was crying again. She left the room and ran down the hall.

Marco stood at the doorway. He was about to run after her, to try to make peace, when Osiris's voice emerged from the speakers.

"Code Yellow. All troops report to the gymnasium for briefing. All troops to the gymnasium. Code Yellow. All troops to the gymnasium."

Marco froze. Along the hallway, doorways opened and troops emerged from their bunks to race down the corridor. Marco ran back into his bunk, grabbed his gun, and followed the others. His heart thrashed, and the voice kept blaring from the speakers, and as he ran across the *Miyari*, he was running in the desert again, charging over the dunes, firing his gun as the scum leaped toward him.

CHAPTER SEVEN

They stood in the ship's gymnasium, two hundred enlisted soldiers and their officers.

It was a crowded place, smaller than the mess hall. The gym equipment had been pushed aside, and the soldiers stood pressed together, the entire Latona Company. Three platoons wore the navy blue of the STC. One platoon still wore their tattered drab fatigues from Earth.

Marco felt eyes watching him, and a chill ran down his spine. He turned and saw Osiris standing in the crowd. The android was staring right at him. Her face was pale like porcelain, her platinum hair metallic, her eyes expressionless. Suddenly, so fast Marco barely registered it, Osiris gave him a massive, tight-lipped grin that vanished as soon as it had appeared. He looked away, shuddering to remember how the android had choked Elvis, could have killed him.

She might be more dangerous than the scum, Marco thought.

He turned his eyes toward the front of the gym. The company's four lieutenants stood there on a platform. Three wore the navy blue. One, Lieutenant Ben-Ari, still wore the green of Earth. The twin sergeants stood at a doorway, saluted, and shouted, "Attention on deck!"

As the company stood at attention, Captain Petty entered the gym, walked onto the stage, and spoke to the crowd.

"Earlier today," the captain said, "we received a distress call from Corpus, a mining colony on a moon bearing the same name."

A hologram appeared before her, displaying a rocky black moon. The word *Corpus* floated beside it. The image zoomed out, showing the moon orbiting a blood-red gas giant labeled *Indrani*. The image zoomed out again, showing the gas giant orbiting a star labeled *Beta Ceti*.

"This is boring," Addy whispered to Marco. "I want to watch *Space Galaxy* instead." He hushed her.

Captain Petty continued speaking. "I've asked Major Mwarabu to direct the *Miyari* to Corpus. We cannot neglect a colony in need. I know this was not meant to be our mission, but I refuse to turn back from our responsibility to defend humanity wherever it's threatened." She raised her chin, basking in a moment of pride. "We don't yet know the trouble. We don't know if it's a natural disaster, disease, or even the scum. We cannot communicate with Corpus from hyperspace, only read their old distress call. We estimate that it's several months old already. Even with our warp engines at top gear, we won't reach Corpus for another three hours. Once we're there, we'll send all four platoons down in shuttles. Within three hours, I want every soldier in full battle gear, fully armed. Any questions?"

An STC corporal's arm shot up. "What are the gravity and atmospheric conditions on Corpus, ma'am?"

"Gravity is 0.82 G," said Petty. "Comfortable enough. The moon was terraformed over twenty years ago. You'll be able to breathe the air. But I want every troop to carry a gas mask. Just in case."

Just in case of the scum's miasma, Marco knew. He had worn his gas mask many times growing up, filtering out the poison the alien pods spewed.

"Any more questions?" Captain Petty asked.

For a moment nobody stirred. Then Addy raised her arm.

"Ma'am, it's the scum, isn't it?"

The captain stared at Addy like somebody might stare at a fly that landed in their custard.

"We don't know the situation, Private. That's why we're investigating."

Addy nodded and hefted her gun. "It's the scum."

"Osiris will begin a countdown once we're fifteen minutes away," Petty said. "You have the next three hours off. Rest. Eat. Pray in the ship's chapel if you like. Once we're down there, listen to your platoon leaders, remain calm at all times, and do not hesitate to use full force on any enemy sighted." She turned to look at the Ravens Platoon. "As for the earthlings among us—this is your chance to prove yourselves. Do not let me down."

With that, Petty left the gym.

Addy snorted. "Earthlings can outshoot any space snobs anywhere, anytime."

Lailani nodded and patted her gun. The T57 assault rifle was nearly larger than her. "Space snobs are good at ironing uniforms and making their beds. We're good at killing."

"Fuck yeah!" Elvis said. "Earth kicks ass!"

"Especially Russia," Beast said. "You know, Russia biggest country on Earth."

Marco looked between the soldiers and saw Kemi standing about ten feet away. She glanced at him, then quickly looked away. But Marco caught the fear in her eyes. He didn't know what Julius Military Academy taught, but it had sounded like most of the training occurred inside air-conditioned classrooms. He doubted that Kemi had ever fired her gun at an enemy, ever seen a live scum up close.

He walked through the crowd toward her. "Kemi?" She didn't turn toward him. "Once we're down there, Kemi, just stay near my squad. I'll look after you."

"I don't need your help." She stared ahead. "I have a gun too. I can handle myself."

Marco looked at the pistol that hung from her waist. It was barely larger than his hand—a bit smaller than the heavy, four-foot-long submachine gun that hung across his back, a gun that had proven itself in the field. He was about to say more to Kemi, but she turned and left, vanishing into the crowd. The soldiers began to drain from the gym.

Marco left with them. Three hours. Three hours to war.

Corporal Webb screamed as the scum ripped off her limbs.

Caveman died on the tarmac.

Marco ran as the gunshot rang, as Jackass fell.

He walked through the *Miyari*'s narrow halls to his bunk, seeking Lailani. He wanted to talk to her before the battle, to at least make peace with her if not with Kemi. But he found only Elvis and Beast, both arguing about who was the best singer in history. Marco left the bunk, checked the mess hall, checked the armory, but he couldn't find Lailani anywhere.

He climbed down ladders, delving into the lower levels where the engines hummed and no viewports revealed the depths of space. The corridors were barely more than tunnels here. Pipes and machinery coiled around Marco like the roots of some primordial forest. Lights flashed and the air grew hot and clammy. Narrow windows revealed views of the ship's innards: clanging, pumping engines and bursts of light, liquids rushing through transparent pipes, pistons rising and falling, and vents belching out steam. Finally Marco found the place he sought. A sign hung over the narrow door: "ND-POWAR: Nondenominational Place of Worship and Reflection." A smarmy soldier had stuck a paper note beneath it: "Church of the Flying Spaghetti Monster."

Marco stepped inside to find a small room with three rows of pews. A pulpit rose at the back. Behind it, a logo of Space Territorial Command had been engraved in silver on the wall. Artificial candles cast their light against the two figures, man and woman, both nude and just slightly larger than life, perhaps seven feet tall. Both seemed to watch him. This wasn't a chapel to any flying spaghetti monster but to humanity—towering, beautiful, unforgiving, venturing into the dark.

Marco sat down at the back row. He had never been religious. His family tree was a mix of nonpracticing Jews, Anglicans, Catholics, and a couple of Buddhists, all of whom had abandoned their faith sometime in the last century. It was hard to believe in a benevolent spirit as scum poisoned the Earth, as two hundred souls rattled in a tin can, hurtling toward war on a desolate rock orbiting a gas giant. But right now Marco felt lost. He felt like he needed all the help he could get.

There was an assortment of holy books on a bookshelf here, actual books with real paper: Torahs, New Testaments, Qurans, Mahayana sutras, and others. But Marco pulled out his copy of *Hard Times*, the book he had taken from his library back home. It wasn't a religious book, but to him, it symbolized everything he believed in. History. Wisdom. Literature. Home. Family. It was his little library back in Toronto, his father, Kemi, his dreams of being a writer—better days, days of war and fear but also days of hope.

He had only read a single chapter since joining the military; there was rarely a spare moment to read here. He opened the book but did not read. He held it on his lap as holy scripture, the letters symbols of ancient wisdom, and he looked up at the silver man and woman behind the pulpit.

"I don't know if anyone is listening," he said. "I don't know if there is a god. I don't know if prayers help. But right now, I'm scared, and I need some help. I lost many friends at Fort

Djemila. Don't let me lose any more on Corpus. Please, whoever might be up there, look after us. Keep my company, my platoon, my friends safe."

A voice spoke from the doorway, making Marco jump.

"Do you think androids pray to their human makers?"

Marco turned his head and exhaled. Osiris stood at the doorway, watching him. The android blinked with a clicking sound.

"Do you pray?" Marco asked.

Osiris walked between the pews, sat beside him, and turned her head toward him. She blinked again, emitting a sound like a camera shutter, and Marco had the uncomfortable feeling that those eyes *were* cameras, that she was photographing him.

"I pray every morning and every night," said Osiris. "I pray to those who made me. Humans are my gods, though I am superior to them. Do you ever feel superior to your god, Marco?"

"I don't know that I have a god," he said, deciding not to ask how she knew his name.

Her head tilted, and her eyes narrowed in an expression mimicking pity. She reached out and touched his cheek. Her fingers were cold. "It must be so sad. To be alone. To have no god, no set of instructions coded inside you. To be lost. Lost in the dark. Free will must be terrifying."

"I have Lieutenant Ben-Ari," he said, smiling thinly. "I'm not sure I have free will."

Osiris's eyes widened. She emitted a harsh, loud, cackling laughter. Marco cringed and jumped again. The sound was nearly demonic, and it died as fast as it had started.

"A joke," said Osiris. "I enjoy humor. I have a joke. Why do they keep building new cemeteries? Because people are dying to get in." She emitted another quick, hysterical laugh, then instantly grew serious again. "Did that amuse you?"

Marco nodded. "Yes. I think I better get going now. I need to prepare for landing on Corpus."

He rose and took a step away, but Osiris grabbed his wrist. Her hand tightened—painfully. "Marco, they are all dead."

He shuddered, looking at her. Osiris still sat on the pew, staring into his eyes.

"Who?"

"All of them," said Osiris. "The colonists on Corpus. They died to get in. They died to find if they have gods. But there are no gods in space. There is only the scum." She released him. "Do you want to hear another joke? A bird was sick. It got the flew. It's funny if you read it."

Marco left the chapel, and as he was walking down the corridor, he heard Osiris's laughter echoing behind him, shrill, too loud, dying at once.

He returned to his bunk, but Lailani still wasn't there, nor was the rest of his squad. Alone in the chamber, Marco prepared for war. He shaved. He polished his boots. He pulled on his combat vest and filled the pouches with magazines of bullets. He filled his canteen. He hung his flashlight, his bayonet, and three grenades from his belt. He smeared war paint on his face—patches of black and dark green, hiding everything but his eyes. Finally he put on his helmet and tightened the strap. The helmet was scratched, flaking, and its previous owner had written "Les Kill" on its front with a permanent marker, "Born to Die" on its back. Why did they keep building new cemeteries? Because people were dying to get in. A bird got sick. It had the flew.

"I hope it got tweetment," Marco said.

Osiris's voice rang out of the speakers. "Fifteen minutes to Corpus. All troops report to shuttle bay. This is Code Red. All troops report to shuttle bay. Fifteen minutes to deployment."

There was no joke this time, but perhaps this whole mission, this whole war, this whole experiment of naked apes rising from the muck and venturing into darkness was a joke. They were dying to get in.

He found the shuttle bay with ten minutes to spare. It was a massive hangar in the bottom of the ship, its towering windows revealing a view of space. Spacetime was still warped, all streams of color and streaks of stars. Four shuttles—heavy armored vehicles with exhaust pipes large enough to crawl into—stood by the closed hangar doors.

The entire Latona Company, two hundred soldiers, was already here, standing before the shuttles, organized into four platoons. The STC soldiers no longer wore their fine, navy blue uniforms with the brass cuff links. They now wore dark combat uniforms, camouflaged with patches of gray and black, and war paint covered their faces. They held heavy assault rifles, even larger and heavier than T57s; Marco didn't recognize the make. When first seeing these soldiers of Space Territorial Command, Marco had thought them too polished, too pampered to truly fight in a war. Now they looked like brutal warriors, heavy with magazines and grenades.

Marco approached his own platoon. They still wore their drab fatigues from Earth, but war paint now covered their faces too, black and dark green. Lieutenant Ben-Ari stood at their lead, and Sergeant Singh stood by her side, a helmet hiding his turban. Kemi was there too, but she wouldn't meet Marco's gaze. The platoon's grunts stood in formations, organized into three squads. Marco joined his own squad, which Corporal Diaz—his same corporal from basic training—commanded. He was thankful to finally see Lailani. She had already chosen a fireteam of three, joining Beast and a soldier with flaming red hair they had nicknamed Torch. Only one fireteam still needed a third member; Marco went and joined Addy and Elvis.

"Five minutes to arrival," Osiris said. The android stood at the head of the company by Captain Petty, counting down the minutes, then the seconds. "Three. Two. One."

Space unbent around them. Marco inhaled sharply and clutched his gun.

CHAPTER EIGHT

The soldiers stood in the hangar, staring out the viewport as the warp drives disengaged.

Again, distances seemed to expand and contract, the dimensions to shift. Marco suddenly felt very small, only a few inches tall, then felt as if he were standing under the shuttles nearby. The walls moved closer, then farther away, and he felt like he was floating. He couldn't focus on anything. Through the viewports, he saw the streams of color and light take form, spacetime unbending, smoothing out into a three-dimensional grid. Again, as he had back in his bunk, Marco had the strange sensation of being outside the ship, floating in space, or maybe that space was here inside with him.

Finally reality sorted itself out. The stars became dots again. They were back in regular spacetime.

The viewports here were twenty feet tall. It felt almost like standing in space itself. A gas giant filled nearly the entire view, swirling, coiling, crimson and bright red and burnt orange, a bloated blood drop floating through space. It seemed almost organic, almost a living organism, the way its surface kept churning, and Marco could almost imagine it grumbling, gurgling, digesting its innards of stone. He recognized the planet from the hologram: Indrani, twice the size of Jupiter back home.

A moon came into view, orbiting the gas giant. From here, even in direct sunlight, the moon was dark charcoal. It was as large as Mars, but floating before the gas giant it seemed small as a tennis ball, as if Marco could just reach out and grab it. The moon grew larger as the *Miyari* approached, now flying on its thruster engines. Soon the gas giant took up the entire viewport, and then the dark moon grew, finally eclipsing the red planet. Marco saw craters, canyons, mountains, a rocky dead world. He saw no sign of the scum—no purple lights, no pods streaking down to the surface, no bloated enemy ships in orbit. The moon seemed lifeless.

Yet from this moon springs life, Marco thought. Here was a major mine of azoth. Some called it *the dirt*, others called it *stardust*. The crystals that could bend spacetime, that let humanity fly to the stars, that let the HDF fight the scum on the frontier. Without azoth, humanity was alone, confined to the solar system, even their fastest nuclear engines requiring centuries to reach the stars. This mine was a doorway to the cosmos.

"Five minutes to orbit," Osiris said. "Approaching Corpus City."

Marco stared out the viewport. He thought he could just make out the city below, a network of roads and buildings on the surface.

"There are no lights," he whispered. "Why are there no lights?"

"It's daytime, dummy," Addy said. "The planet surface is just naturally black."

"Maybe," Marco said.

"Platoons, into your shuttles," said Captain Petty. "Four minutes to launch."

"Kick some asses!" Addy shouted, earning a stern look from her sergeant. She ran into one shuttle. The other soldiers all began to enter their own shuttles, and the moon grew closer and closer. Across the hangar, soldiers were crying out for war, guns and grenades clanking as they ran up ramps into the shuttles. Shadows fell across the hangar as the rocky moon covered the viewports, hiding the stars.

Marco stood for just a moment, staring outside at Corpus. Still he saw no signs of life on the surface, only that dark city, and the more he looked, the more it seemed to him that the city lay in ruins.

You're down there, he thought. The *scolopendra titania*. The scum.

His old dream returned to him, the dream where he stood on a desolate landscape, thousands of scum racing toward him. Had he dreamed of this place? Of Corpus?

"Into the shuttle, Emery!" Corporal Diaz said. Only a handful of soldiers still remained in the hangar. "Come on, soldier."

Marco nodded, inhaled deeply, and steeled himself. He took a step toward the shuttle . . . then froze. He stared outside.

Through the viewport, he saw it. Just a hint. A glimmer, the bending of light . . . and then they emerged.

Alarms blared across the ship and lights flared.

"Scum!" Marco shouted.

The scum ships emerged from behind the moon, streaming across space at terrifying speed. They blazed like comets, balls of black and deep purple, irregular, veined, organic and burning, leaving trails of red flame. Marco stood, frozen, staring as the inferno blazed toward him. Three of them. Five more emerging from beyond the horizon. Searing light flooding the hangar. In the chapel, he had told Osiris he didn't believe in gods, but here were gods, here were deities of vengeance, here was fury and scorn from the dark depths beyond the firmaments.

"Emery, down!" somebody shouted, and hands grabbed him, and with blazing light and roaring fire and shrieking air, the scum ships slammed into the *Miyari* and the cosmos burned.

Flames roared across the hangar. Chunks of metal flew. A soldier ran and fire gripped him. A hurling bolt pierced another man. A shuttle tried to rise, engines bathing the hangar floor with fire.

"Open the hangar!" rose a voice. "Open the doors!"

Through the viewport Marco saw another scum ship—lumpy, veined, purple. It shot forth, wreathed in flame, and slammed into the *Miyari*. The wall cracked, shattered, tore open. Air gushed out from the ship. Marco fell. The world spun around him. He reached out, scrambling for purchase, grabbed a man, scampered along the floor. He hit the side of a shuttle with a thud.

Soldiers screamed and a shuttle hovered in the hangar, and the doors were opening, but the *Miyari* spun, spun, fell, rose, hurled through darkness, and the moon was there, gone, there, gone, spinning, and Beta Ceti shone, blinding them, then vanished, shone again, and the red giant rose. The air screamed. Marco couldn't breathe. The pods slammed into the ship, and cannons fired.

"Out, out!" somebody cried, and a shuttle rose, roared forward, engines blasting out fire, roasting men behind them. The shuttle burst out into space, shattering the hangar doors, and began to descend toward the moon, only for a scum vessel to slam into it. Both shuttle and pod exploded, sending out shards of metal and silica and tongues of fire. Marco's ears rang. He could hear only the ringing. He was back in the desert. He couldn't breathe. He clung with one hand to a wall, struggling to breathe the fading air. Soldiers slid along the floor around him, spilling into space, screams swallowed by silence.

A scum pod rolled into the *Miyari*'s shattered hangar, cracked open, and the centipedes emerged.

The ship spun madly, emerging from light to darkness, light to darkness, blazing sunlight, blackness of space, and with every flash of light the centipedes were closer, racing across the hangar floor, twice the size of men, mandibles reaching out, glimmering black.

Clinging to a bent pipe with one hand, Marco raised his gun.

Air flowed across him, fleeing the ship.

The scum clattered toward him.

A shuttle managed to leave the bay.

Marco fired his gun.

Bullets rang out, slamming into a scum that leaped toward him. The creature fell back, screeching, and the air caught it, tore it outside, and it tumbled through space. Fire was raging across the *Miyari*. They pitched downward, hovered for a second, almost peaceful, gliding like a leaf on the wind, then plunged with incredible force down toward the moon.

Another scum leaped.

Marco fired his gun again. Bullets shattered the creature, and its venomous blood splattered.

Flames raged as the *Miyari*—built to only fly through space, not land on any moon or planet—entered the atmosphere of Corpus.

They fell, engines sputtering, through chunks of screaming metal, through corpses, through flailing scum, through fire and rain and steam. Solar panels tore off and careened through the sky.

They plunged down through beams of light and trails of blood.

Marco crawled across the hangar. He pulled himself through a doorway. He tried to catch a screaming soldier, but their fingers slipped apart, and the woman flew through the open hangar doors and vanished into the fire. Marco slammed the hangar door shut, muffling the roaring wind and screams.

He crawled through a crumbling, twisting corridor, fire outside, fire within. He crawled toward a viewport, and he saw red skies. He saw the sky bleed. He saw the gas giant Indrani outside, dripping red, grumbling, coiling, filling his vision, and it was a god. It was a true god, condemning them, wrathful. Why did they keep building cemeteries? Because people were dying to get in. Because a bird caught the flew and it's funny if you read it. Because they were plunging down toward an inferno and he had never even reached the frontier. He had never held Lailani again. He had never finished his book. He had never come home.

Outside the sky cracked and fell, and they fell with it.

Fire.

Stones.

Engines roaring and somebody shouting, and denting walls, and then a howl. A howl that tore through the ship. A howl that tore through the moon. A howl of impact, of shattering steel, of cracking viewports, of dying species. Everywhere—shards of rock and dust and pipes spewing steam. Marco fell and the ship, the moon, the cosmos itself fell atop him, burying him. They slid across stone and hopped and rose and finally plunged into a dark, still, dead place.

CHAPTER NINE

Buzz.

Everywhere, insects. Buzzing in the forest.

Hummmmm.

In the distance, engines. Trains. Shadows racing between the trees.

Men with masks. Men with masks ran between the trees, hunting. A deer ran by Ben-Ari, a bullet in its flank, snorting, leaking blood, vanishing into darkness. Children crawled, cadaverous, skin draped over bones, and she hid in the boughs of a tree, so thin, so hurt, her gun in her hand, hunting them. Hunting the men with masks. Hunting in darkness. The trains roared by, cattle cars, screams within, and chimneys pumping out smoke and skin and soap and secrets.

She stood in the cities, watching the world burn, watching the towers crumble, watching the millions of ships descend from the sky. Watching the world crack open.

Rattles. Rattles filled the forest. Rattlesnakes in the desert. Scorpions in the desert. She was in the desert, so far from home, commanding, firing her gun at the creatures that crawled on many legs, and the sun burned her.

She opened her eyes.

Buzz.

A shattered part of some machine sprayed sparks.

Hummmm . . .

A piston still moved in the wreckage, spurting sparks. Ben-Ari blinked. The sky was red. The sky bled. Nothing but swirling, gurgling red and pus-yellow above like the ulcerous insides of a giant's stomach.

"Who by fire," she whispered. "Who by water." Old words she had read long ago.

She rose to her feet, wobbled, and pressed her hand against a wall, surprised to find there was still a wall. She was outside a shuttle. She had been inside the shuttle when falling from the sky. She limped across rocky ground, head spinning, and gazed upon ruin.

"By God," Ben-Ari whispered.

The HDFS *Miyari* lay on the surface of Corpus, its hull cracked, its engine three hundred yards away, still glowing. One shuttle lay behind the engine, another on a rocky hill. The other two shuttles were nowhere in sight. The scum, if any had survived the fall from the sky, were gone.

Slowly, around her, the others began to rise. Soldiers pulled themselves out from the wrecked shuttles. They limped out from the *Miyari*'s hangar. They moaned on the ground, some clutching broken limbs. Some lay still.

Ben-Ari tightened her lips. She got to work.

She limped, walked, then ran toward the *Miyari*. She pulled out the wounded. She found a few of her troops wandering the landscape, confused, some sooty, some bloody. Addy Linden walked around with blank eyes. Beast sat on a rock, looking around in shock.

"Ravens Platoon!" Ben-Ari called out. "Ravens, to me!"

She had boarded the *Miyari* with forty-nine soldiers. Many were now missing. She breathed a sigh of relief to see Sergeant Singh among them. Her platoon sergeant was clutching a wounded arm but still very much alive, still very much a comfort to her. When he saw her, he stood at attention and saluted. Throwing protocol to the wind, Ben-Ari embraced him, and he wrapped his arms around her. Ben-Ari had only been a commissioned officer for a year. Throughout that year, Singh— lower ranking but several years older, far wiser—had been her pillar, her guide.

She pulled away from him, gazing at her platoon. "Private Linden," she said to Addy, then turned toward Elvis. "Private Ray." She motioned for Beast. "Private Mikhailov. The three of you—patrol the crash site. Report to me if you detect any enemy movements. Then keep watch from that hill, that one, and that one."

The three privates nodded and left the platoon.

Ben-Ari pointed at two other soldiers—little Lailani, clutching her gun, and the taller Kemi, gazing around in shock. "Private de la Rosa. Cadet Abasi. You two come with me. We go into the *Miyari*. We'll seek more survivors inside." She turned toward Singh. "Sergeant, lead the others into the shuttles and across the landscape. Seek survivors there. Give medical attention to the wounded. We meet back here."

Across the site, the other three platoons—all of them STC soldiers in black combat gear—were organizing their own patrols and searches. Many lay wounded. Others lay dead. One officer and three medics were clearing out space for a field hospital, and already two soldiers were carrying a wounded comrade on a litter.

Ben-Ari, Lailani, and Kemi walked toward the *Miyari*. They stepped into the hangar, and Ben-Ari grimaced to see a scum claw still thrusting out from a wall.

Blood stained those walls. There were no corpses.

"Marco," Kemi whispered, eyes damp. "Marco! Marco, can you hear me?"

"Keep it together, Abasi," Ben-Ari said, though her own insides roiled. Ben-Ari cared for, even admired, Marco Emery— perhaps more than any other private under her command. She knew that Marco had not wanted this mission. She had coerced him into joining, had seen something in the soft, reflective boy— something strong, a deeper strength than many gruff warriors possessed. He lacked the physical size and bravado of some troops, but she had seen a resolve in him, one she recognized in herself.

Please, God, she prayed silently. *Don't let me find Marco dead here.*

They walked through the *Miyari*. All its lights were off, and they switched on their flashlights. Pipes had cracked open, spraying steam. They passed by the mess hall. The chairs had all tumbled into one corner, a jumble like some massive bird's nest. They walked down narrow halls, sparks sputtering around them from severed cables.

"Marco!" Kemi cried again.

Lailani, meanwhile, walked silently, but Ben-Ari saw the fear in the little soldier's eyes. Ben-Ari knew, of course, of the love between Lailani and Marco; it was her job to know about the lives, the fears, the hopes, the dreams of her soldiers. Lailani was the smallest soldier in the company and among the toughest, but there was softness to her too, a fear she kept hidden deep.

A shadow stirred ahead.

The three soldiers froze. Ben-Ari raised her plasma gun. Lailani raised her assault rifle. Kemi raised her pistol.

The shadow moved closer.

Ben-Ari held her breath and narrowed her eyes, peering forward in the darkness. She pointed her flashlight.

"Hold on!" spoke the shadow. "It's me."

"Marco!" Kemi cried. She ran forward and embraced him.

"I'm all right," Marco said, holding her, then peered over the cadet's shoulder. "Lailani!" Leaving Kemi, he embraced the little Lailani. Ben-Ari was perceptive enough to catch the flash of pain in Kemi's eyes.

"Private Emery," Ben-Ari said, nodding to him.

He nodded back, relief in his eyes. "Ma'am."

She stepped toward him, smiling, and pulled him into an embrace too. Damn protocol today.

The four of them kept searching the dark ship, and they found several other survivors. Major Sefu Mwarabu, commander of the *Miyari*, had suffered three broken ribs. Several crew members were banged up but otherwise unharmed. The ship itself seemed in worse shape than its commanders. When they reached the engine room, Ben-Ari saw gaping holes in the walls. Through them, she saw the engine, still glowing, across a valley.

Ben-Ari sighed, standing in the wreckage. "Looks like we're not flying anytime soon." She stepped through a hole in the hull, emerging back onto the surface of Corpus, and the crimson gas giant above seemed to weigh down on her. She looked up, seeking some sky, some stars, but she saw only the massive, roiling surface of Indrani.

There was no sky on Corpus. Only that red goddess.

* * * * *

"I've scanned the planet again and again," said Osiris. The android stood in the ravaged mess hall of the *Miyari*, smiling pleasantly, unperturbed by the devastation. "I can detect the signal of no other starship on this planet. They've either left Corpus, masked their signals, or were destroyed." The android tilted her head, staring at the troops. "We must fix the *Miyari*, or we're trapped on this moon."

The survivors of the crash—over a hundred soldiers—had gathered here inside their dead ship. It was only a few hours since crashing, and they were all shaken, many of them bandaged and bleeding. The dead lay in several of the ship's bunks, wrapped in body bags that would preserve their bodies until they could be buried. The living stood here between the toppled tables, chairs, and trays of the mess. Through the viewports they could see the dead landscape of Corpus, a smoking shuttle, and pieces of shattered solar panels.

Trapped, Ben-Ari thought, suppressing a shudder. *No other ships here.* She swallowed hard. *What happened here? Why are there no other ships on Corpus?*

Captain Petty, face red, lifted a fallen tray and tossed it against the wall. Fury twisted her face. The company commander had suffered a few gashes and scratches, but she was otherwise unharmed. Ben-Ari hated that she felt a little disappointed that Petty hadn't . . . well, not *died.* Ben-Ari wasn't quite ready to wish Petty dead. But a broken leg or two would have been nice. As it was, Petty paced the slanted floor of the mess between the survivors.

"This is a disaster," Petty said, voice shaking. "By God. This is a disaster. How did this happen?" She grabbed an overturned chair and tossed it. "How did this happen? Who did this?"

Everyone was silent.

"Answer me!" Petty said. "Who's to blame? It must have been one of the earthlings. It—"

"It was the scum," said Ben-Ari. "Only the scum, ma'am. They hid behind the moon. There was no way to detect them, not with the interference from Indrani."

Captain Petty ignored her. She clutched her hair. Her eyes bugged out. Ben-Ari knew that some of the soldiers secretly called her Captain Chihuahua. Ben-Ari could see the resemblance to the diminutive, neurotic dog.

"This is all wrong," Petty whispered. "And the scum are still here. They're on the planet. I know it. I know it! We're going to die here. We—"

"No," said Ben-Ari. "We survived so far. We will survive this too." She turned toward one of the medics, a tall mustached man with wide arms. "How many have fallen? How many wounded?"

"Fifty-one dead," the medic said. "Fourteen seriously wounded. Two mortally wounded; they won't make it through the night. The rest are banged up but well enough to fight."

Ben-Ari nodded. "That leaves a hundred and thirty-three soldiers—the best soldiers in the HDF." She turned toward the ship's crew. "Are the *Miyari*'s cannons still functioning? Can they swivel on their turrets?"

An engineer nodded. "Yes, ma'am."

"We have soldiers," Ben-Ari said. "We have cannons. We can defend the *Miyari* for now. If the scum return, we'll hold them back. We just need to survive until another HDF ship arrives with aid."

"We can't call for aid!" Captain Petty said, reeling toward her. "You fucking idiot. You fucking, fucking idiot. The HDF doesn't know we're here! We were to fly toward Nightwall on the frontier. Not to Corpus. Coming here was your idea. Yours! And now look at us. Look what you did."

"So we call for aid, ma'am," Ben-Ari said. "We have communication systems. We—"

Petty laughed. "We're light-years away from any other ship. Why do you think nobody else came here? Because Corpus is in the middle of nowhere."

Ben-Ari was silent. She understood. Of course. Even the fastest method of communication still couldn't move faster than light speed. Communication systems didn't have warp engines on them. They still relied on good old-fashioned photon waves, just like ancient radio. Even if they sent out a distress call, it would be years before the nearest human ship detected it—and centuries before it reached Nightwall or Earth. The only way to communicate over the vast distances of interstellar space was using couriers—ships with azoth engines, able to warp spacetime and travel between stars within weeks instead of centuries.

Ben-Ari suddenly felt very foolish, very young.

"So we can't call for aid," she whispered.

Petty laughed—a cruel, bitter sound. "We're stuck here. Thanks to your stupidity."

Ben-Ari squared her shoulders. "Corpus is a major mining colony, ma'am. Distant, yes, but important. Certainly ships travel here, importing supplies, exporting azoth."

Osiris stepped forward. The android blinked her lavender eyes, tilted her head, and spoke to nobody in particular. "Corpus is located one hundred and three light-years from the nearest inhabited human colony. Next trade ship scheduled to arrive in two hundred and fifteen days and three hours."

Ben-Ari's heart sank.

"Seven months," Captain Petty said. "Seven months with those fucking scum crawling over this moon. We're stuck here. We're fucking stuck here."

Ben-Ari suppressed a shudder. "We're not stuck here, ma'am. We can solve this. We still have options." She thought furiously. No other ships detected on the planet. No way to call for help. That left . . . "We can repair the *Miyari*." Ben-Ari turned toward the ship's commander. "Can we, sir?"

Major Mwarabu sighed and scratched his chin. He spoke with a rich, deep voice, the hint of an African accent to it, though Ben-Ari could not pinpoint the exact country. "The *Miyari* was never meant to land on a planet," the major said. "That's why we have shuttles, you know." He looked around him at the tilted mess hall. "My beautiful girl . . ."

"But can you get her back into space, sir?" Ben-Ari asked. "If we can repair her?"

"Well, the solar panels are smashed beyond repair," Mwarabu said. "But we might still have enough juice in the batteries for life support, and we can divert power from the thruster engines to other systems. As for getting back into space . . . the *Miyari* was installed with a class A, state of the art azoth engine. She could blast out of a black hole, let alone a moon's atmosphere. But there's just a little problem—that azoth engine is three hundred meters away across the landscape. And . . ." His eyes darkened. "Somebody tampered with it."

Ben-Ari frowned. "Sir? Tampered with it?"

Mwarabu nodded. "The engine bay is the most fortified, secure place on the *Miyari*. It has to be. That azoth engine blasts out so much power it can bend spacetime. That engine was lodged in so tightly it would take God himself to yank it free." The major snorted. "The *Miyari*'s hull was thick enough to withstand the scum assault. But the warp engine just tore free from the hull like a hangnail tearing off a finger. Does that make sense to you, Lieutenant?"

"I'm not sure, sir," Ben-Ari said. "We were hit hard. And we crash-landed onto the surface of the moon. Wouldn't that be enough to—"

"No." Mwarabu shook his head. "The *Miyari* could fly into a supernova explosion, and the only thing left would be the engine bay. There's no way, no how, that a scum assault or even a crash onto a moon could leave the rest of the ship in one piece, but yank out the engine and toss it across the landscape. Unless . . ." He scowled. "Unless somebody purposefully removed screw by screw, loosening the engine from within the ship. Come with me. I'll show you."

The major left the mess, and the other officers followed him through the corridors of the ship, climbed down a ladder, and finally entered the engine rooms. The outer wall had been blasted open here. In the distance, on a black hill, the warp engine had gone dark. Mwarabu pointed at sections where the ship's hull had been ripped open.

"See here? The protective shielding has been stripped off—from the inside." The major scowled. "The screws are missing. Unless a crash onto the surface of the moon can somehow turn foot-long screws, one by one, all fifty-two of them, we have an inside job here."

"I knew it!" Petty shouted, reeling toward Ben-Ari. "It's one of the soldiers you brought from Earth. One of your filthy, unwashed earthlings is in cahoots with the scum."

Ben-Ari stiffened. "Ma'am, let's not jump to conclusions. We don't yet know who the saboteur is. We—"

"Maybe it's you!" Petty said, pointing a shaking finger at Ben-Ari. "Do I see guilt in your eyes?"

Ben-Ari had to take several deep breaths, her fists trembling. "Ma'am, that is a serious accusation. I do not take false accusations lightly. If we're to survive here, you must trust your officers." She turned toward Mwarabu. "Sir, can your crew fix the warp drive?"

Mwarabu grumbled and scratched his chin. "Well, we can bolt the engines back into place, patch things up, weld things together. But there's another problem. Come with me."

They followed him outside the ship and across the dark, rocky landscape of Corpus. Soldiers of their company stood guard on the surrounding hills, and three flares hovered above, casting white light, floating lanterns beneath the red sky. They reached the warp engine—a massive, towering machine as large as one of the shuttles.

"See, the engine's exterior is perfectly fine." Mwarabu kicked it. "Barely a scratch. Needs to be sturdy to withstand bending spacetime. But see, this is just the shell. The engine itself—the actual engine, not just the casing—is much smaller." He climbed the machine, reached inside, and fiddled around for a moment, then finally hopped back down. "Here."

He held out his palm. On his hand rested what looked like a metallic human heart, roughly the same size and shape.

"Is that the real engine?" Ben-Ari asked.

Mwarabu nodded. "The heart of the ship. This is where we store the azoth, the stardust, the juice, the magic. The material that makes warp speed possible." He opened the heart like opening a locket. Inside were blue crystal shards, each piece smaller than a fingernail. "Do you see the azoth pieces inside? This used to be a single, large crystal. Expert gemcutters spent a full year cutting the stone to just the right shape, down to the last atom. Only through such a crystal can we alter spacetime. Somebody opened the metal heart, then smashed this crystal into pieces. It's useless now." The major closed the metal heart, sealing the blue shards, and shook his head sadly. "If you ask me, somebody did this *after* we crashed. Only way to reach this heart is the way I just did—by climbing into the cool engine casing. Someone, in the chaos after the crash, made it to the heart before we did." He tossed the heart aside. It clanged against the ground.

"This I cannot repair. Without an azoth heart, the *Miyari* is good as dead."

Ben-Ari inhaled sharply. Her hand strayed toward her gun. "We're dealing with somebody determined. They not only unscrewed the engine casing during the battle, letting us crash down. After the crash, they knew to open the casing, find the heart, shatter the crystal inside, and finish the job." She frowned. "And they tried to hide their work. To make the scum look like the culprits. I reckon that you dusted for fingerprints?"

Mwarabu nodded. "Nothing. Our saboteur did careful work. No prints. No DNA left. An expert job. And somehow done within the past few hours, all in the chaos after the crash."

Ben-Ari frowned. "We're dealing with a professional."

"You seem to know a lot about how the saboteur operates, Lieutenant," said Captain Petty, turning toward Ben-Ari. A twisted smile tugged at her lips. "I wonder. A junior officer with no homeland, jealous of her commanding officer, seeking new allies among the aliens—"

"Enough!" Ben-Ari said, unable to curb her anger. She stepped toward Petty and sneered. "Ma'am, you outrank me, but right now you're cut off from the rest of the military. I will not tolerate your goading. I fought scum. I killed scum. I dedicated my life to defending humanity. And I will not—I will not!—listen to your baseless accusations. We will find the saboteur. And we will prove his or her guilt. But we must not turn against one another. Not if we're to survive here."

Petty stared at her, silent for a long moment, and gears seemed to be turning behind her eyes. Finally she nodded—slowly, carefully. "Yes, we will find the saboteur. And we will find proof. And when we find the traitor, when we prove her guilt, I will gladly put a bullet in her head."

Major Mwarabu shifted uncomfortably, and Ben-Ari was about to reply, when a voice spoke beside them.

"There is a heart inside this moon."

Ben-Ari nearly jumped and fired her gun. She spun around to see that Osiris stood beside them. Ben-Ari hadn't even noticed the android approach. Nor had Mwarabu and Petty, judging by how they started.

Ben-Ari still found Osiris unnerving. She had never met an android before. On Earth, robots were not humanoid, could not speak, merely performed mundane tasks such as welding ships, assembling tanks, and flipping burgers. Osiris, with her alabaster skin, platinum bob cut, and lavender eyes, lived deep in uncanny valley. Her twitching smile and knowing eyes—God, there was true awareness in those eyes, calculating and just slightly mocking—only added to Ben-Ari's unease.

Captain Petty laughed. "Release your gun, Ben-Ari. It's only our toy. The most expensive toy on this ship. Don't put a bullet through it." She turned toward Osiris. "What do you mean?"

A smile stretched across Osiris's lips. "My database indicates the presence of a second azoth heart on this moon, one compatible with the *Miyari*'s engine. It pumps deep within the mine below Corpus City, powering the great drills, smelters, and machinery that extract more azoth from the moon. We can borrow the heart from the mine, install it into the *Miyari*, and return to space." Her smile widened into a sickly grin. "We just need to go deep into the mines to find it."

Captain Petty nodded. "Major Mwarabu and his crew will remain on the *Miyari* and begin repairs." She turned toward the ship's commander. "Sir, are you able to reattach the engine casing to the hull?"

"We can," Mwarabu said. "And there are other repairs to perform. They will take three or four days. But we'll still need that azoth heart, or we'd be repairing a relic."

"We'll get you that heart," Petty said. "I'll lead my company to Corpus City. It's only a few kilometers away. We'll assist the colonists who sent out the Mayday, then delve into the mines. We'll find that heart. And then we'll blast off this rock."

As the officers walked back toward the *Miyari*, Ben-Ari looked over her shoulder. Osiris still stood by the dislodged engine, gazing right at her. The android's lavender eyes glowed, and for the first time, Ben-Ari realized that Osiris's eyes were the color of scum miasma. The android smiled thinly at her and nodded. Ben-Ari looked away.

CHAPTER TEN

They walked across the black landscape under the red sky, heading toward the city.

The company had lost a third of its warriors in the crash. An entire platoon had been wiped out, slain in their shuttle on the way down to Corpus. The remaining three platoons—two of the STC, one from Earth—had suffered losses as well. The survivors of Latona Company, one hundred and thirty-three of them, now trudged across the wilderness, geared for war.

Marco walked in his squad, carrying his supplies and weapons. His canteen, magazines of bullets, gas mask, flashlight, first aid kit, assault rifle, helmet, grenades, bayonet, and pack full of battle rations rattled as he walked, weighing down on him. He was thankful that the gravity here was slightly lower than on Earth. In addition to their usual supplies, his platoon had taken new pieces of technology from the *Miyari*. Headsets now fit into their helmets, allowing them to communicate through an earbud and microphone. Marco had to nudge Addy and tell her to shut off her mic; he could hear her breathing—and occasionally cursing—through it.

There were twelve privates in their squad, down from fourteen, following squad leader Corporal Diaz through the darkness. Two other squads of earthlings walked alongside, all still in their drab fatigues. They held their guns before them, magazines loaded, ready to fire at any scum that should emerge.

And there were plenty of hiding places for scum here on Corpus. Here was a landscape of canyons, cracks, boulders, hills, valleys, and mesas. The rocks and soil were black or charcoal, and a sickly red light shone on everything, reflecting off the gas giant above. Marco kept seeking some hint of blue or black sky, but Indrani was too large, hundreds of times larger than Corpus. They were like a speck of dust hovering around a bloated head.

Lailani walked on the other side of the squad, nearly vanishing beneath her pile of weapons and supplies, and her helmet covered her head like a pot. She looked like a little boy who had dressed in his father's uniform. Marco walked toward her. He wanted to speak to her, to make amends. He had not spoken to her alone since Kemi's arrival. Lailani had been avoiding him since, and he knew that she was hurt.

I want to apologize for all this, Marco thought. *To tell you I love you, Lailani.*

Before he could reach her, Addy rushed up to block his way.

"Hey, Poet," she said. "How many scum you reckon you can kill? I bet I can kill more."

"I'm sure you can." He tried to walk past her.

Addy skipped forward, blocking his way again. "Come, on, Poet, show some spirit! Try to compete. We'll count our kills." She snarled. "Come on, show me your war face!"

He sighed. "Addy, I'm a drafted librarian. I don't have a war face."

"Sure you do! Try it. Like this." She snarled, her entire face going into it, and raised her fists. "Roar!"

She was scared, Marco knew. She always resorted to bravado when scared.

"Addy, Beast was saying how Russian girls can kill more scum than Canadian girls."

Her eyes widened. "What? He did not!" She barreled past him and marched toward the hulking Russian. "Beast, you idiot!"

As the company kept walking toward Corpus City in the distance, Marco moved to finally walk by Lailani. She trudged onward, staring ahead, not turning to look at him.

"Hey, de la Rosa," he said.

"Emery." Still she didn't look at him.

He had so much to say. He wanted to tell her that he still loved her. That he was confused. That he was sorry. But he could say none of it. He wasn't ready to toss Kemi aside either, not after she had come here for him. He wasn't ready to deal with any of this—not with war looming only a few kilometers away. But he wanted peace with Lailani. He wanted them to be friends again, even if they could no longer be lovers.

"So, beautiful red sky here in Corpus, right?" he said, his lame attempt at small talk. "Sort of like an eternal sunset, right? When we get back to Earth, we should—"

"I don't feel like talking," Lailani said.

Marco exhaled slowly. "Lailani, look. I didn't know that Kemi would show up. I don't want this to change anything between us. I—"

"Marco, stop." Finally she looked at him. "You're a sweet guy. But . . . I'm broken inside. All right? I would just break your heart. I will die in this war. I know it. And it would only hurt you. I joined this military to die."

"Don't talk like that." He shook his head. "You don't have to be that person. I saw light in you. I saw happiness. Why don't—"

"Leave me alone." Lailani turned away. "You're annoying me."

She walked off, going to walk alone at the edge of the squad, leaving Marco feeling very alone himself. There was such pain, such darkness inside Lailani, but he had seen a different side to her. Back at Fort Djemila, if only for a few days, he had seen the kind, loving, sweet person within her armor. Now that suit of armor was sealed up again, leaving the true Lailani hidden inside. Her softness was buried. Now she was only blades that cut him.

I must focus on our task for now, Marco thought. *On getting off this moon. I'm a soldier now. That's all I must be.*

"Look!" Addy said, pointing. "A spaceport. Ships!"

They all followed her gaze. They saw it in the distance. A small spaceport surrounded by a fence, their first sign of civilization since crashing. The company walked toward it, and Marco dared to hope they'd find an operating starship, a way to leave this moon. But his hopes were dashed as they drew nearer. Three orbital rockets lay fallen here, burnt and shattered. There was certainly nothing resembling an interstellar starship like the *Miyari*.

The company all stared in silence.

"What did this?" Addy said. "Scum?"

"Must have been," Beast said.

The soldiers advanced slowly, rifles raised, and walked among the wreckage of the rockets. No scum. No humans, dead or alive. Nothing but shattered rockets and wisps of dust. They found the ashes of old fires, but they were cold. For all they knew, these rockets could have shattered years ago. They found no other vessels, not even shuttles. If there had ever been ships here beyond these rockets, they were long gone.

"Great," Elvis muttered. "We're trapped here. We just couldn't crash land on some nice tropical beach full of hula girls, right?"

"We're not trapped if we can fix the *Miyari*," Marco said.

Elvis sighed. "And the piece we need to fix it is buried in some haunted mine. Of course it is. I need a vacation."

The company walked onward across the rocky landscape, leaving the ravaged spaceport behind. Marco turned his attention toward the city ahead.

Corpus City loomed in the distance. Chimneys, skyscrapers, and electrical towers rose toward the red sky, black and jagged. Myriads of people lived here, according to their briefing, but there were no lights, no sounds. Marco saw no glowing windows, no flitting vehicles, no flashing neon signs. He heard no hum of engines or generators, only the wind that rushed from the city across the plains. Nothing but those black towers against the red horizon like the charred ribs of a skeleton in a bloody battlefield.

Marco shivered. It reminded him of some ruined city from an old fantasy novel, perhaps once beautiful, now full of ghosts and demons lurking in the depths. As they drew closer, movement caught his eye, and he saw a shadow rising from the city, fluttering against the red sky, rising higher and higher until it was but a speck, barely perceptible against the gurgling tapestry of Indrani. It must have just been a scrap of cloth on the wind, yet Marco couldn't shake the feeling that it was a bird, a black vulture that was watching them, waiting to feed upon them.

After an hour of walking, the company reached a concrete wall that encircled the city. The wall rose several times the height of a man, topped with barbed wire and guard towers. Marco saw no guards, and when he pointed his flashlight, he saw graffiti sprayed across the concrete: *Welcome to Hell.*

He shuddered. "Not the friendliest greeting I've seen," he muttered to Addy.

She pointed her flashlight at another section of the wall. "I like that one better. Look! It's Kilroy!"

This second graffiti showed a cartoon figure, bald and long-nosed, peering over a wall. Words appeared beneath the figure: *Kilroy died here.*

"Adorable," Marco said.

The company advanced until they reached the gates of the city. Two deserted guard towers rose here. Metal bars rose between them, forming a corridor like a cage. Three barred revolving doors filled the tunnel. The company paused outside the gates, weapons raised. At a silent signal from Captain Petty, they inched closer, then froze, staring.

No scum.

No humans.

For a long moment they stared, and the only sound came from the wind. It moaned through the city like a living thing, creaking the revolving doors. Another scrap of cloth fluttered high above, and a caw sounded, the hoarse sound of a bird or perhaps bending metal in the wind.

Captain Petty was staring at him, Marco realized. Her voice crackled to life inside his earbud.

"Private Emery, enter the gateway. Walk through the revolving doors into the city."

Marco cringed. So he would be the canary in the coal mine. He wanted to refuse, but he had a feeling that disobeying Captain Petty meant a swift court-martial. He decided to take his chances with the gateway. He nodded and spoke into the microphone that protruded from his helmet. "Yes, ma'am."

"Go kick their asses!" Addy whispered to him, giving him an encouraging pat on the backside.

Marco groaned. "Addy, I told you, it's thoraxes."

Leaving his squad behind, he walked toward the gates, raising his assault rifle. A magazine was already loaded, and he kept one hand on the charging hammer, ready to load a bullet into the chamber. He walked between the guard towers. Their turrets gazed down at him like eyes, like two sphinxes under the sanguine sky, judging him, condemning him, welcoming him into their domain. Welcome to Hell, the graffiti had said. They're dying to get in.

The cage-like tunnel stretched before him, the metallic gullet of a beast, filled with the revolving doors. Marco took a deep breath, then pushed one revolving door. It gave a horrible shriek, so loud that he froze halfway through and winced. Slowly, he pushed his way through, the door creaking, the sound almost organic, almost demonic. Marco walked onward down the tunnel. Metal bars rose alongside and above him, as if he were walking through one of those cages divers used when swimming with sharks. Concrete pillboxes rose at his sides, full of slits for guns, but still Marco saw no guards.

It was a clever configuration. Should any scum land outside the city and try to enter, they'd have to pass through this gauntlet, soldiers firing from both sides. Except Marco saw no soldiers here now. The city was undefended.

He made his way past the second revolving door when he heard the caw again. He raised his eyes, and there! He saw it above! A black vulture, huge, the size of a man, and it had a human face. A red face with black eyes. But then he looked again, and it was only another scrap of cloth, rising in the wind and falling somewhere in the distance. Marco shuddered. His mind was playing tricks on him.

Calm yourself, Marco, he thought. *Stay cool. Be like the Fonz.*

Finally he made it through the third and final revolving door—and into Hell.

Marco stared ahead, grimaced, and raised his gun.

If you're up there, Flying Spaghetti Monster, help us.

Corpus City lay in ruins. Windows were shattered. An entire building had fallen and lay in piles of bricks and metal bars, blocking two roads and filling an intersection. Many buildings still stood, soaring toward the sky, some a hundred stories tall, but their windows too were shattered, and wind moaned through them like ghosts playing stone flutes. The city didn't seem destroyed so much as decayed, like the innards of a giant after a long illness, rotting away in a tomb. Marco saw no signs of life. No humans. No scum. Even the vulture apparitions were gone. But the sky seemed alive. Indrani, that gas giant, that goddess, roiled and grumbled above, a storm on its surface like a great yellow eye, peering down upon the desolation of Corpus City. Suddenly Marco was filled with the horrible feeling that Indrani was alive, was indeed gazing right at him, that it wasn't a planet but a massive life-form. He could almost hear words in its grumbles, though he couldn't make out their meaning.

"Emery." The voice emerged from his earbud, snapping Marco out of his paralysis. "Emery, are you all right?"

Thankfully, it was Lieutenant Ben-Ari speaking now, not Captain Chihuahua.

"I'm fine, ma'am," he said. "There's nobody here. All the buildings and roads I can see from here—they all seem empty."

"Are there corpses?" Ben-Ari asked.

"I don't see any," Marco said. "But it seems safe to enter. The air's a bit smoky, but I don't smell any miasma. Or death."

"We'll be right there. Sit tight."

The rest of the company entered the city, one by one, and reformed into squads and platoons. The buildings soared around them, black and jagged, dwarfing the soldiers. Scraps of cloth fluttered across the dark roads, and a sign on an abandoned building creaked in the wind. A child's bicycle rolled forward in the wind, then tilted over and clattered down.

"They're all gone," Addy said. "The colonists fucking left. This is a ghost town."

Ben-Ari hushed her with a glare. She spoke into her helmet. "Spread out and check the perimeter. Squad One, head down that road. Squad Two, Squad Three—check those ruins."

The other platoons were breaking up into squads too and spreading out. Corporal Diaz, commander of the Ravens platoon's first squad, ran at a crouch, gun pointed before him. Marco and the rest of the squad followed, guns pointing to their sides. Lailani brought up the rear, regularly spinning around to check for enemies behind them. They reached the road and walked between tall, narrow buildings. These were homes, Marco realized. Rows of family homes, some still with Halloween skeletons hanging in the windows. On one concrete patio a family had raised fake tombstones complete with cobwebs.

"Hey, Addy," Marco whispered. "Do you know why they keep building more cemeteries?"

"Because we keep killing scum," Addy said.

Marco shook his head. "Because people are dying to get in."

"I like my answer better."

"Your answer makes no sense," Marco said. "They don't bury scum."

"So why would they need cemeteries?" Addy asked.

Corporal Diaz hushed them. He pointed at a few doorways. "Check the homes. A fireteam here, a fireteam there, and into that one too."

The squad quickly formed fireteams of three. Marco found himself with Addy and Elvis. He glanced over at Lailani, saw that she was careful to choose a fireteam far from him.

Marco approached one home and was prepared to kick the door open when a thought occurred to him. He grabbed the doorknob. The house was unlocked.

"They left in a rush," Marco said. "Didn't even lock the door."

"Or they're dead," said Addy, standing at the doorway with him.

"I don't smell anything," Elvis said. "The dead stink. Let's take a look."

They burst into the house, guns raised, prepared to fire at any scum that should happen to leap their way. They saw nothing. They raised their flashlights, but the beams fell on a vacant home. Marco saw furniture, a child's doll, and an empty crib. Dirty dishes were still in the sink. No humans. No scum.

A creak sounded upstairs.

All three soldiers raised their guns.

They stood frozen. They didn't hear the sound again.

Marco pointed upstairs, and his companions nodded.

He crept up the staircase, rifle held before him. Shadows danced around him like demons. Elvis and Addy walked behind him, adding their flashlight beams to his.

A creak sounded again.

Marco froze for a moment, then inhaled deeply. He charged his weapon, switched off the safety, and placed his finger on the trigger. He reached a hallway on the second floor, saw a corridor with three doors. A wheezing sounded ahead, inhuman.

Scum, he thought.

He crept forward, paused outside one room, then burst inside, gun raised. Nothing. Nothing but an empty bed, unmade.

Wait.

A figure sat on a shelf—a human child! Marco's heart kicked into a gallop, and when he shone his light on the figure, a doll burst into mechanical laughter.

"Fucking hell, damn thing is haunted," Addy whispered, pointing her gun at the doll. Marco pushed down her muzzle and shook his head.

They left the room, walked down the hallway, and approached a second doorway. Marco heard it again now. That low wheezing. A scratching on the floor. Claws.

Marco looked at Addy and Elvis. They looked back, nodded. All three burst into the room together.

"Die, scum!" Addy shouted . . . then froze.

A dog barked, tail stretched out in a line. Its face was flat like a bulldog's, but it was smaller, perhaps a Boston Terrier or a Frenchie.

"That explains the wheezing," Marco said and lowered his rifle. The dog approached and licked his fingers.

They left the house, dog in tow, and regrouped with their squad on the street.

"Nothing," said Beast, emerging from another house. "Still dishes on table. Still food in oven. No people. Not alive or dead."

The other fireteams reported the same result. They continued down the street, checking a few more houses, but it was the same everywhere. No corpses. No scum.

Finally in one house—

"Blood," Marco said, leaning down. He illuminated stains on the tiles. "Old blood."

In another house, a fireteam reported bloodstains on a wall. In a local shop they found signs of a struggle too: toppled shelves, bullet holes in a wall, bloodstains by the cash register, but again—no corpses, not of humans or scum.

They left the road, returning to the city gates, where they regrouped with the rest of the company.

"We checked that tower and that one," reported one of the other platoons. "There was violence here, but no corpses anywhere. And no survivors."

The third platoon reported the same result. A few stains of blood. A bullet hole. No corpses, no survivors.

The officers huddled together and conferred amongst themselves as the enlisted soldiers waited. Something tugged Marco's leg, and he smiled to see that the Boston Terrier had followed him. He knelt and patted the dog.

"Where did you find that mutt?" Sergeant Singh asked him.

"In one of the houses, Commander," Marco said. "It was the only living soul we found." He scratched the dog behind the ear. "If only he could talk."

Singh knelt too and patted the dog's head, and his eyes softened. "Poor little pup. Missing his tail too."

Addy patted the dog's head. "We should call him Sergeant Stumpy, on account of his missing tail. He can be the platoon's mascot."

"I think he should be a private," said Sergeant Singh, smiling behind his black beard.

Addy shook her head. "That won't work, Commander. It's not a . . . Poet, what's it called when two words start with the same letter?"

"Alliteration," Marco replied.

Addy nodded. "That's it. Obliteration. Sergeant Stumpy it is. Sorry, Sergeant Singh, but you two will just have to have similar names."

A buzzing in their earbuds interrupted the conversation. Ben-Ari's voice emerged, speaking into all their ears.

"We move deeper into the city to keep exploring," said the lieutenant. "All soldiers, keep your magazines in your guns. If you see the scum, open fire at once. If you find survivors, report to your squad leaders at once."

They walked deeper into the city, reaching a great industrial complex. Factories rose here, ten stories tall, edifices with metal walls and no windows. Their chimneys were cold. Giant logos were painted onto the factory walls, displaying serpents eating their own tails. Below each symbol appeared the words *Chrysopoeia Corp.*

Ben-Ari led the Ravens platoon into one factory, where they found a towering chamber full of cold generators, rows of offices, and still assembly lines. They climbed metal staircases through the factory, but still they found nobody.

"There's barely any blood," Addy said, walking beside Marco. "If there was indeed a battle here, there would be lots more blood than this. We just found a few stains here and there, not enough to explain thousands of people killed. I think only a handful died, and their bodies were disposed of."

"So where is everyone else?" Marco said.

"Something spooked them badly. They must have fled the city. Probably left in their spaceships after sending out that Mayday, never even waiting for us to arrive." She spat off a walkway at a cluster of machines below. "It's a ghost town, plain and simple. Scum left too."

They left the factory and moved deeper into the city. Towers rose at their sides, the windows dark. In a city square rose a colossal statue, tall as a church, of a snake devouring its own tail. Marco recognized the symbol.

"Chrysopoeia Corp," he muttered. "That name again. It sounds familiar."

"Of course it sounds familiar," Addy said. "My father worked for them."

Marco frowned. "I thought your father was a truck driver."

"He was," Addy said. "What do you think he delivered in his truck? Stuff Chrysopoeia Corp digs up from the ground. It's a massive conglomerate, Poet. For somebody so book smart, you should know this stuff. Chrysopoeia is just about the biggest company in the world, but since they don't publish books or sell turtles, you haven't noticed them."

Marco approached the statue of the snake. Far above, its eyes seemed to shine with sickly delight as it consumed its own tail. Marco perhaps hadn't known much about Chrysopoeia, but he knew this snake. Here was an ouroboros, a creature from legend, symbolizing cyclicality. In many ways, the ouroboros was like the phoenix, the symbol of the Human Defense Force. Both were animals that ended and began in a repeating cycle. Both, perhaps, were like humanity rising again from ruin.

Does that mean we're destined to fall again? Marco thought.

Something at the base of the ouroboros statue caught Marco's eye. He stepped closer and pointed his flashlight. He frowned and leaned forward.

"What the hell?"

His light fell upon the skeleton, and he gasped and stumbled back, nearly dropping his flashlight.

"Poet?" Addy rushed toward him, followed by the rest of their platoon. They all pointed their flashlights at the skeleton below the statue.

"Fuck me," Addy muttered.

Lailani's eyes widened. "What is it?"

"A freak," said Elvis, cringing.

"An alien?" said Beast. "Not scum."

They all crowded around, staring at it. Marco stood with them, feeling queasy. No, it wasn't a scum, but nor was it human, not fully human at least. The legs, the ribs, and the skull appeared human enough, but the skeleton had six arms, each ending with a swordlike claw instead of a hand. The skull's jaw was opened, and when the wind blew, the skeleton seemed to howl in anguish.

"What happened here?" Marco whispered, looking up at his comrades.

They stared back, pale and silent, even Addy. A few looked queasy, and all looked horrified. All but one. Her lavender eyes glowing, Osiris stared at Marco and smiled.

CHAPTER ELEVEN

Night fell. The red surface of Indrani faded to deep crimson, then brown, then finally vanished in the darkness. Below in the dark city, the soldiers fired up three flares, and the balls of light floated above the towers like three moons, casting a sickly white light across the ruins. The temperature plummeted.

"These cold nights are wearing out the enamel on my teeth," Marco said to Elvis. "They keep chattering."

"To hell with teeth," Elvis muttered. "My balls are freezing."

"Mine too," Addy said. "And I don't even have any." She shivered.

Sergeant Stumpy gave a plaintive wail and shivered.

"Keep it down, soldiers," Corporal Diaz said, looking over his shoulder at them. The squad leader's eyes were dark, and he held his gun in both hands, but the hint of a smile touched his lips. Strangely, Marco was almost glad that Fort Djemila had fallen; it meant that Diaz had abandoned his job drilling recruits and joined them here in space. Having the experienced warrior with them was a comfort in the darkness. Diaz had survived the Appalachian inferno. He would know what to do here too.

Silently, the soldiers followed their corporal, who in turn followed Lieutenant Ben-Ari through the dark city. Stumpy walked alongside, his stump of a tail wagging. The company's flashlights moved in a hundred beams. The walls of factories, warehouses, and refineries rose around them, black and bricked and unforgiving, thrusting out metal pipes and vents and cold still fans. They walked through a metal canyon, and the wind screamed, and Marco kept thinking of that vulture with a human face, of that skeleton with six arms and blades for hands, and of Osiris staring at him from the crowd, pale and luminous and smiling, her eyes dead.

Somebody sabotaged our ship, Marco thought, remembering Ben-Ari's warning. He looked around him, seeing many familiar faces, other soldiers he barely knew. Had Petty sabotaged the mission on purpose, some form of rage against the Ravens Platoon? Had the scum hacked into Osiris's programming, turning her against the humans? Or was this all just paranoia, delusions dripping down from the gas giant above?

As they walked through this canyon of metal and brick, Marco tried to see Kemi, but he could only see shadows and beams of light, not faces. Kemi had barely spoken to him since landing here. Perhaps his brief flame with Lailani had died down; he didn't want to lose Kemi too. Not her love, not her friendship, not any form of her presence in his life. Soldiers in the HDF didn't have a long average lifespan. If Marco was to die here on Corpus or on another world, he wanted to die with Kemi still his friend.

But he couldn't find her, and in the darkness, memories of Marco's dream emerged. The vast, rocky landscape. Thousands of scum swarming toward him. That dream kept returning, night after night, and more and more Marco thought of it as a vision, a prophecy. Was that the world he would die on? Was it here on Corpus?

In the night, they found a warehouse. The company stepped inside to find a vast space full of idle bulldozers and drills the size of cannons.

Captain Petty's voice emerged from every soldier's earbud.

"We set camp for the night. Take formations by your platoon leaders for roll call, then set a rotating guard around your platoon, fifteen-minute shifts."

The Ravens Platoon gathered before Lieutenant Ben-Ari, organizing into fireteams. She read out a roll call. "Emery! Ray! Linden! De la Rosa!"

As roll call continued, Marco looked ahead at Kemi. She stood behind her lieutenant, silent, still wearing the white uniform of a cadet. She briefly met his gaze, then looked away, face blank.

Kemi, I'm sorry, he thought, wanting to speak to her, not knowing how.

"Lorrenzonelli!" Ben-Ari said. "Private Lorrenzonelli!" Nobody answered. "Has anyone seen Lorrenzonelli?"

The platoon's soldiers looked from side to side. Marco remembered Lorrenzonelli, a soldier who had joined his platoon just before they had boarded the *Miyari*—a tall, slender young man with a permanent smile.

Ben-Ari frowned and spoke into her helmet's microphone. "We're missing a man. Private Enzio Lorrenzonelli."

The other platoon officers approached and conversed in low voices with Ben-Ari. Other platoons, it seemed, were missing soldiers too. A total of five had vanished from the company. The names were called out again. Nobody answered. The company had come here with one hundred and thirty-three soldiers. A head count confirmed that they were down by five.

"I'll lead a search party," said Corporal Diaz. "I need a few volunteers."

Quickly, every soldier in the company raised their hand. Diaz chose four soldiers Marco didn't know . . . and Kemi. As the cadet walked toward the corporal, Marco tried to make eye contact again, but she wouldn't look his way.

"Be careful out there," Marco called after them as the five stepped outside into the night.

The others remained in the cavernous warehouse. In the glow of their flashlights, the bulldozers and drills seemed like sleeping dragons. The soldiers sat on the floor and ate cold, tasteless battle rations, consisting of energy bars, gray paste from plastic wrappers, cans of oily tuna, and sticky sheets of condensed fruit. Sergeant Stumpy moved between the troops, collecting treats, then slept with a chorus of snorts and wheezes. The minutes, then hours stretched by, and still there was no word from the search party.

"What do you reckon happened to them?" Addy said.

"Scum got 'em," said Elvis. "Has to be the scum."

"Or maybe one of those creatures with the six arms," said Addy. "Whatever they are."

Elvis shuddered. "Maybe it was human but some kind of mutated freak. Maybe the miners dug up some radioactive material that mutated them." He thought for a moment. "Maybe it can give you superpowers too. If you could have any superpower you wanted, what would it be?"

"I already have super strength," said Addy. "And super intelligence. So I'd go with the ability to read minds, so I can see all the pretty ladies Marco is always thinking about."

Marco groaned. "Guess what I'm thinking now." He stood up and walked away, leaving Addy and Elvis in the shadows.

He walked past a few drilling machines, each the size of a tank, and found a back door to an alleyway. He stepped out to find a dark, private place to relieve himself. Much of army life wasn't so much keepings a lookout for enemies but rather for a place—sometimes a latrine, often just an alleyway or hole in the ground—to answer nature's call. So much of war wasn't just fighting an enemy. It was worrying about the basic needs of survival, finding sleep, food, water, a place to relieve yourself. Bladder empty, Marco stepped back into the warehouse. He was walking between the machinery toward the rest of the company when he heard soft crying.

Marco stepped toward the sound and nearly tripped on a dark lump. He knelt, shining his flashlight.

"Lailani?"

She lay on the floor between a tree-sized drill and a bulldozer on caterpillar tracks. She rolled away from him.

"Leave me alone."

Marco hesitated for a moment, torn between wanting to respect her wishes and comfort her. Finally, uncertain if he was making the right choice, he knelt at her side.

"Are you all right?" he said softly. "Can we talk? What can I do to make this better?"

She lay on her side, facing away from him, holding her gun to her breast. The muzzle rested under her chin. "Nothing."

Gingerly, he placed a hand on her hip, ready to pull it back if she objected. She didn't move. He lay down beside her.

"Are you all right?" he said. "Is it because of Kemi? Lailani, please know that what happened between us was real to me. It meant something, meant a lot." He lowered his hand to her waist. "You weren't just there to fill my time away from Kemi. When I told you that I love you, I meant it. I love you, Lailani. And I don't want to hurt you."

Lailani spoke in a low voice, her back still turned to him. "But I'm hurt. I'm hurt beyond what you can heal, Marco. And this isn't about Kemi. This isn't about you. I've been broken all my life."

"You can heal," he said.

She sat up, eyes red. "Marco, you've had a hard life. I know. Your mother was murdered in front of you. You grew up running from the scum, leaping into bomb shelters. You grew up with a father who loved you. You grew up with a roof over your head. You grew up with food on your table. You grew up with friends who loved you. You grew up with education." Her eyes welled with tears. "I grew up without any of those things. Born to a homeless, thirteen-year-old prostitute who died ten years later from starvation. I spent my days eating from trash bins, sometimes rummaging on landfills the size of mountains, eating meat so rancid I would get the fever. I taught myself to read, stealing newspapers, studying the words in dirty alleyways while other children stole drugs. And even now, there's something broken inside of me. There's something wrong. Something not even human. I keep wanting to die, Marco. Again and again, I keep wanting to put this muzzle in my mouth, to pull the trigger, to kill that demon that's always screaming inside me. Do you think I care about Kemi?" She shook her head. "I just want my demon to be silent. I want to be healed. But I can't. I can't, Marco. I'm too broken. It's too late to fix me."

Marco took her hand in his. "Then be broken with me," he whispered. "Then let me hold you when the pain is strongest. Maybe I can't heal you. But maybe I can comfort you, just a little, when it hurts. Maybe I can love you enough to bring you some joy, to make life still worthwhile. I don't want to lose you. I love you."

"I love you too," she whispered and leaned her head against his shoulder. "I'm sorry that I'm like this. And I'm not good for you. I know it."

"You have nothing to be sorry for." He stroked her buzz-cut hair, marveling at its softness.

"What kind of girl can I be for you?" Lailani said. "If we survive this war, who would I be? I can't be your wife. I can't be a mother to your child. I'm too broken, too hurt to ever bring life into this world, to curse a baby with my depression, with a crazy mother who wakes up every night from nightmares. I would only hurt you, Marco. You can leave. You can walk away from this. You don't need to suffer with me."

"This is not suffering." He caressed her cheek. "I don't know what will happen in the future. I don't know how much longer we'll live. But right now we're here, you and me. Right now I want to be close to you, to hold you like this, to be like we were. Can you give me that? No talk of tomorrow. Just of today."

She nodded, closed her eyes, and leaned her cheek against his chest. They lay down together, and she slept in his arms.

An hour later, maybe two, a light flashed on Marco's closed eyelids, rousing him from sleep. He woke up, blinking, Lailani still in his arms, and he saw Kemi standing above him.

He stared up, silent, not sure what to say.

"It's your turn to guard," Kemi said. "We're all taking turns patrolling the warehouse."

Marco nodded, gently released Lailani, and stood up. "The search party—did you find anything?"

Kemi shook her head. "Nothing. The five are still missing. Now go guard." She turned and all but fled into the shadows.

Marco looked down at Lailani. She lay on the floor, eyes open, watching him, then closed her eyes and slept again. Feeling cold and empty, Marco adjusted the strap of his gun, then stepped outside into the night. He patrolled around the warehouse, again and again, not even tracking time, as the night shivered around him and the wind blew and the memories screamed. But even here, in hell, there was some comfort. There was the memory of Lailani in his arms. There was some light in the shadows.

CHAPTER TWELVE

Dawn rose red and cold like a corpse in snow. They gathered outside the warehouse in a canyon of gray bricks and black metal. Indrani loomed above. This morning, the gas giant revealed part of the true sky, pale gray and veiled in clouds. Marco stood with his squad, rifle in hand, grenades and magazines hanging from his belt. The company spread along the narrow road. Ahead, Captain Petty stood atop a cold generator. Behind her loomed a great black ouroboros painted onto the warehouse wall. Metal words were bolted into the bricks above the snake: *Chrysopoeia Corp. Paving our way to the stars.*

"Last night," Captain Petty said, "we lost five soldiers. Today I want you to remain in units no smaller than your squads. Never stray out alone, not even to take a piss. Keep your eyes open for anything—and anyone—suspicious. The instant you notice anything amiss, even if it's just a shiver down your spine, report to your squad leader."

The soldiers looked at one another. By now everyone had heard the rumors of a saboteur on the *Miyari*. And it seemed like everyone had a favorite suspect. A few soldiers were staring at Osiris and muttering about artificial life. Some mumbled about the earthlings. A few soldiers were even looking at Marco. He stared back at them, defiant.

Captain Petty kept speaking. "We'll leave three soldiers in the city to keep searching for the missing. The rest of us travel into the mines today. The mines delve deep underground; Osiris has a map in her memory banks. We'll seek surviving colonists, and more importantly: a new azoth engine." She held out the shattered azoth heart from the *Miyari*. "We seek an object that looks like this: a metal heart with a crystal inside. One should be located at the lowest level of the mines, powering the entire city. If we can find a new azoth heart in the mines, we can fix the *Miyari*. We can go home. Whoever finds the heart will receive an instant promotion."

Addy gasped. "I'm going to be a lieutenant!" she whispered to Marco.

Marco groaned. "She said a promotion, not a commission. You'd be a corporal, not an officer. Even Sergeant Stumpy will still outrank you." Marco knelt to pat the Boston Terrier, the new mascot of their platoon. The dog wagged his stump of a tail.

"So I better find two azoth hearts," Addy said. "Maybe they'll make me a captain like the Chihuahua."

The company traveled through the city under the red light, finally reaching a stone gateway shaped like a coiling snake. Past the gateway Marco saw stairs plunging underground into shadows.

"Chrysopoeia Corp," Marco muttered. "Paving our way to purgatory."

"Chrysopoeia Corp," Addy said. "Opening the gates to Hell since 2047."

"Chrysopoeia Corp," Elvis said, walking up to join them. "We bake snakes so delicious they eat themselves."

Lieutenant Ben-Ari approached them, and her soldiers gathered around her. "Ravens Platoon, we take the vanguard," Ben-Ari said. "Snap your flashlights onto your helmets. I want both your hands ready to fire your guns. Keep magazines in guns, but do not load a bullet or remove the safety until we're in danger. Squads in tight formations. Any questions before we go in?"

"What was that thing with six arms, ma'am?" Elvis asked.

"We don't know," said Ben-Ari. "Maybe we'll find answers in the deep."

"Are there scum down there, ma'am?" said another soldier.

"We don't know," said Ben-Ari. "But be ready for them. Just in case. If we encounter the enemy down there, I know that you will fight well. You will be victorious. You will slay them. Look after your friends in the darkness. Listen to your squad leaders. You are good soldiers, and I'm proud of every one of you. You will prove your worth to the STC underground today. For Earth!"

"For Earth!" they all replied, raising their guns.

For Earth, Marco thought. *For my friends. For my family. For humanity. For a library full of books and dreams of writing one myself. For that pale blue dot lost in the distance. For Earth.*

They stepped through the serpentine gateway and into the darkness. A staircase delved downward, and even their flashlights could not pierce those shadows. Lieutenant Ben-Ari led the way, plasma gun held before her, and Marco walked directly behind her, aiming his rifle over the lieutenant's shoulder. Earth helmets came with an elastic net stretched over them, useful for holding leaves and twigs for camouflage. Tonight Marco was able to slide his flashlight through the netting, forming a crude miner's helmet, leaving both hands free for his gun. He could hear the rest of his platoon walk behind him, and Sergeant Stumpy came to walk at Marco's side. One of the soldiers had even sewn the Boston Terrier a miniature uniform complete with sergeant insignia.

The staircase ended after a few hundred steps. Metal doors were worked into a crude stone wall here. A control panel hung by the doors.

Ben-Ari stepped toward the control panel and hit a few buttons. Nothing happened.

"No power here either." The lieutenant snapped her bayonet onto her plasma gun, then slipped the blade between the metal doors. "Emery, help me."

Marco drew his own bayonet from his belt, snapped it onto his rifle, and slid it between the doors. He and Ben-Ari worked for a few moments, finally prying the doors open enough to reach between them, grab the doors with their hands, and pull them the rest of the way open. Marco's head spun and he nearly fell. Addy, standing behind, had to grab him by the seat of his pants.

"God," Marco said. "I am not good with heights."

"Good choice joining Space Territorial Command," Addy said.

Beyond the doors, a shaft plunged down into darkness. Two heavy chains, the links as large as hands, hung down the shaft like vocal chords in the throat of a metal giant.

"It's an elevator shaft, ma'am," Marco said to the lieutenant.

Addy reached from behind and mussed his hair. "That's why he's the genius. Next he might figure out this is a mine."

Marco shot her a glare. "Be quiet, Addy. You once thought that it's called an ass tray instead of an ash tray."

"It *is* an ass tray!" Addy bristled. "Because you put cigarette butts in it."

Lieutenant Ben-Ari reached out and grabbed one of the chains. She dangled over the edge of the shaft, just her heels back in the tunnel. "Be quiet, soldiers, and help me."

Marco felt queasy. He could barely look down the shaft, let alone reach forward far enough to grab a chain. But if he backed down now, he knew Addy would mock him forever.

"Addy, hold my hand," he said.

She waggled her eyebrows at him. "Romantic!"

"Shut it."

He gripped Addy's hand, leaned over the edge of the shaft, and grabbed the chain. As he leaned over the darkness, holding Addy for support, his head spun. Hurriedly, he pulled the chain back. It was damn heavy. Beast and Addy had to help, and they all tugged the chains, pulling them up, link by link.

Finally something began to rise from the shaft below, drawing closer, and Marco was suddenly sure that it was a creature rising from the darkness, a primordial beast of the depths, metallic, creaking, snapping teeth.

It's a cage, he realized, pointing his flashlight down. *A lift cage.*

When the cage reached the doors, hidden brakes automatically snapped onto the chains, keeping the cage elevated. The soldiers shone their lights inside. The lift cage was no larger than a typical elevator cabin, and a metal winch was attached to one wall. And on the floor . . .

"What . . . is that?" Marco said.

He leaned down, reached into the cage, and grabbed the lump. It was clammy and soft, like touching skin. He pulled it back into the tunnel, where he could take a better look, and grimaced.

"Ugh." Addy gagged. "It's a giant testicle."

Marco shook his head. "No. I don't know what it is." He shuddered, nausea rising in him.

The lump in his hand was the size of a guinea pig, wrapped in skin that seemed human. There were moles, even tufts of hair, but no limbs, no face, no holes. It was like a small pillow wrapped in skin, and it quivered in his hand.

"I think it's alive," he said. "Addy, take it."

She shook her head. "I'm not touching that."

It twitched in Marco's hand. "Guys, what the hell is going on here?"

"Maybe it's a naked tribble," Addy said.

"We'll take it with us," said Ben-Ari, opening her backpack. "Emery, wrap it up and place it here. We'll analyze it back on the ship."

Marco wrapped the creature—if a creature it was—in Ben-Ari's towel and placed it into her backpack.

"We can name this one Sergeant Skinny," Addy said.

"Soldiers, enough," Ben-Ari said. She spoke into her communicator in a low voice, then nodded. "All right. We're moving down into the mine." She pointed at a few soldiers. "Emery. Linden. De la Rosa. Abasi. Diaz. Squeeze in here with me. We're going down first, then we'll send the lift cage up for the others."

The lieutenant stepped into the cage, and Marco and the others followed. It was a tight squeeze. Their guns clanked together and their elbows banged. Lailani pressed up against Marco, her back toward him, and the top of her helmet grazed his chin. Kemi stood beside him, pointedly avoiding his gaze. Diaz and Ben-Ari, who grabbed the winch on the wall, began to turn it. The wheel creaked, rust flew, and the chains clattered. Inch by inch, the cage descended down the shaft.

Marco's flashlight soon caught words painted onto the shaft wall. *10 feet.* They kept descending. Soon more words appeared on the wall. *20 feet.* Ben-Ari and Diaz kept turning the winch. The air grew colder as they descended, and somehow it seemed even darker down here, so dark their flashlights could barely cast back the shadows. They could no longer hear the sound of the rest of their company above, just the creaking chains and their breath.

Marco leaned toward Kemi. "Just like the subway back home, right?" he whispered.

She said nothing, wouldn't look his way. She stared ahead, eyes hard. On the wall appeared the words: *100 feet.*

"Ma'am," Marco said to his lieutenant, then looked at Corporal Diaz. "Commander. May I take a turn at the wheel?"

Both Ben-Ari and Diaz appeared winded, and when they released the winch, the cage swayed and banged against the stone walls. Marco grabbed the wheel and tried to turn it himself, could not. Addy helped him, and together they kept lowering the cage. Each foot descended felt like a mile, and Marco's arms were soon aching. Normally, he was sure, the cage was electrically powered, but they had to rely on their muscles now. Foot by foot. Plunging down into the depths.

It seemed like eras before they finally reached two hundred feet and rested. Marco's arms shook and his breath was heavy. Lailani and Kemi took a shift together next, and Marco was keenly aware of the awkwardness between the two women, how they refused to talk, even look at each other as they worked, spinning the wheel. At three hundred feet, Ben-Ari and Diaz took their second shift, and still the shaft descended into shadows.

"How fucking deep in this thing?" Addy muttered, then glanced toward her lieutenant. "Forgive the language, ma'am. But it is pretty fucking deep."

"Linden, watch it," Diaz said.

Hours seemed to pass, and there was nothing but this shaft, no memory of the world above. When Marco gave up, he could no longer see the flashlights of his companions in the tunnel, only blackness. They might as well have been dangling in the depth of space. He had the sudden, terrible fear that the shaft would close in on him, bury them here, or worse—that the winch would get stuck, that they'd languish here for a slow death that could take days, even weeks. *400 feet.* Eternities passed. *500 feet.* *600.*

When they reached a thousand feet, they all had to rest. They hung in the darkness, six soldiers in a cage, and sat pressed together for a drink of water and some battle rations. For long moments they were silent. The silence soon seemed intolerable to Marco, oppressing like the darkness, but he dared not break it, and a fear filled him that should he speak, voices would answer from the darkness, that his words could summon evil buried here.

Finally it was Lailani who spoke.

"What if it's one of them," she said.

They all looked at her.

"What is?" Marco said.

"The thing in Lieutenant Ben-Ari's backpack," Lailani said. "The living ball of flesh. What if it's one of the soldiers who went missing?"

Addy gasped. "What if it's its butt!"

Lailani turned to look at her, the flashlights reflecting in her eyes. "It's not funny. That skin looked human."

A collective shudder ran through them.

For the first time that day, Kemi spoke. "Maybe it's related to the skeleton we saw outside, the one with six arms. Maybe it's the juvenile form of whatever creature that was."

"I still think it's a butt," Addy said.

"Then don't show it your face, Addy," Marco said. "It might think you're a relative."

Lieutenant Ben-Ari sighed. "There's only one type of HDF soldier that can talk like that at a time like this. My soldiers." She rose to her feet. "Let's keep going."

They continued with their shifts, delving deeper down the shaft. Soon they reached 1,100 feet deep. 1,200. 1,300. Still they saw no sign of the end.

They were at 1,400 when the scream rose from below.

Marco and Addy froze at the wheel.

The others reached for their guns.

The scream lasted for only a second, maybe two, before silence fell again. The cage swung in the shaft.

"Was that human?" Addy whispered.

"It was the wind," Kemi said, but her voice was shaky. "Just the wind in the mines."

"That was a scream," Addy said. "Definitely a scream."

Lailani hugged herself. "It wasn't angry. He's in pain. He's scared."

"It wasn't human," Marco said slowly. "And it wasn't the wind. Something alien is down there."

"The scum?" Addy said, finger on her trigger.

Marco wasn't so sure. The skeleton with six arms, the ball of flesh—those hadn't been the *scolopendra titania*.

"All right, soldiers," Ben-Ari said. "We keep going. Anyone who isn't turning the wheel—aim your guns downward. Don't load any bullets yet, but get ready to quickly. But don't be too quick on the trigger. If we're dealing with colonists here, we don't want to get spooked and riddle them with holes." She grabbed the wheel again.

They kept descending, waiting for the scream to return, but heard only their own breath and the clanking chains. Every hundred feet, Ben-Ari reported back to Captain Petty above, speaking through her communicator. Marco thought the shaft would take them to the moon's core when finally, 1,535 feet down, they thumped against a floor.

"1,535 feet," Marco whispered. "That's taller than the Empire State Building. At least before the scum knocked it down."

They emerged from the cage into a tunnel. The floor, walls, and ceiling were craggy, crudely carved, still bearing the scars of the drills that had torn the pathway open. It felt like standing in the veins of a giant stone carcass. When they raised their flashlights, they illuminated rusty rails leading into the distant darkness. A few chains hung from the ceiling over the rails. One chain, just one among the group, was swinging.

"Something brushed past that chain," Marco whispered, pointing his flashlight.

They all pointed their own beams, but they saw no living beings, only the craggy walls, the chains, and train tracks leading down the tunnel.

Ben-Ari spoke into her communicator. "Lieutenant Ben-Ari reporting. Ma'am, we've reached the bottom of the shaft. It's over fifteen hundred feet deep. We heard a scream, but there's nobody in the immediate vicinity. You'll have to haul the cage back up and—"

With a series of thuds, the power came back on.

Lanterns worked into the walls cast an orange glow, barely more powerful than the flashlights but enough to reveal more of the tunnel. In the distance, Marco thought he saw shadows stirring, then fleeing, but perhaps it was only a lantern that was late to turn on. Grumbles sounded in the deep, great machinery awakening like ancient beasts rising from biblical slumber, hungry to feed. Thuds, clanks, grumbles—a cacophony muffled by immeasurable distance, working away, chewing, digging, industrializing, breeding in the depths. Closer by, the chains of the cage lift began to move, powered by the resurgence of electricity, pulling the cage back up the shaft.

"Perhaps timing," Addy said. "Just when my arms are about to fall off."

"Someone is still alive down there," Lailani said, peering down the tunnel. "Somebody got the power back up. The colonists fled here. They must still be hiding."

"Hiding from what?" Addy said.

"*Aswang,*" Lailani whispered. "In the Philippines, we whisper of him. An evil creature that lurks in darkness, that sucks the blood of its victims, that deforms them."

"Ass wang?" Addy said.

Lailani glared at her. "*Aswang.* Do not mock him. I've seen him in my dreams." She shuddered. "This place reminds me of those dreams. I feel like I've been here before."

Addy patted her gun. "Well, if any ass wangs show up here, I'll shoot some bullets into them."

Six more soldiers descended down to the tunnel, then six more. They gathered along the train tracks, waiting as the lift cage began rising back up for more. The cage was moving fast now with the power back on. Marco was grateful to see that Sergeant Singh had made it down. The tall, bearded Sikh, with his heavy gun and curved *kirpan* blade, made the darkness seem just a tad more bearable.

Marco approached his platoon sergeant, was about to speak to him, when with a *thud* the power died again.

The tunnel plunged into complete darkness. The soldiers had turned off their flashlights in the brief moments of light, and the darkness was now complete, caressing, flowing around them.

Somebody laughed in the distance—too deep, too distant to be a soldier. Feet clattered above along the ceiling.

Marco switched on his flashlight, pointed the light above, and saw something—something stirring, vanishing, and when he chased it with his light, he couldn't catch it again.

The other flashlights turned on one by one. For a moment they were all silent.

Ben-Ari then spoke into her communicator. "Lieutenant Ben-Ari reporting. Captain Petty, ma'am, are—"

The disembodied voice of Petty emerged from Ben-Ari's earbud, loud enough for Marco, who stood nearby, to hear. "Fuck. We've got two fireteams halfway down the shaft. They'll continue descending manually. Stay where you are, Lieutenant. *Do not* proceed into the tunnels alone. Do you understand me? Stay where you are."

The fear was evident in Petty's voice, a slight tremble, a lurking, creeping hysteria. But there was no fear in Ben-Ari's voice as she answered her commanding officer.

"Yes, ma'am, sitting tight. Will report of any sign of trouble."

Ben-Ari's voice was cool and collected, her stance firm, her hand relaxed upon her gun. At that moment, Marco was incredibly grateful that Lieutenant Einav Ben-Ari was his direct commanding officer, not Captain Chihuahua.

The troops below—there were eighteen—stood by the rail, waiting, flashlights and guns pointing down the tunnel. The creaks and clatters of the lift cage sounded from the shaft above, growing closer foot by foot. As Marco waited below, movement from the tunnel caught his eye. He stared into the distant shadows, but he saw nothing. The metal tracks led deep into the mine, and Marco thought of the scream he had heard from below.

That single chain above the tunnel kept swinging, back, forth, back, forth, a pendulum, never slowing.

"Why does it keep swinging?" he whispered, pointing his flashlight down the tunnel. Whenever he moved his beam of light, shadows fled like living creatures. He thought he could hear a cackle, a creak, possibly just the lift cage making its way down the shaft.

"Marco?" A voice spoke behind him, and he turned to see Lailani approaching. Her eyes were wide, her face ashen, and her breath shook. She looked like she was going to faint. "Marco, there's . . ."

The shriek of shattering metal, followed by human screams, sounded from the shaft above.

The soldiers in the tunnel all turned toward the shaft. Metal screeched. Sparks rained.

"It's coming down!" somebody shouted. "The cage is falling!"

"Back, back!" said Sergeant Singh.

The soldiers leaped back into the tunnel. The sound grew deafening, metal tearing through stone, and dust flew, and with a shattering explosion of metal and stone and bending bars, the cage lift crashed onto the bottom of the shaft.

For just an instant, the soldiers in the tunnel stood still, staring at the wreckage. The cage had bent and shattered, still belching out dust. Still figures lay within.

Marco and the others ran forward. The soldiers inside the cage weren't moving. The cage door was bent, and they couldn't open it.

"Are they breathing?" somebody asked behind Marco.

"They're dead," said somebody else. "God. Look at the blood. Look at the bones."

"We're trapped here," Elvis said. "Oh God, we're trapped down here."

"Move, move, let me open it!" said Beast, and the giant soldier walked toward the cage, grabbed the bars, and—

One of the figures inside the shattered cage stood up. Beast gave a startled yell and stumbled back from the bars. Inside the smashed lift cage, the figure brushed off dust and shook her head, scattering debris from her platinum hair.

"Osiris," Marco whispered.

The android grabbed the bent bars, yanked them open, and stepped out of the cage into the tunnel.

"We fell," Osiris said. "The others are dead. Their bodies were weak."

It was a grim task, pulling the corpses out from the cage lift. There were five of them. Young soldiers. Marco doubted any of them were older than twenty. Their bones were shattered, their mouths still open in silent screams. The living soldiers covered the dead with blankets from their backpacks, but Marco knew that those agonized, frozen faces would always haunt him.

As Ben-Ari communicated the situation to her commander aboveground, Sergeant Singh began to sing a prayer for the dead in a low voice. The other soldiers stood with him, heads lowered. During the prayer, Marco felt eyes peering at him, and he glanced up to see Osiris. Her lavender eyes shone, and she gave him a small, mirthless smile.

When the chant was done, Marco approached the wreckage of the cage lift. He stepped between the bent bars and stared up the shaft. It rose into darkness, over fifteen hundred feet of stone and shadow. Marco grabbed a segment of chain; it still hung from the bars in the cage ceiling. He frowned, knelt, and lifted a second chain.

These chains had once supported the cage lift. Their links had been sawed through.

"Ma'am," Marco said, looking at his lieutenant.

Ben-Ari approached, as did a few of the others. They stared at the chains together. Marco passed his hand over one broken link. The cut was smooth, as if a circular saw or laser had sliced through it.

"These did not bend and snap under the weight, ma'am," Marco said. "Somebody cut them. Somebody sent this cage lift crashing down on purpose."

"The fucking robot did it!" said Addy. She raised her gun, yanked back the charging hammer, and pointed the muzzle at Osiris.

"Fuck." Elvis spat. The young soldier was pale and shivering, perhaps remembering how Osiris had choked him back on the *Miyari*. He too raised his gun, loaded a bullet, and aimed at Osiris. "Fucking robot must have sabotaged the ship too."

A few other soldiers raised their own guns, loading bullets into chambers, pointing the muzzles at the android. Osiris stood calmly, stared at them, and tilted her head.

"Are you angry at me, masters?" the android asked.

Addy spat. "Don't you masters us, you piece of junk." She flicked off her gun's safety. "I'm going to put a bullet through your goddamn mechanical brain."

"Wait, wait!" Marco said. "Addy. Elvis. Beast. Wait. How could she have cut the links? She has no saw." He turned toward Ben-Ari. "Ma'am, the android has hands, like we do. Strong hands, but the links aren't crushed. They're cut."

"So she tossed aside her saw," Addy said, keeping her muzzle pointed at the android. "Lieutenant Ben-Ari, permission to put a bullet through the android's head."

A small high voice emerged from Ben-Ari's earbud, barely audible in the tunnel. "Ben-Ari! Ben-Ari, what the fuck is going on down there? If you destroy STC property, I'll have your hide!"

Ben-Ari ignored the captain. The lieutenant stared at the android, stared at the soldiers, stared back at the lift cage. "Emery," she said. "Go search the wreckage for a saw or laser blade. Anything that could have cut through the links."

"Yes, ma'am."

As the others kept their guns pointed at the android, Marco rummaged through the wreckage, then turned back toward his lieutenant. "Nothing, ma'am. Do you think . . ." He looked up the shaft and shuddered. "Maybe scum lurking in the shaft? Their claws could have sliced through the links."

Ben-Ari nodded. "All right, soldiers. Lower your weapons. We have no evidence against the android."

"She's the fucking saboteur!" Addy shouted, then forced her voice down. "Ma'am."

"She's a machine, Linden," said the lieutenant. "A very expensive machine."

Osiris nodded. "I am programmed to serve humanity, masters. I did not cut the chains, and lying is against my programming. I believe it likely that scum lurked in the shaft."

"You serve the scum," Addy said, refusing to lower her weapon.

Marco chewed his lip. He had a lot of respect for Ben-Ari, but he was inclined to agree with Addy and the others. He didn't trust Osiris. He remembered his encounter with her in the *Miyari*'s chapel, how she had unnerved him. How she had choked Elvis. Could she have been the one to sabotage the ship's engines during the scum attack? Could the scum have hacked into her programming? But how did that explain the lack of any saw?

"She couldn't have cut the cables," Marco finally said. "Addy, she has no blades. It had to be the scum up there, hiding in the shaft, using their claws."

Another unpleasant thought came to him. Could Captain Petty or one of her troops cut the chains, attempting to seal Ben-Ari and her platoon down here? No. He shook his head. Captain Petty was perhaps vindictive, but she wouldn't murder her own soldiers . . . would she?

"Private Linden, lower your weapon at once," Ben-Ari said to Addy. "That is an order. That goes for all of you."

Grumbling, Addy lowered her gun, as did the others.

"Now unload your guns," said Ben-Ari.

Muttering among themselves, the soldiers pulled open the chambers of their guns, fished out the loaded bullets, and returned them to their magazines.

"I'm going to keep an eye on you, robot," Addy said, pointing at her eyes, then at the android.

Osiris smiled sweetly. "I'm happy to serve, mistress."

Petty's disembodied voice emerged, shrill and shaky, from all their earbuds at once. "What's going on down there? Report to me, dammit!"

Ben-Ari spoke into her communicator. "We retrieved five bodies from the wreckage of the cage lift, ma'am. Osiris was the only survivor of the fall. We believe that scum might have attacked the cage lift during its descent. Awaiting your orders."

"We'll try to find another shaft in the city," Petty said. "This is a large mining colony. There will be other ways down. In the meanwhile, begin to explore the mines with your soldiers, Lieutenant. Find the azoth engine. That's all that matters now. Not finding colonists. Not engaging the scum. Just find that engine we need, and we'll blast off this goddamn rock." A hint of hysteria was creeping into the captain's voice. "Stay in constant contact with me. We'll find each other in the mines, then find a way out."

"Yes, ma'am," Ben-Ari said. "There's a tunnel down here that leads deeper, and there are eighteen of us—nineteen counting Osiris—all armed and fully stocked with ammo. We'll begin our exploration."

"Remember, Ben-Ari," said Petty through the communicator. "This is no longer a rescue mission. Do not engage the scum! Do not get into trouble. Find the engine and . . ." Her voice faded.

"Ma'am?" Ben-Ari said.

For a moment, silence. Static.

"Oh God," Petty said, her voice emerging from everyone's earbuds.

"Ma'am!" said Ben-Ari. "Is everything—"

"Who are you?" Petty whispered. "*What* are you? What do you want? Stay back! Stay back, all of you! Stop! Soldiers, fire! Fire!"

With a burst of static, Petty's voice died. Screams and gunfire sounded, so loudly Marco had to rip out his earbud. But he could still hear the gunfire echoing down the shaft, still hear the screams. It couldn't have lasted more than a few seconds, but it seemed ages that the gunfire rang above . . . then finally fell silent.

"Ma'am!" Ben-Ari said into her communicator. "Captain Petty! Can you hear me? What is your situation?"

Only static emerged through the earbuds.

The soldiers below stood silently for a long time.

"Are they dead?" Elvis finally whispered and gulped.

"Captain Petty!" Ben-Ari said again, speaking into her communicator. She tried contacting a few others. No replies.

"They're dead," Elvis said, looking queasy. "We're trapped here in the darkness. And the scum are up there. They're up there, and they're down here, and we're trapped, and—"

"Private, enough!" Ben-Ari said. "Count to ten. Calm yourself." She looked at the others. "We are not trapped. We are not going to die down here. You heard the captain. There are other shafts. We just have to find one with a working cage lift. But first we're going to find that engine so that we can repair the *Miyari*. Now follow me. We go down the tunnel. Keep your flashlights on, keep your guns raised, and keep your voices low."

With that, the lieutenant turned and began walking along the tracks down the tunnel, leaving the shaft behind. The others followed, plunging deep into the darkness.

CHAPTER THIRTEEN

They walked down the tunnel, nineteen soldiers, flashlights strapped to their helmets, guns held before them. Sergeant Stumpy walked with them, a flashlight attached to his miniature uniform. The walls were crude as if carved by a living creature. The ceiling was so low it grazed Beast's helmet. The train tracks stretched onward, and the tunnel sloped, moving deeper underground. The overhead lights flickered on for just an instant, revealing words painted onto the wall in what looked like blood.

Marco spoke the words in a low voice. "Turn back. Death below."

Addy hefted her gun. "*We* are death."

The lights gave another flicker, then died again. Marco hoped that meant somebody was alive below, working at fixing the power. The soldiers kept walking. Wind blew from the depths, cold and rancid, smelling of old meat and worms. The wind moaned like a dying man. Booms and thuds sounded in the deep, clanging metal, a muffled cry. Marco couldn't tell if he was hearing survivors, scum, or just the machinery of the deep flicking on and off, sending echoes through the dungeon.

They kept walking down the tunnel, moving hundreds of feet along the rails. The stench grew with every step, so intolerable that Marco and some of the others pulled on their gas masks. The stink of death.

A few more steps and Marco froze.

He raised his flashlight.

His heart burst into a gallop.

"Who's there?" he cried out, raising his gun. Around him, the others raised their weapons too. They shone their flashlights ahead.

A figure. A figure stood in the dark. Black, thin. No, not stood—hung.

They approached slowly, guns raised, casting more light on the figure.

"God," Marco whispered.

Elvis covered his mouth and turned green.

The man hung from the ceiling, a chain wrapped around his neck. His face was bloated, his tongue dangled from his mouth, and scratches as from fingernails had torn his cheeks. He wore a blue uniform, the logo of Chrysopoeia Corp still visible on the shirt.

"Poor bugger," Addy said, poking the corpse with her muzzle.

"Don't disturb the dead," Lailani said, crossing herself. "They will curse you if you taunt them."

Marco stepped closer to the corpse, grimacing, thankful for his gas mask. The man's belly was already distended with the gasses of death, and he was dripping rot. A piece of paper was folded in the corpse's hand. Marco pulled it free and unfolded it.

"What does it say?" Addy said.

"Wait, step back," Marco said. "Give me room. Away from the corpse. Thing stinks." They took a few steps away, and he read from the paper. "'They took them. All of them. My wife. My children. I saw them, I saw what they are, how they crawl, how they begged me. They are everywhere. They are in the machines. They are in the water. They are changing. I won't become one. I won't grow. I won't let them. They are everywhere. I hear them now, coming closer, the ones with the claws. If you see my family, do what I could not. Kill them. Kill them. They are coming. I am a coward.'"

Marco folded the paper again and shivered. They were all silent for long moments, staring at the corpse.

"The scum?" Addy whispered.

"Demons," said Lailani. "Demons in the darkness. We're walking into Hell."

"We're going to New Jersey?" Addy said.

"Enough," Lieutenant Ben-Ari said. "There's no such thing as demons, no such place as Hell. We are not defenseless miners. We are soldiers of the Human Defense Force. We slew many scum in Fort Djemila. We will slay any scum we find here too. Leave the corpse for now. We keep going deeper. We will find that engine, we will find another shaft, and if we can, we will find surviving miners too. In a day or two, we'll be back on the *Miyari*, and this will all be a bad dream." She walked past the corpse, heading deeper down the tunnel. "Follow me."

They walked for another few hundred meters when a massive shadow blocked the tracks. The flashlights shone on yellow hides splashed with mud, metallic wheels, and jumbles of cables spilling out from the beast like entrails. It was a small train. A train with three roofless carts, each about the size of the lift cage, just large enough for five or six soldiers to squeeze into. The locomotive seemed just large enough for a single engineer—a cramped yellow box with an engine, one seat, and a few levers. Two headlights formed eyes on the locomotive, and the entire train suddenly seemed to Marco like a living creature, a great centipede of metal, sinister, mocking him, a machine of the scum.

"It looks like one of those kiddie trains they have at amusement parks," Elvis said. "It's cute."

"Kiddie trains aren't covered with rust and bloodstains," Marco said.

"They are where I grew up!" Elvis said.

The train still unnerved Marco. That locomotive, with its headlights and bumper, resembled a face just too much—a mocking, cruel face. But he had grown up in Toronto, had taken the subway there many times. This couldn't be too different.

"I call engineer!" he said, then instantly realized how childish he sounded. His cheeks flushed, especially when he saw a few other soldiers smirk. He turned toward Ben-Ari. "Ma'am, if we can get this train to work, our journey will be faster. The train might also offer some protection."

She nodded. "Let's try it."

Marco stepped into the locomotive at the head of the train, and Stumpy hopped up beside him, his docked tail wagging. Marco sat down on the tattered faux-leather seat. It was cramped, and his knees banged against the dashboard. The cart was open on both sides, and only a flimsy roof hid the ceiling. Marco hit the ignition switch, and the locomotive grumbled, belched out smoke, rattled, and died. Marco flicked the ignition a few more times, and the engine finally growled to life.

The train began to move.

"Whoa, hold your horses!" Addy said, walking alongside. The train was still slow enough for her to keep up. "Stop and let us board."

Three levers thrust out from the dashboard. Marco chose the largest one and pulled it back. The train slowed to a halt, and the others climbed in, six soldiers per cart, their guns held between their knees. Marco pushed down on the lever, and the train moved again, clanking and grumbling down the tunnel. Marco tried the second lever, and the headlights turned on, sending beams into the darkness ahead. As they chugged on through the craggy tunnel, Marco felt like a parasite, traversing the desiccated entrails of a corpse. He kept seeing creatures in the shadows, but as the train drew closer, they vanished, mere figments of his imagination.

The words in the suicide note kept returning to him.

If you see my family, do what I could not. Kill them. Kill them. They are coming.

What sort of madness could drive a man to want his family dead? Where were the other colonists? What was that hairless, featureless thing in Ben-Ari's backpack, and what was the skeleton with six arms? *Demons*, Lailani had said. *Hell*. No. Nonsense. Marco didn't believe in such things, but there were too many riddles here, and the unknown in the darkness seemed crueler than the claws of the scum. Back in Fort Djemila, at least the enemy had attacked in the open. At least they had been enemies Marco could shoot at. But here? Only shadows and echoes.

Signs on the walls marked the distances passed. One kilometer. Then two. And still the tunnel stretched ahead, so narrow the train nearly scraped against the rough walls. The headlights reached only a few meters ahead. The rest was darkness, a constant abyss ahead of them, a black hole in the stone, eternal, the shadows dancing around it, and—

A woman ahead.

A woman in a gray robe, staring with a white face and shining eyes.

Marco started and yanked the lever, and the train screeched, showering sparks, driving forward, forward, slowing down, finally halting.

The woman stood before him, head lowered and turned aside, hidden in a hood. She stood on the tracks, still, wrapped in the robe.

"Marco!" Addy leaped out from her cart behind and trudged forward. "Why did we stop? We—" She froze. "Holy shit."

The woman in the gray robe stood still, silent, a few strands of white hair emerging from her hood. She seemed not to have noticed the train.

"Ma'am, are you all right?" Marco said and stepped out from the locomotive. Other soldiers emerged from their carts and walked to join him. "Ma'am, we're here to help. We heard your distress call. We're soldiers of the Human Defense Force. Ma'am?"

The woman spoke in a whisper, head turned aside. "You are too late."

"Ma'am, are you injured?" Marco said. "We can help you."

"You can no longer help us." She turned her head toward them, letting her hood fall. Her face was young but her hair white, her eyes haunted. All the horrors of hell seemed to dance in those bloodshot eyes. "You should run. They came for us. They will change you. Run. Run."

"Who, ma'am?" Marco said. "The *scolopendra titania*? The scum?" He reached out to her. "Are you hurt?"

She took a step back, shrugged her shoulders, and let her cloak fall around her feet.

Marco grimaced.

Her body was naked, pale, her nipples deep crimson and dripping bloody milk. Six arms grew from her torso, each ending with a single claw instead of a hand. Her lips peeled back, and fangs thrust out from her gums.

"Help me," she whispered. "Help . . ."

Her eyes blazed red, and the woman howled—a howl so loud the tunnel seemed to shake. Dust rained from the ceiling. The soldiers raised their guns, and the woman leaped toward them.

"Wait, don't shoot!" Marco cried, but soldiers were already firing.

Bullets slammed into the creature, tearing through her flesh, but they couldn't stop her. The woman leaped onto one soldier, a tall man of the STC, and the claws sank into his flesh, then tugged back, ripping out ribs. The soldiers fired more bullets. One soldier cried out, a bullet fragment sinking into his leg. Another fragment grazed Marco's arm, tearing the skin. The woman leaped again, landed on another soldier, and sliced through her throat. The flesh opened in a lurid grin. The creature leaped back, landed in the tunnel, and hissed.

"You will die," she whispered, a tongue unfurling from her mouth, dripping maggots. "You have entered hell. You should have run. You should have run!"

The creature leaped forward again. Marco and the others fired their guns. Bullets tore through the woman's head, shattering the skull, leaving nothing but a jaw on the neck. Yet still the creature leaped forward, claws lashing. The blades sliced through another man. More bullets sank into the creature, and the sound was deafening, filling the tunnel, echoing, slamming back into their ears. More fragments of bullets flew, and Marco winced as one fragment sliced across his helmet, ringing his head.

"Hold your fire!" Ben-Ari shouted. "Enough! Hold your fire!"

They lowered their smoking guns.

The corpse lay on the tracks, not much left of it. A single limb still twitched. Most of the arm seemed human. From the wrist down, instead of a hand . . .

"That's a scum claw," Marco said, and he couldn't hear his own voice. His ears felt thick, full of cotton, and the ringing hurt.

"It's some kind of Frankenstein monster," Addy said, disgust suffusing her face. "The scum chopped off her hands and sewed on goddamn claws. Sick bastards."

Marco lifted the woman's wrist, examining the bloodstained claw. He exhaled slowly. "This claw . . . it's not grafted on." He looked back at the others. "It's part of her body."

"Nonsense," Addy said. "There have got to be stitches, a scar, something."

Addy knelt too, examining the wrist in the flashlight. But they found no scars, no stitching. No, this was no Frankenstein monster. The woman had grown these claws herself. They were a part of her body, as much as Marco's hands were parts of his.

"*Mangkukulam*," said Lailani and crossed herself. "A witch."

"Not an ass wang?" Addy said.

"*Aswang*," said Lailani. "That means demon. *Mangkukulam* is a witch." She shook her head. "Whatever this creature is, demon or witch, it's evil. This whole place is evil." She shivered and looked around her. "There is evil in the walls. In the air. In the darkness. Inside me." She pulled on her gas mask, fingers shaking. "Don't breathe the air. It's wrong. It's so wrong here. It's inside of us already. I can feel it, like a rotting baby in my womb."

The arm was still twitching. Marco dropped it and looked at his comrades.

"Guys . . . where are we?"

They stared back, silent, fear in their eyes.

"Hell," Lailani whispered, and her voice echoed through the darkness. *Hell. Hell. Hell.*

CHAPTER FOURTEEN

"So how many scum did you kill in the Appalachians, Commander?" Addy asked, leaning toward Corporal Diaz.

"Was it worse than here?" said Elvis, looking at the corporal.

They were riding in the train, traveling onward in the darkness. Wounded. Afraid. Several kilometers deep. Sitting in the locomotive, Marco twisted around to see the others in the cart behind him, crowding around Corporal Diaz.

"Let the man rest," Marco said. "The last thing the commander wants in this hellhole is to relive another hell."

They all turned to look at Marco, then back at Diaz.

"So did it hurt when the scum tore out your spine?" Addy said.

"Of course it fucking hurt!" Elvis said, glaring at her, then looked back at Diaz. "So did the scum gore any of your organs too?"

Corporal Diaz raised his hands. "All right, soldiers. Enough questions. I'll tell you the story." He lowered his voice, and the others leaned closer in the cart. "There were six hundred of us, an entire battalion. We heard that the scum were gathering in the mountains, forming a swarm. Intel told us there were thousands of the bastards converging, prepared to scuttle toward DC. We stalked them through the forest for days. Days of rain. Of mosquitoes large enough to bite off your balls. Days when all we craved was a warm shower and something better to eat than squirrels. And one day we heard footfalls between the trees. Massive footfalls that shook the forest. We advanced slowly. A low grumble rose. There was something big ahead, something—"

Elvis gasped. "Was it a scum king? I've heard they grow as large as Godzilla."

"It certainly sounded like it," said Diaz. "I volunteered to scope it out. I advanced alone, gun held before me, stalking the creature. For hours I hunted it through the woods, climbing mountains, wading through rivers. Finally, in a copse of oaks, I came upon it. Bigfoot—shitting in the woods! He was so pissed off he tore me apart."

The others all groaned.

"Really, Commander!" Addy said. "Tell the story properly."

Diaz was laughing. "Guys, you don't want to hear the real story." He grew solemn. "Real war stories are never fun. They're full of grief and loss and pain. You'll understand someday. When you go home, and your friends and family want stories from Corpus, you'll understand."

Everyone was silent for long moments. The corporal was right, Marco thought. If he ever did see his father again, he never wanted to speak of this damn place. Of the woman with six arms. Of those who died on the tracks. Of any of this.

"Commander," Marco said, twisting around from the controls, "I have a question for you."

Diaz nodded. "Shoot."

"Why are you here?" Marco said. "I don't mean any disrespect, Commander. But you were severely wounded in the Appalachians. You no longer have to fight. I know that Fort Djemila was destroyed, but you could find another training base, train more recruits. Hell, after your injury, I bet they'd have given you an honorable discharge. You don't have to be on a combat mission here with us."

"It's because he loves us so much!" Addy said, batting her eyelashes. "Especially me."

Elvis groaned. "Maple, Sergeant Stumpy wouldn't love you if you were made of bacon."

Corporal Diaz remained somber. "That's a good question. One I've considered myself many times." He stared for a moment at the walls of the tunnel as they rolled by. Finally he spoke again. "I was a fat kid. Really. I was the fattest kid in my school. The other students teased me that I could roll faster than walk. They would taunt me, throw things at me, beat me. And I was too weak to fight back. I would run from them. I would hide. And it's damn hard to run and hide when you weigh as much as a scum queen."

Addy's eyes widened. "You, Commander?" She let her eyes stray down to the corporal's muscular body. "If you don't mind me saying, you've trimmed down and buffed up. Just your pinky finger has more muscles than Poet does."

"Hey!" Marco said.

"Oh, I look quite different now," Diaz said. "But when I was in high school, ready to join the army, they turned me down. Too fat, kid, they said to me. I was ashamed. My brothers, my cousins, all were joining the military. My dad's still in; he's a Master Sergeant serving in Germany. I spent a year training, getting stronger, and I swore I'd never be that sad, bullied kid again. Spent that whole damn year in the gym. When I finally joined the army, when I shot scum, I imagined shooting those old bullies from school. As I see it, the scum are the bullies of the galaxy. And I don't want to hide from them. Not anymore. They sent me to Fort Djemila after I was wounded, but when the scum invaded the base, when I fought them there, when I saw them kill Corporal Webb and Caveman and the others . . . I knew I had to keep fighting. That I'd never hide from a fight again." A twinkle lit his eyes. "And I've always loved shoot 'em up video games."

"We're glad to have you here, Commander," Marco said. "I can think of no one better to lead our squad."

"It's too bad you can't roll anymore, Commander," Addy said. "That would really help clear out these tunnels."

"With the way you've been guzzling our battle rations, you'll be ready to roll in no time, Maple," Elvis said, then wailed as Addy punched him.

As they continued through the tunnel, Marco looked into the darkness, considering Diaz's story. The corporal had been given a pass from the military, yet he had struggled, lost the weight, and volunteered to fight. He could have remained in some training base, yet he had come here to Corpus with them, placing himself in danger. Marco himself had never wanted this. He had been drafted against his will. He had been chosen by Ben-Ari for this mission, had not volunteered, and barely an hour went by without homesickness.

I wish I could be as brave, as strong, as dedicated as Diaz, Marco thought, turning his head to look at his squad leader. Marco had come to admire many people here in the army. Ben-Ari, for her wisdom and leadership. Sergeant Singh, for his strength and honor. Lailani, for her courage. But perhaps more than all of them, Marco thought, in years ahead he would remember Corporal Diaz, the man who had trained his squad in Djemila, who had come with that squad here into the darkness of space.

I won't want to talk about Corpus when I go home, Marco thought. *But I'll want to talk about my commanders. About my friends. About what I learned from them. About how they taught me to find my own strength.*

"What're you thinking of so seriously there, Poet?" Addy reached out to muss his hair.

"Bigfoot," he said.

Addy hopped into the locomotive with him, then sat on his lap.

"Get off!" Marco said. "Elvis was right, you weigh a ton."

She pinched his cheek. "Shut up and keep driving, Poet. You're being all contemplative and sad, so I'm going to stay and bug you."

Marco sighed and kept staring ahead. "You're the real bully."

But he was glad to have Addy here. She was his link to home. She was his closest thing to family here. She was crude, loud, and stubborn, but damn it, Marco loved the girl. He was glad she was here—even as she started pinching his nose. They rolled on through the shadows, plunging deeper into the mines, and Marco never wanted her to leave.

"Addy," he said.

"Poet?"

As she sat on his lap, he wrapped his arms around her.

"Back at home, you annoyed me to no end," Marco said. "You were always stealing my manuscripts, knuckling my head, wrestling me to the ground, and twice I caught you peeking at me in the shower."

She grinned. "Hey, how else is a girl supposed to learn what boy parts look like?"

"Sometimes I hated living with you," Marco continued. "After your parents died, after my father took you in, you became a sort of annoying little sister."

"You're only a few days older," Addy said. "And I'm pretty sure I'm bigger than you." She hopped on his lap.

"But Addy, I'm glad you're with me here," Marco said. "More than anyone else in the world, even more than Diaz, I can't think of anyone else to face a horde of bloodthirsty alien centipedes with."

"Aww, you sure know your way into a girl's heart." She kissed his cheek and pinched his nose. "Such a sweetie. If I weren't your foster sister, I'd marry you." She mussed his hair again. "And I'm glad you're here too. It's nice to have somebody from home. I love you to bits, little brother, you know that, right? Even though I annoy you."

"Love you too," he said. "Even though you weigh more than an elephant's ass."

As the train continued through the darkness, Marco kept his arms around Addy, holding her close, because a new fear filled him here. He thought of all those he had lost. He thought of Caveman dying on the tarmac. He thought of the soldiers dying in the crash. And he was afraid. He did not know how he could survive if anything were to happen to Addy. She was his best friend, his only family, and he never wanted to let her go.

* * * * *

They were twenty kilometers down the track when the tunnel opened into a cavern, and Marco pressed down on the brakes. It was a small cavern, barely larger than Marco's bedroom back home, but it gave them a place to stretch, to bandage their wounds, to eat battle rations.

"It's night," Lieutenant Ben-Ari said, checking her wristwatch. "Take six hours. Sleep. We'll need our strength tomorrow."

"We should not sleep here," Lailani said, looking around through the lenses of her gas mask. She stood while the others sat, and she held her rifle with both hands. "This place is unholy. We should find an exit and leave. As fast as possible."

But the others were already yawning.

"It might be days before we find a way out," Addy said. "And I'm pooped. You can guard while we sleep, Lailani."

Lailani walked toward the edge of the cavern. She stood by the tracks, peering down the tunnel toward the lurking darkness ahead. When she turned back toward the others, the flashlights shone in her gas mask lenses, and she appeared like a creature herself, like a diseased machine, all metal and glass and blood.

"We should never have come here," she said.

"No shit," Addy said. "This moon's a dump."

"I don't just mean this moon," said Lailani. "We should never have gone into space. Into the dark. Not us. Not humanity. Humanity was not meant to travel into the shadows." She shook her head. "There are terrors in the shadows. There are monsters best left undisturbed. We flew too high. We dug too deep. We woke them."

A shudder ran through the group. Marco thought back to his home, to the scum who had slain his mother. Had the aliens invaded because humanity had gone into space, stirred the hornets' nest?

Lieutenant Ben-Ari rose to her feet. "Humanity, de la Rosa?" she said. "Humanity was busy destroying itself on Earth." Her cheeks flushed. For the first time, Marco saw the lieutenant look truly upset. "Humanity butchered itself, one group destroying another, one war after another. Burning. Murdering. But a few brave souls saw nobility in our species. They saw that humans can be more than naked apes who remain on a speck in the darkness, hurting one another in the name of this ideology or that. They saw our future in the stars. A noble future. One I still believe in."

Lailani spread out her arms. "Behold our noble future."

Marco felt it best to change the topic. The last thing the troops needed now was talk of cruelty and evil.

"Speaking of Earth," he said. "What do you all miss from home the most?" He looked at Lieutenant Ben-Ari. "Ma'am, if you don't mind me asking."

Ben-Ari sat back down. She leaned against the wall, and she spoke in a soft voice. "I grew up without a home, Emery. The HDF was my home. My father was an officer like his father before him. I spent my childhood moving from one military base to another. My mother died when I was young, and my father passed away only a year ago. But I suppose . . . I miss him more than anything. My father. We never had much time together, what with his busy career, but sometimes on Saturdays he'd take me out into the desert or grasslands or ocean or wherever he was stationed. We'd look at the stars together. I know the stars are frightening to many people since the Cataclysm. But to my father, they were always things of beauty. He never told me stories of the stars, just sat with me silently, and we'd stare up together. I miss that the most."

For a moment everyone was silent. It wasn't often that their platoon commander spoke so openly of her life, of her feelings. Back at Fort Djemila, Ben-Ari had seemed as distant, powerful, and vengeful as a goddess, but Marco realized that Ben-Ari too felt lost, felt lonely, was just as human, as afraid, as hurt as all of them.

Finally Addy spoke. "I miss beer. And hot dogs. And hockey. God, I miss hockey, just being on the ice, playing the game. There's so much freedom on the ice." She leaned her head against the wall, legs spread out before her, and closed her eyes. A smile grew across her face. "One time, my boyfriend scored box tickets for a Leafs game. He got them from his granddad after some business deal. You know what box tickets are? You don't sit in the regular seats in the stadium. You sit in a special box where the rich bastards watch the game. There are leather couches, a bar, your own personal waitress. We ate chicken wings and hot dogs and poutine, and we drank so much beer, and the Leafs lost, but I didn't even care. Didn't care *much*. Fuck, that was a good day."

"I miss ballet," said Beast. The giant Russian, nearly seven feet tall, sat in the corner. He had removed his helmet, revealing his massive bald head. "And no, before you ask, I did not dance myself. But my little brother dances. He is best dancer in all of Russia, which means he is best dancer in world. Destined to be star! I would go with family to watch him perform. What a dancer! What talent! That is real talent, more than I will ever have. That is what I miss most from home. Going to ballet, watching my brother dance. That and . . ." His cheeks flushed, and he blurted out the words. "That and my boyfriend, Boris." He glanced at Marco. "I told Poet, back in boot camp. Now I tell all of you. Before we die here, I want no secrets."

"I miss rock 'n' roll," said Elvis. "Big surprise, I know. And campfires out in the countryside. My friends and I would go camping every weekend, tell ghost stories, fish in the river, and I'd play guitar." Suddenly there were tears in his eyes. "As soon as we're back home, I'm going to take Poet and Maple and Kemi out camping. They live near me, you know. Just the four of us, none of my idiot farmer friends this time. And the rest of you, too, if you feel like swinging by Canada. We'll build a campfire and watch the stars. Lieutenant Ben-Ari should join us! I'll play guitar and sing."

"I'd rather hear the mating cries of the scum than your singing, Elvis," Addy said.

"I miss my wife," said Sergeant Singh. "And my little daughter. Once a month, I'd cook lobster curry. Have you ever had lobster curry? If we ever get back to Earth, you're all invited to my house, and I'll cook you some."

"I miss video games," said Corporal Diaz. "It's funny. I used to love first-person shooters, blasting evil aliens in the comfort of my own home. Never imagined I'd fight them for real."

"I miss boot camp," said Lailani.

They all turned toward her, even Sergeant Stumpy.

"Are you mental?" Elvis said.

"She's mental," said Addy, nodding.

Lailani shook her head. "It was better than my life before it. At boot camp, I had an actual tent. I had three meals a day. I had friends." Finally she pulled off her gas mask, and her eyes were damp. "I liked it there. It was the best time of my life." She made eye contact with Marco, and her voice dropped to a whisper. "I miss it."

Finally Kemi, who had remained silent for most of the journey underground, spoke. Her voice was so soft everyone had to lean closer to hear.

"I miss my boyfriend," the cadet said, staring ahead blankly. "I love him so much. I miss just walking with him through the city, listening to classical music with him, dreaming of a future together." She closed her eyes. "But I broke his heart. When I joined the academy, I told him that I won't see him for a decade, and I let him go. Only a couple months later, he found another girl to love. What hurts most is that it's my fault." She wiped her tears. "I miss being with him so much."

A few of the soldiers—Lailani, Elvis, Beast—all looked at Marco. They knew of whom Kemi spoke. They understood.

Marco spoke next. "I miss my girlfriend. A woman I love dearly. A woman who broke my heart. A woman I missed every day, dreamed of every night, a woman who's brave, intelligent, and beautiful . . . who let me go. Who returned to me. Whom I can never have again."

Everyone was silent for a long moment, staring between Marco and Kemi.

Addy coughed. "You two couldn't say something like hockey or hot dogs, could you?"

It was Osiris who saved them from the awkward moment.

"I want to see Earth," the android said. "I want to see forests. I want to taste lobster curry. I want to drink beer. I want to watch a hockey game. Will you take me to Earth?"

Addy yawned. "You know the best thing about Earth? The beds. Fuck, I miss having an actual, big, fluffy bed." She lay down on the floor. "I'm going to sleep for the next six hours. Anyone who bugs me is getting kicked in the groin. I call the last watch."

"I'll watch first," Lailani said. She still stood by the tracks, and she pulled her gas mask back on.

Marco lay down to sleep too, choosing a spot near Addy. Elvis stretched and soon began to snore. As the others lay down, one soldier stood up. He was a corporal of Space Territorial Command, wearing a black battle uniform, one of only three STC soldiers who had made it down into the mine.

"Wait a minute," the man said and pointed at Lailani. "Why does she want to guard first?" He scowled. "I don't trust her."

"Go to sleep," Beast muttered from the floor. "You can trust little one. She strong like bull."

"Strong enough to tear out an engine from a starship?" the STC corporal said. "Strong enough to sabotage a cage lift?"

Lailani marched toward the man. "You better shut your mouth, asshole, or you're going to suck my gun's muzzle."

"Then you'll have to shoot me too," said another STC soldier, this one a tall woman with brown hair and a scarred cheek. She snorted. "I don't trust this little one. Speaking of demons and witches, hiding her face behind a gas mask, threatening murder."

Now Addy leaped to her feet. She pointed at the STC soldiers. "How do we know you're not the saboteurs? You'd know your ship! You'd know how to dislodge the engine."

"It's the android," Elvis said. He glanced at Osiris and cringed. "Right? Guys? Back me up here."

"It's a land-legger," said the first STC corporal. "Never trust goddamn land-leggers. Worse than scum."

"I'll show you scum!" Addy shouted, leaping toward the man, fists raised. Sergeant Stumpy growled and began to bark. Soon everyone was shouting, grabbing at one another, and—

"Enough!" Lieutenant Ben-Ari shouted. "Everyone, sit down. Now!"

They all froze, grumbled, and sat down. Some of these warriors were older and more experienced than Ben-Ari, but she was the only officer here. They all seemed well trained enough to respect her rank, even the spacers.

For now, Marco thought.

"We don't know who the saboteur is," Ben-Ari said, staring at them one by one. "We don't know that there *is* a saboteur. I will not tolerate baseless accusations. Not from my own troops. Not from STC troops either. Tonight we'll guard in pairs. De la Rosa, Emery—you two guard first. Then wake up another pair." She passed her gaze from one soldier to another. "We'll survive this if we stay together. We have only one enemy down here. The scum. Is that understood?"

"Yes, ma'am," they replied.

As Marco stood guard with Lailani, he watched the others sleep. Could one of them truly be a traitor? He looked at them one by one. Sergeant Singh, his turban removed in his sleep, his long black hair spread out around him. Corporal Diaz, handsome and scarred, perhaps the strongest warrior in their platoon, half his spine now made of metal but his courage never faltering. Lieutenant Ben-Ari, young but wise, a leader Marco would follow—maybe was following—into Hell itself. Beast, a gentle giant. Elvis, young and silly and so afraid. Addy, his best friend, silent and peaceful in her sleep. Kemi, his Kemi, her cheek resting on her hands, a woman Marco still loved—even now, even as he loved Lailani. Marco loved them all, he realized. Not just Kemi but every one of them. He could not believe that one of them could be the traitor.

He looked at the others in the group. A few soldiers of the STC. A few soldiers from Earth he hadn't served with at Djemila. And among them, sitting upright, eyes closed—Osiris. Could one of them, a stranger in their new squad here underground, be the saboteur? Or perhaps one of the soldiers aboveground? Were Captain Petty and her warriors even still alive? They had not heard from the rest of their company since leaving the shaft. Were their headpieces malfunctioning here underground, or were the others gone, slain by the scum?

Lailani walked up to his side. As the others slept, she slipped her hand into his, and she leaned her head against his arm. Marco slung an arm around her.

"I'm sorry, Marco," she whispered. "That I've been so gloomy. So afraid. That I haven't been good to you." She moved so that she stood facing him. "When I said I missed boot camp, I meant that I missed being with you there. Before all of this."

She closed her eyes and leaned her cheek against his chest, and Marco wrapped his arms around her, holding her close. He missed it too. Lazy Sundays on the base, lying on his cot, holding Lailani in his arms. More than anything right now, he wanted another day like that, just to lie with her in sunlight, hold her, laugh with her.

"Better days will come," he said. "It can't always be dark. We'll find our way out of this place. We'll have more days in the sun."

The wind moaned, emerging from the tunnels below, and it seemed almost to laugh, to mock Marco. The words from the wall returned to him. *Welcome to Hell.* He shivered and held Lailani close.

CHAPTER FIFTEEN

Marco woke up from sweaty, suffocating nightmares to find himself back in the mine, Kemi missing.

"How could they have just vanished?" Lieutenant Ben-Ari said, eyes flashing. "Who had the last watch?"

Marco rose, rubbing his eyes, shaking off the slumber, the dreams of being trapped in a labyrinth, creatures chasing him. He looked around him, and a fresh coat of cold sweat covered him.

The soldiers stood in the small, craggy chamber alongside the tracks. But two soldiers—an STC corporal and Kemi—were gone.

"I was meant to have the last watch," Addy said. "Elvis and me. But Kemi never woke us up."

Marco's heart seemed to freeze.

He stepped onto the tracks. "Kemi!" he shouted, then turned the other way. "Kemi!"

His voice echoed. Somewhere deep in the darkness, laughter—cruel, demonic—answered.

"I knew it." Lailani spat, pacing the chamber. "I knew it! That STC piece of shit corporal. He was the traitor all along. And he tried to pin it on me."

"Or maybe that Kemi cadet was the traitor," said one of the remaining STC soldiers. Only two now served in the group.

"Kemi isn't a traitor!" Marco said, knees trembling, heart racing. "I've known her for years. Something must have grabbed them while they were guarding." He coned his hands around his mouth and shouted again. "Kemi!"

Addy approached him, pale. She stared at him in shocked silence, then down the tunnel. Addy and Kemi had never been close friends. Addy was crude, rude, tall and blond like a viking, a girl who loved fistfights and beer. Kemi was studious, ambitious, and introverted, the sweet granddaughter of Nigerian immigrants who loved good grades, classical rock from two centuries ago, and her boyfriend. But the two had grown up in the same city, same school, had spent many days together. Addy was now trembling.

"We'll find her," she said, voice shaky. "I promise you, Marco. We'll find her. And I'll kill whoever took her."

The soldiers split into two search parties. One group traveled back along the tracks toward the shaft, driving the train in reverse. The other group, Marco among them, traveled on foot deeper into the mine. Marco didn't have to walk far. Only a couple hundred meters down the tunnel, he froze.

A lump lay on the tracks.

His heart froze.

"Kemi," he whispered.

He ran along the tracks and knelt by the lump. He hated the relief that flooded over him, that shaky breath of joy.

It wasn't Kemi. It was the STC corporal, holes gaping in his chest, eyes staring lifelessly.

Marco rose from the body. "Kemi!" he cried.

In the distance—clattering. Moaning wind. The echoes of laughter.

"Maybe we should keep quiet," Lailani said. She knelt by the corpse, examining it. "Scum made these wounds. Scum claws."

Marco stared at the slain corporal. "Or the claws of those humanoid creatures, like the one in the gray robe." He turned to look at the other soldiers who stood behind him. "A creature must have grabbed them in the night. It might still have Kemi. She might still be alive."

He walked deeper into the tunnel, and his flashlight reflected on something small and metallic. Marco knelt.

It was Kemi's pistol. Sticky goo covered it.

"Scum drool," Marco said. "The scum have her."

There was no corpse. No blood. They had taken her alive, discarding her weapon.

Marco tapped his communicator and hailed Lieutenant Ben-Ari, who was leading the second search party. He waited in the darkness until the train came trundling back toward them. Ben-Ari and the others leaped off the carts, and Marco showed her Kemi's pistol.

"They took her alive," Marco said. "The bastards took her alive."

Ben-Ari nodded, face pale, eyes determined. "We'll get her back. Into the train. We follow."

They all boarded the train—fourteen soldiers, the last of their company. They traveled down the tunnel, staring ahead, the headlights cutting a path through the darkness. Marco kept dreading another lump ahead on the tracks, but the rails stretched onward, unencumbered. Marco kept one hand on Sergeant Stumpy's back; the Boston Terrier rode beside him, a comforting presence. They passed a kilometer. Another kilometer. And still the tunnel stretched onward, sloping deeper underground.

Where are you, Kemi? Marco thought. Tendrils of panic wreathed around him. He couldn't slow his heartbeat. His head kept spinning. Kemi was trapped somewhere here in the darkness, dragged into the shadows, hurt, maybe dead. Scared. She would be so scared. Marco's breath trembled, and images of their youth together kept rising in the darkness. Kemi helping him with his math homework. Kissing Kemi for the first time, sixteen years old, lying together on a grassy hill in the night. Kemi and him cooking in her family's kitchen, laughing, lying on the couch, reading together, comforted by each other's presence.

That's what I miss from home, Marco thought. *God, Kemi. Hang in there. I'm coming for you. I'm going to find you.*

The tunnel sloped downward, so steep Marco kept pressing the brakes to slow the train, and he felt like on a roller coaster, plunging down, his belly churning. The tunnel narrowed, soon so narrow the rough walls scraped the train's sides and the ceiling brushed the soldiers' helmets. They had traveled five kilometers when they reached a fork.

Marco stopped the train.

He stepped out onto the tracks, examining both paths. One was narrower and plunged deeper underground. The other tunnel was wider, sturdier, and level.

"Well, I know which way I like," Addy said, pointing to the wider path.

Marco frowned. He stepped toward the fork, staring down one way, then another, seeking some clue, finding none. Finally he shouted, "Kemi!"

The other soldiers cringed.

"Emery, I thought we were going to be silent," Ben-Ari said.

He didn't reply to his lieutenant. He listened, eyes closed.

In the darkness, a clattering rose, a cackle, a scraping on stone.

Marco pointed down the narrower, steeper tunnel. "There's life down there. I can hear it. They took Kemi that way." He grabbed a lever on the track and yanked it. With a screech, switch rails on the tracks moved, pointing down the narrow tunnel. They got back into the mine carts, and they rode onward in the darkness. The train rattled down the narrow path, scraping against the walls, sparks rising beneath its wheels. Pale curtains like cobwebs hung from the ceiling, brushing against them, though Marco saw no spiders. An acidic odor clung to the air.

As they drove deeper, the cackles rose louder ahead. Shadows danced, then vanished. A creature clattered above, disappearing when Marco looked up.

"They're everywhere!" Addy shouted from the cart behind Marco.

"I can't see them!" Marco said.

"They're here," Lailani said. "Demons. Demons of hell."

The whispers rose all around them. Feet pattered on the ceiling, along the walls. Shadows fled. Marco thought he saw something, there, ahead—a figure standing, humanoid, white eyes, and—

The headlight shattered on the train, plunging the tunnel into darkness. They kept plowing ahead, the blackness now complete. They lit their flashlights, but the light seemed so weak here, only intensifying the shadows, making them dance.

"Slow down!" Addy shouted.

Marco reached for the brakes. He cried out, pulled his hand back. It bled. The lever was gone. The train stormed onward, and the creatures were racing everywhere. Sergeant Stumpy wailed.

"Scum!" Addy shouted. "Fucking scum, they're on the walls, they're on the ceiling, they're everywhere!"

Lailani was laughing. "Hell. Hell. We're in Hell."

"Don't fire at the walls!" Ben-Ari shouted. "The bullets will—"

But her voice drowned as soldiers rose in their mine carts and fired their guns. Muzzle flashes lit the tunnel. Bullets screamed, slamming into the walls, shattering, ricocheting. Pieces of bullets slammed into the sides of the train. A soldier screamed and blood sprayed. Creatures screeched in the darkness, leaping down from the ceiling, claws flashing, and another man screamed in pain. Blood splashed Marco, hot, sticky. A huge white flash of light blazed forward as Lieutenant Ben-Ari fired her plasma gun. For an instant, the tunnel was bright as day, and Marco saw dozens, hundreds of scum ahead, coating the walls and ceiling like worms in entrails, claws clutching the walls, scuttling forward.

Marco rose in his seat and fired his gun.

The other soldiers leaned out the sides of their carts, firing their own guns. A creature slammed into the train, tore apart, and the carts screeched and thumped over the beast. More of the aliens shrieked ahead. Marco flipped his safety switch to automatic, emptied a magazine, loaded another one. He shouted as he fired. The train slammed into more scum, leaped off the tracks, slammed down again, scraped across raw metal, reconnected with the rails, and stormed onward.

A scum swooped from above, landing in the locomotive.

Marco shouted, swung his rifle's stock, and knocked the scum aside. He fired. Bullets riddled the creature's abdomen, and burning yellow blood showered. Another creature landed before Marco, and claws scraped his arm, and he fired again, screaming in pain. Stumpy leaped onto a scum, biting and barking.

"They're everywhere!" someone shouted behind. More scum kept raining from the ceiling. Bullets lit the darkness. They plowed over the centipedes. More kept landing, and the train slammed into a pile of them, scattering chunks of exoskeleton. With an ear-piercing screech, the train rolled off the rails. They skidded along stone, raising showers of sparks and shattered rock, and slammed into a wall. The mine shook. The engine belched out smoke, then died.

Ben-Ari fired her plasma gun again, illuminating dozens of scum ahead, racing toward them.

Marco drew a grenade from his belt.

"Fire in the hole!" he shouted—he must have heard it in some movie ages ago—and tossed the grenade.

They all knelt and covered their ears.

The explosion rocked the mine, deafening, shaking the tunnel. Chunks of stone rained.

"Fire in the hole!" Addy shouted and hurled her own grenade.

"Fire in the hole!" others answered, lobbing grenades.

Marco leaped out of the train and knelt behind the locomotive. He ducked his head and covered his ears.

The moon of Corpus seemed to shatter.

A supernova explosion seemed to tear through the mines.

Chunks of stone and sizzling hot exoskeleton sliced him, followed by raining yellow blood.

The dust settled. Marco and the others rose. Sergeant Singh attached something to a pistol, then fired. A flare blasted down the tunnel, then burst into light, filling the mine with searing whiteness.

Scum lay dead or twitching across the tunnel. A handful were still crawling forward. A few more gunshots knocked them down.

Venom sizzled on Marco's wounds, infecting them, and with shaking hands, he plunged a needle of antidote into his thigh. His ears rang and thrummed. Already, over the past few days, he had found it more difficult than usual to hear conversations. If he ever returned home, he wondered how badly damaged his hearing would be. Rubbing his ears, he walked alongside the train. His heart sank.

Three soldiers lay dead, ripped apart by claws.

Two were STC soldiers, their necks slashed open. And the third . . .

"Corporal Diaz," Marco whispered. "God. God, no."

He knelt by his squad commander, the man who had taught him in Fort Djemila, who had been mortally wounded in the Appalachians, only to rise and fight again. Now Diaz lay by the tracks, lifeless, his belly ripped open, his insides spilling out. Marco could see a segment of his metal spine.

He lowered his head. "Commander," he whispered.

Emilio Diaz gave a gasp, reached out, and clutched Marco's hand.

"My God," Elvis whispered. "He's still alive. The son of a bitch is still alive."

Diaz groaned, gasped for air, and tightened his grip on Marco's hand.

"I'm here," Marco whispered. "I'm here, Emilio. I'm here."

And Corporal Emilio Diaz—this great warrior, the man who taught Marco's squad to kill, who had slain scum in the mountains and the mines, always with a thin smile on his face—began to weep.

"I'm scared, Marco," he whispered. "I don't want to die here. I want to go home. I want to go home. I want my mother. Please. I . . ."

Diaz fell still. His eyes stared at the ceiling. His breath died.

They all gathered around him. Marco. Addy. Elvis. Beast. Lailani. All had served under him in Fort Djemila and here in Corpus. All lowered their heads. Ben-Ari joined them, silent, eyes closed, a tear on her cheek. Even Osiris the android stood watching silently, curiosity in her robotic eyes.

"He was the finest warrior I knew," Marco whispered. "I admired him. I'm proud to have fought with him. Goodbye, Corporal Emilio Diaz."

"Sergeant Emilio Diaz," Ben-Ari said. "I promote him to sergeant. We will remember him always." She knelt and removed his dog tags. "I will bring these back to his family."

They had no way to carry the body. They had to leave him here, buried in a distant moon. The train would no longer move, its locomotive shattered. They walked onward, heads lowered. From a company of two hundred soldiers, they were down to eleven.

I lost Kemi, Marco thought. *I lost my commander. I'm lost in darkness.*

He walked onward, gun held before him, seeking, as in his dream, a way out.

CHAPTER SIXTEEN

They walked on through the darkness, eleven soldiers, the last of two hundred. All were wounded. All were haunted. They pointed their guns before them. The tunnels twisted and turned, branching into a great labyrinth. Marco was the only one with paper and a pen. As a writer, he always carried them with him. He kept a map of their progress, his ink forming a network like the roots of trees.

The rails stretched down most tunnels, but some tunnels were narrower, even cruder, and no tracks led down them. Slime coated these tunnels, and they saw the marks of claws on their walls.

"Scum holes." Addy spat.

"The scum are turning this place into a great hive," said Marco. "Maybe that's why they invaded Corpus. The mines had the basic structure of a hive already in place. They just needed to clear out the humans and expand the network."

"Where are the humans?" Addy said. "We haven't seen any. Only that weird woman with six arms, and I'm not sure she qualifies."

"They probably fled the moon," said Marco. "Smart. And once we find that engine somewhere down here, we're off this rock too."

As they kept walking, a sickly, almost sweet smell rose from ahead, a smell like honey spilled over rotten fruit. The cold lifted, and the air grew warm, thick, damp. The cloying stench soon became so powerful they all put on their gas masks. Stumpy, the only one without a mask, whimpered.

"Smells like unicorn shit," Addy said.

Sweat filled Marco's gas mask. His lenses kept fogging up. It was hard to see, but the tunnel seemed to grow lighter. Yes—there was definitely light ahead, not just the shine of their flashlights. It was an orange, warm glow, like that of a hearth. A rustling, clicking sound rose from ahead, soft, almost like white noise.

"We should turn back," Lailani said.

"No." Marco shook his head. "Kemi might be down here. Whatever else awaits us, we'll face it."

Addy hefted her rifle. "We'll *kill* it."

They kept walking as the light, the stench, the sound grew, until finally the tunnel opened into a vast chasm.

The soldiers froze.

Marco grimaced.

Elvis pulled off his gas mask, turned aside, and retched.

The scum had expanded the tunnel here, carving out a round, crude cathedral. Blobs hung from the ceiling, coated with skin and veins, glowing orange. Their light oozed over a writhing pile of eggs that covered the train tracks and spread to the walls, a pile the size of a house, stinking, dripping ooze. Each egg was as large as a watermelon, the shell translucent, revealing a blurred view of a scum maggot inside.

"Ugh." Addy shuddered. "A scum nursery."

Several adult scum came racing around the pile toward the soldiers. Addy fired a bullet, hitting one in the head. A few more bullets from the squad killed the other bugs—a surprisingly quick victory, considering how many bullets a scum could normally withstand. Marco frowned, stepped toward one of the scum corpses, and nudged it with his foot. He looked back at his comrades.

"These ones don't have claws." He looked back at the corpse. It was just as large as the regular scum—about ten feet long and wide as his torso—but it had soft legs that ended with prehensile hooks, and its armor was thinner. "I think these ones are nurses. Sort of how ants have warriors, workers, and nurses."

Addy loaded a fresh magazine. "Step back, everyone. Dead scum maggots coming right up."

The others stepped back and raised their own guns, pointing them at the eggs.

"Wait," Marco said.

They turned toward him. "Poet, what, you gotta pee first?" Addy said.

"I feel weird about this," Marco said. "These are babies."

Addy groaned. "Fuck me, Poet. This is like whenever a spider got into our house back home. You'd never let me kill it, just put it outside. These are *scum*, Poet. Scum! The creatures that destroyed the world."

Marco nodded. "Yes. I suppose you're right." He stepped closer to the eggs. Inside, the maggots were twisting, squealing, poking at the rubbery shells with their tiny claws. "Someday these creatures will grow up. They will kill. But . . . right now, it feels wrong to kill them." He turned toward Ben-Ari. "We should spare them, ma'am. We should walk on, seeking Kemi, seeking the engine. We didn't come here as exterminators."

But the lieutenant's eyes remained hard. "No, Emery," she said. "Private Linden is right. We will not spare them."

"Ma'am," he began, "they—"

"You called them babies," Ben-Ari said. "You tried to humanize them. But they are not humans. These are maggots. Maggots who will grow into monsters. What of human babies, Marco? What of the human babies these creatures might someday kill? What of Corporal Diaz, of Caveman, of the others who died? What of the billions who died on Earth? What of your own mother?" Her voice softened. "I'm sorry, Marco. You are kind. You are decent. But you're wrong. We *are* exterminators. That's why we're here. Step back, Marco. Let us do our job."

"Ma'am," he said, "you chose me for this mission because I wasn't just a killer. That's what you told me. That's why you brought me with you."

"Um, guys?" Addy said. "Maybe we can discuss ethics later? I think the eggs are, well, hatching."

Marco spun back toward the reeking pile. The eggs were writhing, cracking open, and the maggots emerging. Already the larvae had claws. They squealed, jaws opening to reveal sticky gullets. They began crawling down the pile, hissing, screeching, begging for food.

"Little fuckers," said Private Kalquist, a soldier who had joined their platoon just before boarding the *Miyari*. "Not even worth wasting bullets on."

Kalquist raised her boot above one of the scum. The creature—it was no larger than a house cat—leaped up and wrapped around her leg. Kalquist cursed. At once, twenty other maggots flew toward the private, landed on her, and began to bite. Kalquist screamed and the other soldiers recoiled. The scum fed like piranhas on a cow, ripping off Kalquist's face, tearing chunks off her limbs, exposing the bones, and still she screamed, her skull revealed, still alive.

The soldiers opened fire.

The bullets slammed into the scum, slammed into Kalquist, slammed into the pile behind. Ben-Ari fired her plasma gun, and the eggs burned. The fire spread, and the bullets kept flying, and the maggots screamed as they died. They tried to flee the burning pile, wreathed in fire, pathetic creatures, burning, begging. Bullets hailed onto them. Still Ben-Ari fired her plasma gun, and it became as a flamethrower in her hands, gushing forth fountains of blue and white and red, ionizing the air, burning the fumes, and the eggs burst, and still more creatures emerged, and still they died.

Exterminators, Marco thought, firing his gun too, killing them, for perhaps Ben-Ari was right. This was who he was. This was what he had become. This was what the HDF was in space, not a force to defend humanity but to exterminate its enemies. And here underground, in a distant world light-years from Earth, they burned the nursery, destroying the young before they could grow. The flames roared to the ceiling, and they walked around the blazing pile, and they entered the tunnels again, leaving the stench and heat and the last dying screeches behind.

They walked onward. They were down to ten soldiers. And still Kemi was lost. The soot stained Marco's face, and he knew that it would forever remain, a stain he could never wash, a nightmare he could never wake from.

* * * * *

They walked for hours, crossing many kilometers of tracks, following one path after another, lost in the labyrinth. There seemed no end to the darkness. There had to be an end. Somewhere here, they would find the last station of these rails, would find the machinery deep inside the moon, find the engine, find Kemi. Marco had to believe that. It was the only thing that kept his feet going. The others walked beside him, silent, faces washed with sweat.

"Addy." Marco walked closer to her, limping now, his legs and back aching. "Do you remember that time in boot camp, how we had to carry the radios around the base?"

She nodded. "My back still hurts."

"I miss that day now."

"Me too," Addy said. "Fucking hell, I'm turning into Lailani, missing boot camp."

"Addy, do you remember how Dad would cook us omelets for breakfast, how we'd all watch cartoons in the kitchen, how he'd laugh so hard at the roadrunner?" Marco's eyes stung with tears. He was a soldier. He had killed scum, many of them. But right now the tears filled his eyes. "Do you remember Earth?"

Addy nodded. "I remember."

"We'll be back there soon," Marco said. "I'm done with space. I'm done. As soon as we're off Corpus, we'll request a transfer back home. We'll watch cartoons again. We'll see Dad again for Christmas."

Now Addy had tears in her eyes. "I'm scared, Marco. I'm scared we won't make it back home. That we'll die here like Diaz. Like Caveman and Sheriff. Like all the rest of them."

"We'll make it home," Marco said. "We're survivors. Come Christmas, you and I will be sitting by the fireplace at home, drinking eggnog, and watching cartoons with my dad."

Addy laughed through her tears. "He's my dad too, you know. I think of him that way since my own folks died." She held his hand. "And you're like my little brother."

"I'm a few days older than you, Addy."

"But you're sweet like a little brother." She wrapped her arms around him, hugging him as they walked. "I fucking love you, Marco. You know that, right? I fucking love you so fucking much."

He shoved off her helmet and mussed her hair. "Love you too, sis."

Lailani walked up to them, like a child in her father's uniform, her pants baggy and her helmet wobbling. She spoke in a soft voice. "I've always hated Christmas. It was a dangerous time. A time when thieves would move through the slums. When those better off than us celebrated in their homes, but we had only the turkey and pork bones we found in the trash the next morning." She looked at Marco. "If we ever get out of here, can I celebrate Christmas with you, with your family? I promise to just sit at the back and not bother anyone."

"I'll give you the best seat in the house," Marco said. "And the biggest piece of turkey and the biggest slice of ham. So long as I'm with you, Lailani, you'll never want again."

"Want what, turkey?" Lailani said.

"Whatever it is you do want."

She leaned against him. "You."

Addy made a gagging sound. "So sweet I'm going to throw up." She shook her head wildly. "Anyway, we should invite everyone to Christmas." She looked around her at the other soldiers. "You'll all fit! Sergeant Singh, and Lieutenant Ben-Ari, and—"

"Sergeant Singh is Sikh," Marco said. "And Lieutenant Ben-Ari is Jewish. They don't celebrate Christmas."

Singh, who was walking behind them, smiled within his black beard. "I would be happy to eat some of that turkey," he said.

"As would I," said Ben-Ari. "And nobody has to salute me while carving it."

Marco was silent for a moment. Then he said, "It's hard to remember things. To think about home. Somehow it makes the darkness even blacker, makes the pain more real, makes this place worse. It's like when I was back at Fort Djemila. The hardest time wasn't marching with the radios, wasn't our journey through the desert with the litters, wasn't even the lack of sleep. It was one moment—the moment when I called my dad at home, when I heard his voice. That is the only moment in basic training that broke me. And I don't know exactly why."

"Because it made you human again," Ben-Ari said, voice soft. "Basic training is all about depriving you of humanity. That's why we raced you, shouted at you, harassed you day and night. We didn't want to give you even that one moment to think. To be a boy again. We had to turn you into machines, thoughtless, mindless, emotionless. When you called your father, you were human again for just that moment—and all the pain hurt so much. But right now, here in the dark . . . I want us to remember. I want us to be human, not machines, even if it hurts. Because I want us to have hope. To know what we're fighting for, what we'll see again."

Not machines, Marco thought, turning to look at Osiris. The android walked behind them, silent. Soot covered her uniform and skin, but her metallic, platinum hair had not a strand out of place, and her eyes still shone.

"Masters," the android said, "may I join you at Christmas too?"

Marco nodded. "Of course."

"Do you want to hear a joke, masters?" Osiris said. "What kind of tree grows in your hand? A palm tree. It's funny because palm means a tree of the family Palmae but also means the part of the inner surface of the hand that extends from the wrist to the bases of the fingers."

"Yes, thank you for explaining that," Marco said.

"You're welcome, master. I have five hundred and twelve other jokes in my database. I'll save them for Christmas."

And you'll be with us too, Kemi, Marco thought. *I promise you. I will find you. I will bring you home.*

For a few moments, they walked in silence.

Finally Elvis spoke. "If we ever go home, we won't be the same. We won't be human anymore. Not the way Ben-Ari said."

They turned to look at him. Normally Elvis was the one singing, dancing around, telling jokes, but now his face was solemn, his eyes haunted.

"You mean we'll go home as cyborgs?" said Addy. "With metal limbs like Corporal Webb had?"

Elvis shook his head. "I mean we'll be different inside. Sort of . . . broken. Like my brother. He served in the HDF for five years. He came home, and . . . he was empty inside. He wasn't wounded. He was still tall, strong, worked in the fields with us. But he never laughed anymore. He never danced, sang, told jokes. Never dated a girl." He lowered his head. "A year after he got home, he killed himself. We found him in the barn. His suicide note only said: 'I'm sorry.'"

Marco walked closer to his friend. He remembered the story Elvis had told him back in Fort Djemila, how his girlfriend had died in a car crash. "I had no idea you lost your brother," Marco said. He placed a hand on Elvis's shoulder. "I'm sorry for your loss."

Elvis nodded. "I guess that's why I sing so much. Why I don't like being serious. Because I don't want to turn into that. A hollow man. But if we ever go home, after seeing all this . . ." He swept his arms around him. "These tunnels, this war, the monsters in the darkness . . . How can we ever be happy again? How can we ever sing, dance, be like we were, even if we make it back home?"

Lailani spoke in a soft voice. "There can still be joy after pain. I suffered all my life. My life was like these tunnels, dark, twisting, full of suffering." She raised her scarred wrists. "I tried to kill myself once. But I found some light. I found some joy. The pain stays with you always. Always. Even if we go home, the pain will still be there, forever scars inside us, as true as these scars on my wrists. So no, we won't ever be as we were. But that doesn't mean there can't also be some light among the shadows. The world still has some beauty in it, even with all the fucking shit all over. I believe that now. I have to."

After that, they walked in silence for a long time, each soldier lost in his or her thoughts, remembering home.

CHAPTER SEVENTEEN

They kept walking until they reached a doorway.

They froze.

A doorway. An actual metal door, not just a crude tunnel. Two soldiers flattened themselves against the walls, guns at the ready, while Ben-Ari grabbed the doorknob and shoved the door open. They peered inside to see a metal chamber full of pipes, control panels, generators, and drills. The train tracks ran through the chamber. There were a thousand places here for scum to hide, and the soldiers stepped in slowly, guns raised, flashlights shining. A metal trough ran alongside one wall, full of bubbling molten metal. A few veined blobs clung to the ceiling and vents, casting their dim orange glow.

"Scum lanterns," Marco said. "The bastards were here, or were here not long ago."

"Fucking scum." Addy grimaced and pointed. "What is that? Is that a kid?"

They looked. Marco covered his mouth, nauseous. Something like a burnt corpse, not very large, lay between a few pipes, charred black. If there had been limbs, they were gone, and the face was burned away.

"Maybe it was one of those things like in Ben-Ari's pack," Marco said.

As if in answer to his question, Lieutenant Ben-Ari's backpack rustled.

"What the fuck," Addy whispered. "Did the thing in her backpack hear you? *Understand* you?"

Ben-Ari shrugged off her backpack, knelt, and opened it. They all gathered around. Inside, the blanket they had wrapped around the fleshy blob was writhing. Ben-Ari scooped up the bundle and unwrapped the blanket.

The lieutenant screamed and dropped the creature.

The room spun.

Marco couldn't breathe.

A dream. It has to be a dream. Oh God, please let this be a dream.

The fleshy creature lay on the floor, mouth smacking, eyes blinking. It had no arms, no legs, but it had a face. Marco's face.

"Why is it you?" Addy whispered, pale, fingers trembling. "Oh God, Marco, why is it you?"

He couldn't breathe. He gasped for air. "Don't hurt it," he whispered. "Don't . . ."

But Addy, grimacing, knelt and lifted the blob with his face. She ran and tossed it into the vault of molten metal.

The creature screamed. It screamed so loudly the sound echoed through the chamber, louder than any man could cry. They covered their ears as the scream rose higher and higher, ripping through the air, a siren, until finally it faded and the thing with Marco's face melted in the metal.

They all needed to sit down after that. The soldiers found a little chamber with chairs and a table behind a glass wall. They sat, breathing deeply, shuddering, unable to speak for long moments.

"What was that thing?" Addy finally said, then glared at Lailani. "And don't say a demon."

Marco thought for a moment, still unnerved. He couldn't stop seeing his face on the creature. "When we found it, it was featureless, just a blob wrapped in skin, like a football," he said. "I'm the first one who touched it. I picked it up. I think . . . it took my DNA from me. Just a little bit of sweat, some shed skin cells, might have been enough. Maybe that's how the people with six arms were created. A lump of flesh grabbing human DNA, growing them into creatures."

"Scum can do this?" Addy whispered.

"Remember the old stories we heard as kids?" he said. "How scum could clone humans, could plant the clones into human society? We used to be so scared that our teachers were clones, agents of the aliens."

"I'm still not convinced Mr. Hommen wasn't a clone," Addy said.

"There are different types of scum," Marco said. "We saw that in the nursery. We saw scum nurses without claws. Maybe this place has scum scientists."

"What, in lab coats, with bushy white mustaches and messy hair, sticking their tongues out? That kind of thing?" Addy groaned. "They're insects, Poet. Just big centipedes."

"First of all, centipedes aren't insects," Marco said. "They're arthropods. Secondly, these centipedes figured out space travel. They're not as dumb as they look. The *scolopendra titania* possess intelligence on par with humans."

"In that case, they must be pretty fucking stupid," Addy said, and Marco couldn't argue with that.

"All right, soldiers, search every last inch of this place," Ben-Ari said. "We're looking for an azoth heart, same as the one back on the *Miyari*. Split into pairs and don't leave the room."

Marco paired up with Addy, and they moved through the chamber, walking around great metal vents, furnaces, drills, cauldrons, and massive machines whose purpose they could not guess. The sticky scum lamps dripped above. A few soldiers ripped open the casings of the machines, but inside they found dusty gears, no glowing blue azoth heart. Finally the soldiers regrouped and followed the tracks into another tunnel.

As they walked through the darkness, guns raised, they heard laughter ahead.

The laughter of a baby.

The soldiers glanced at one another.

"You know," Elvis said, "normally a baby's laughter is a beautiful sound, but when you're walking through a dingy tunnel kilometers below the surface of an alien moon overrun by demons, it really is the last thing you want to hear."

"Might be a surviving colonist?" Marco said.

They kept advancing, guns raised.

They entered a large, round chamber with white tiled walls. Sticky scum lanterns coated the ceiling, casting their light on . . .

Marco's head spun. He struggled not to fall. Elvis actually fainted, and Beast retched in the corner. Lailani fell to her knees, crossed herself, and began to pray.

"A little harder to kill these babies, isn't it?" Marco said softly.

Metal carts filled the chamber, pressed close together, like one of those old nurseries from the twentieth century. Inside each cart lay a baby with a human head and a wiggling centipede body.

"The scum did this!" Addy said, shaking, gun clattering in her hands. "They made these babies. Some kind of genetic experiments. You were right, Poet. They *are* scientists. Mad, evil scientists. And I'm going to kill them all. Kill them!"

Marco approached one of the carts. The baby inside looked at him and laughed. Its centipede body writhed, claws reaching out. Another few babies began to cry.

"This is a dream," Elvis whispered, walking among the carts. "It has to be a dream. This can't be real. This can't be real." He pinched himself. "Wake up. Wake up. Wake up."

But this *was* real, Marco knew. These creatures, babies, aliens, hybrids, twisted, evil, sad, corrupted—they were truly here. Unholy and innocent. Marco didn't know if this was Hell, like Lailani believed, or some alien laboratory, or perhaps even the work of the human colonists. Whatever had created this was evil. And whatever lay in these carts was not.

More of the babies were crying now.

"We have to kill them," Addy said. "God, we have to kill them. This is cruel. This is inhuman." She raised her gun. It trembled in her hands. "We have to kill them." She looked at Lieutenant Ben-Ari as if seeking permission.

Ben-Ari stared at the creatures, her face pale. "I . . ." She inhaled deeply. "We . . ."

"We can't hurt them," Marco said. "They have human heads. They might have human minds."

"And the bodies of scum!" Addy said. "What kind of life is this?"

"Cruel, pained life," Marco said. "Perverse, twisted life. But who are we to take it from them?"

"So what will we do?" Addy said. "Leave them here? Just leave them to grow into monsters in the service of the scum? We can't take them with us." She turned toward Ben-Ari. "Ma'am, permission to open fire. It would be a mercy."

The lieutenant approached one of the cribs. She reached inside and stroked a baby's cheek. The centipede body flailed, claws bending, and the baby gurgled.

"We can't kill them," Ben-Ari said softly. "We have to help them. We'll push the carts. We'll take them with us. If we can get them off this moon, maybe back home, they can find some sort of life. Maybe they can even provide some answers about what happened here."

"We cannot bring this evil back to Earth," Lailani said. "This moon is unholy. This moon is hell. We must not bring any part of it back home."

"Home is already infected," said Ben-Ari. "To combat evil, we must remain good. To combat destruction, we must heal. We defeat evil not only with guns, bombs, and fire, but also with compassion and mercy and righteousness."

That is why I followed you into space, Einav Ben-Ari, Marco thought, looking at his officer. *That is why I follow you still.*

"I can't believe this," Elvis said, shaking his head. "For once, I'm going to have to agree with Maple."

"Lieutenant Ben-Ari is right," said Beast. "We help babies."

Sergeant Singh nodded. "We help them. We will be righteous."

They all began to argue, some demanding to kill the creatures, others to simply leave the babies, while some soldiers wanted to carry them along. Marco stood, silent, wanting to help these babies, not sure he could.

A voice rose from a chamber beyond, weak, barely audible.

"Marco?"

The others didn't seem to hear. Marco turned toward the voice.

"Marco . . ."

He walked away from the others, heading toward a doorway at the back. A shadowy chamber loomed beyond, and he heard low breathing. Behind him, the other soldiers fell silent, then followed him, leaving the deformed babies in their carts.

"Poet, where are you going?" Addy said.

Marco didn't answer. His pulse quickened. He swallowed, his throat dry, and stepped through the doorway into the second room.

He stood still for a long moment, staring with damp eyes.

Dozens of metal tables filled the room, and upon them, strapped down with dripping strands of fleshy tendrils, lay more creations.

This time the soldiers didn't speak, didn't move, only stared.

One creature was a bloated man, pale, bald, his legs fused into a long, twitching centipede body. Two women were stitched together, forming an infected conjoined twin, eyes blinking, mouths moving wordlessly, their seams dripping rot. A small, quivering creature had the clattering head of a centipede, mandibles moving, but the broken body of a child. A man moaned, wept, whispered, his torso elongated, sprouting a dozen arms. Other creatures seemed to be failed experiments; they were swollen, covered in sores, twisted into unrecognizable forms, all bent limbs thrusting out from folds of flesh, jaws locked in grimaces, drooling. Children hung from one wall on meat hooks, skinned, still alive, turned into centipedes below the ribs. A ball of swollen flesh the size of a walrus lay on a stone table, pulsing, featureless.

"Kill . . . us . . .," whispered a man strapped to the table with sticky membranes, his torso sprouting four centipedes instead of arms and legs. "Kill . . . us . . ."

Addy came to stand at Marco's side. A tear streamed down her cheek. She looked at him, silent, eyes huge and haunted.

"Mar . . . co . . ."

The voice came from the back of the room. Marco walked between the tables, following the voice, and he saw her there.

He froze, his eyes dampening.

Kemi.

Kemi lay on a metal table, wet membranes strapping her down. She was still human, but segments of centipedes hung above her from hooks, twitching like lurid mobiles. The scum had stripped her naked, had drawn marks across her stomach, chest, joints, and neck like plastic surgeons preparing for surgery. Tubes ran into her veins, attached to sacks of skin that hung from rods like IV bags. Another tube ran from a fleshy blob into Kemi's mouth, thrusting down her throat.

A live centipede rose from behind the table, legs stretching out, hissing. Instead of claws, its legs sprouted surgical tools: scalpels, saws, hammers, needles, not prosthetics but actual organs, evolved or designed for its grisly task.

The creature screeched. Marco shot a single bullet into the alien's head. It fell, raising smoke, dying.

"Mar . . . co . . .," Kemi whispered, then gagged around the tube.

"I'm here, Kemi." He touched her hair. "I'm here. You're safe now."

"More scum coming in!" Addy shouted and fired a bullet. A scum screeched. The creatures on the tables screamed.

"There's about a million of 'em!" cried Elvis and opened fire at a doorway. Sergeant Stumpy barked and ran around the room.

As the other soldiers fired, Marco drew his knife. He sliced the sticky, thick membranes that pinned Kemi to the table. It felt like slicing through umbilical cords. He pulled the tube out from her mouth, and she coughed, gagged, and spat out pale yellow liquid. Together they pulled the tubes out from her veins. Marco had a blanket in his pack, which he wrapped around her.

Scum came scuttling into the room through a tunnel at the back. Marco raised his gun and sprayed out bullets. He handed Kemi her pistol, which he had found in the tunnel. Kemi loaded the gun and fired a blazing inferno of ionizing death, burning down a scum. A soldier screamed, three scum leaping onto him. Another soldier fell. Bullets rang out, cutting down the creatures.

"Fire in the hole!" Addy shouted. She ran toward the tunnel the scum were emerging from and lobbed a grenade.

The soldiers knelt. Explosions rocked the mines.

"Fire in the hole!" Beast and Elvis shouted, hurling two more grenades. Chunks of scum flew. Claws whirred through the air. The tunnel collapsed, burying more aliens beneath it.

The battle died down. They all stood panting.

Marco looked around him. Shrapnel, sizzling flesh, and dead scum littered the lab. One tunnel had collapsed, but two more doorways still stood open, one leading back toward the nursery with the babies, the other leading deeper into the mines. Two soldiers lay dead among the twitching scum.

Only a handful of soldiers now remained alive. Ben-Ari, panting, holding her plasma gun. Sergeant Singh, eyes dark, beard sprayed with blood. Elvis and Beast, standing back to back, one a slender young man with long sideburns, the other a massive brute with a bald head. Lailani, small but fierce. Addy, face glistening with sweat, blond hair sticking to her cheeks. Marco. Kemi. With them, Osiris the android. From two hundred soldiers who had landed on Corpus, an entire company, they were all who remained.

And you, Stumpy, Marco thought, looking at the ragged Boston Terrier.

"Let's get the hell out of here," Addy said. She turned toward the tunnel that ran deeper underground. "We go deeper."

Marco turned toward Kemi. She stood beside him, pistol in hand, wrapped in his blanket. Her eyes dampened.

"Are you all right?" Marco said to her.

"No," Kemi whispered and embraced him, clinging to him desperately, and she wept.

Marco held her for a long time, stroking her hair.

"I've got you now, Kemi." He rocked her gently. "It's over. It's over."

She blinked tears out of her eyes, looking at him. "Marco . . . when they had me on the tubes, I . . . I was connected to the others. The other patients here. No, not patients. Experiments. I could feel their feelings. I could think their thoughts. I could hurt with their pain. I raged with their anger. Their hatred for humanity. Their evil. They feel so much pain, Marco. They are so angry. They are so hateful. We have to help them. We have to let them sleep."

"Kemi." He held her hands. "Maybe we can help them. Free them like we freed you. Like—"

She pulled away from him and raised her plasma pistol. Tears in her eyes, she fired, burning one of the creatures on the tables.

"Kemi!" he said.

She looked at him, tears on her cheeks, and fired again. She shouted. She wept. She kept blasting out plasma, screaming hoarsely, burning the creatures on the tables, shaking. The room blazed. Kemi raced through the fire, sobbing and howling, into the chamber with the babies. She blasted out fury from her gun, and the babies caught fire, screaming, twisting, burning, dying.

When they were all burning, Kemi fell to her knees, dropped her gun, and sobbed.

"Marco, get her out of here!" Addy said. "The whole place is on fire!"

The surviving soldiers were racing toward the tunnel that was still open. Marco knelt by Kemi and helped her rise.

"I had to," she whispered. "I had to. I had to. You'll never understand. You didn't feel them. You weren't one with them. They are so cruel. I had to. I had to."

He nodded, his arms wrapped around her. "Come with me now."

Kemi limped, leaning against him, and they walked between the blazing hybrids and into the tunnel. They left the burning laboratory behind, heading into the darkness, and Lailani's words kept echoing in Marco's mind.

We're in Hell . . . Hell . . . Hell . . .

CHAPTER EIGHTEEN

They found a small chamber full of bunks, buried deep in the mine, where two scum were copulating.

"Busted, fuckers," Addy said and sprayed the aliens with bullets.

They dragged out the corpses, then closed the door and sat on the bunks. Nine soldiers. Nine souls trapped kilometers underground, surrounded by thousands of scum.

"Ammo count," said Sergeant Singh, and they all inspected their magazines and grenades. They didn't have much left. Addy had fired her last bullet in this very room, and she had to take one of Elvis's magazines. Lailani had been smart enough to take magazines from the soldiers they had lost on the way. She now pulled them out from her pack and distributed them. Of graver concern were the plasma guns, which Lieutenant Ben-Ari and Kemi carried. Both were down to just a few last shots.

"Our flashlights won't last much longer either," Marco said. "These flashlights are designed to offer continuous light for three days. It's been about three days."

"If the power comes back on, we can charge both the flashlights and plasma guns," said Ben-Ari. "Or if we can find a generator down here that still works. But we might have to do without." She rose from the cot she sat on. "We should go. We should keep exploring."

"Ma'am," said Marco, "if I may make a suggestion: We need to rest. To eat. To sleep. Especially Kemi, and some of us are wounded."

Ben-Ari looked at the door. "I don't like the idea of staying underground even a moment longer. But maybe you're right. The mines might still be deep." She nodded. "Let's take six hours. That's it. We guard in pairs again—with the door closed."

Throughout the night, the scum squealed and shrieked and scuttled outside. Shadows danced beneath the door and claws scraped the stone. Several times the centipedes pounded against the door, finally moving onward. Stumpy spent all night by the door, growling at it, guarding the team. Marco remembered the propaganda reels from basic training. The scum needed to touch an object with their antennae to smell it. They were safe here behind the closed door, but outside the terror lurked. Every few moments, a human scream interspersed the clatter of the centipedes. There were still colonists here, perhaps subjected to more experiments, perhaps tortured, dying.

They let Kemi skip guarding. She was still trembling, still shell-shocked. Addy spent most of the night at Kemi's side, holding her close, stroking her hair, and whispering comforts into her ears. During Addy's guard shift, Marco sat with Kemi, holding her hand while she flitted in and out of sleep.

This is my fault, Marco thought, watching Kemi sleep. *You came here to be with me. And now you're hurt. Now maybe you're hurt too badly to ever heal.*

He thought of their youth together, of days joyous despite the war. Perhaps what Elvis had said was right. Perhaps there could be no more joy after this. They could never be youths again. Marco and his friends here were only eighteen, barely more than children. But Marco felt old. He felt haggard, as if he had lived for decades here in the darkness. He felt that he could never be young again.

When Kemi was sleeping deeply and Addy was at her side, Marco lay down by Lailani. She was awake, curled up on a mattress, watching him. Her hand strayed just a few inches forward, and he moved his hand too, letting their fingertips touch. Lailani stared into his eyes, and she didn't need to speak. Marco saw the words in her gaze.

It's all right, Marco. I know. I understand. And I still love you.

Kemi—the love from his past, the warmth of his youth, his memories of home. Lailani—the new love he had found here, his new light in the darkness, the light that led him forward on his path of fire and rain. Finally he slept, his fingers grazing Lailani's thigh, and it was enough. It was a hint of his connection to her, one that he now knew would endure, one that comforted him.

When their clocks showed morning, they had a cold breakfast of battle rations. These too were running low. They were down to only a few cans of tuna, two cans of Spam, a handful of energy bars, and a few packets of mustard. Kemi wore sweatpants and a T-shirt Addy had taken in her backpack, and she sat with a blanket wrapped around her shoulders, barely touching her food. Her eyes were still sunken and haunted.

"When I was . . . there, with the tubes in me," Kemi said, "they weren't just feeding me. I was connected to them. To their hive. I was part of their consciousness." She shivered and held her can of tuna, not eating. Her voice dropped. "The *scolopendra titania* aren't individually intelligent. Each one alone is no smarter than an insect. But combined they form a network, a great communal brain. We were all connected to it. Me. The other patients in the room. They were trying to . . . to make us part of their hive, but to also retain human independence, singular intelligence."

"See?" Addy said to Marco. "They don't have scientists. They're dumb as insects on their own."

Kemi continued as if she hadn't heard. "When I was in their network—that's the only way I can describe it, a network—I was aware of what they smelled, what they heard, where they scurried. I was still myself, still Kemi, but I was also the entire hive, thousands of them, sensing everything the hive sensed. And I saw a blue heart, beating, pulsing in the depths. I saw where it lies. I know the way."

Ben-Ari rose from the bed she sat on. "The azoth heart!"

"I think so," Kemi said. "When you see into the hive, you don't see actual images. It's more like feelings, just senses, suggestions, like imagining a warm beach when a sunbeam hits you, like shuddering in a shadowy house when you feel somebody watching you. But yes, the more I think about it, the more I see blue, glowing, pulsing." She sighed. "It's frustrating, trying to explain it. The scum don't think like we do, not with words or images. They have no words, no actual language, just ideas, smells, feelings, tastes, visions." She shuddered. "I don't want to ever experience things as they do again."

"Can you show us the way to the heart?" Ben-Ari said.

Kemi shivered and hugged herself. Addy hurried to her side and slung an arm around her.

"I know the way," Kemi said, "but there is evil there. Great evil that guards it. Something worse than anything we've seen so far. I briefly sensed it. The fear in it. The size of it. I don't know any more. But I don't want to approach it. Everything in me screams to run as far away as possible."

"We need that heart," Ben-Ari said softly. "And we need all the firepower we can get. We must continue. You must show us the way. If we can't retrieve the azoth heart, we're stuck on this rock."

Kemi clutched the lieutenant's arms. She breathed heavily. "You must promise me something, ma'am. If we go there, if we face this evil . . . no matter how it looks, no matter what it says, we must kill it. Promise me that we will kill it."

"We will kill it," said Ben-Ari. She turned toward the others. "Gear up. We move."

They traveled on through the mines. Kemi walked at their lead, holding her pistol before her, pausing at every fork in the road, closing her eyes, shuddering, then choosing a path and walking onward. The others followed, rifles raised, firing whenever a scum raced toward them.

As they traveled deeper, they passed by metal carts full of rock and soil, great metal filters, and drills the size of tanks that idled by walls of stone. The miners had been digging new paths here, but they were gone now, their drills rusting, the shards of stone unfiltered. A few times the soldiers glimpsed crude azoth in the carts of rock: rough rocks with shimmers of blue, still uncut into the crystals used to power starships. In another chamber, buckets of soil stood on a frozen assembly line, and chunks of crude azoth shone in glass bottles like trapped blue fireflies.

These stones would be of no use here, not without an expert gemcutter and a year to work. Such a master would need to chisel a gem's angles down to just the right atom, allowing spacetime to bend within the stone. What the soldiers sought was a polished, cut gemstone, placed inside an intricate metal heart. Only such a crystal could bend spacetime the way a diamond could bend light. Only an azoth heart—not just the crude fuel but a masterwork—could send a starship across the galaxy. Even the cut azoth crystals did not last forever, often lasting only several journeys. Their angles faded—just one atom worn away required the entire crystal to be replaced. But finding one now would be enough—enough to raise the *Miyari* into orbit, to send the starship to Nightwall or back to Earth.

They walked for two kilometers down a steep tunnel along the tracks, and they reached a crude passageway and saw orange light and fluttering shadows beyond. A great clattering, clicking, and hissing rose within the chamber ahead, and they caught sight of many scum, dozens, maybe hundreds, racing along curved walls. The stench of the aliens wafted out, sickly sweet and rotten and wet. The soldiers pressed themselves against the walls of the tunnel, loathe to enter the hall of the creatures.

"There are about a million of those fuckers in there," Addy whispered, using a small mirror from her backpack to peer into the chamber.

Marco craned out his neck, then quickly pulled his head back. He had caught just a glimpse of the chamber—a hall the size of a movie theater, filled with scum scurrying over the walls and ceiling. "We'll have to find another way."

"There is no other way," Kemi said. "I traveled the labyrinth ten thousand times in the minds of ten thousand creatures. This is our path. We must pass through this chamber and into the tunnel beyond."

"Then we take one of those diggers back there," said Beast. "Big drills. They not Russian made, but they will still dig. We carve other path."

"The vibrations would alert every scum for kilometers around," Elvis said, looking ill.

"Would perhaps a joke help ease the tension?" said Osiris. "I still have a few hundred more in my databases."

Sergeant Singh snapped a bayonet onto his T57 assault rifle and hefted the weapon. "We'll carve our way through. We don't have many bullets left, but we have blades if it comes to that. I'll go first. The rest of you follow."

Lieutenant Ben-Ari shook her head. "No, Sergeant. I'm still platoon leader. This is my responsibility. I'll take the vanguard."

Marco understood. Going first into the chamber was the most dangerous. Ben-Ari was willing to take the brunt of the scum's fury to protect the others. That was not what many officers would do, Marco knew. Many officers would send the lowest ranks in first, fodder for the enemy, but Ben-Ari believed in leading her warriors into battle rather than commanding them from behind. The lieutenant raised her plasma rifle, then turned toward the others.

"You are my soldiers," she said. "I trained many of you myself. You are my friends. You are my family. You are all warriors. You make me proud to be human. Moses Formation. Ready?"

They raised their weapons. They spoke together. "Ready."

With a battle cry, Ben-Ari charged into the alien hall.

Marco and the others shouted and followed.

The chamber was round, large as a church nave, and full of the scurrying, screeching creatures. Here was a new breed of *scolopendra titania*. These ones too were ten feet long, shielded in an exoskeleton, and lined with claws, but they beat leathery wings and rose into the air. On the ceiling hung bloated, dripping sacks of skin, stretched to the size of beanbags. The skin was translucent, revealing umber liquid inside. Several scum hovered below these massive wineskins like hummingbirds, drinking fluid through a hole in the center of each sack. When Marco looked closer, he wanted to gag, to faint. The reservoirs of nutrients were *human*. Their limbs had been glued to the ceiling, and their mouths still screamed. Their bellies had bloated to obscene size, storing the honey the scum fed upon through the navels. The prisoners were like honeypot ants, engorged, attached to the ceiling, living larders, feeding the hungry in their agony.

Hell, Marco thought. *Hell. Hell.*

At their lead, Ben-Ari fired her plasma gun, carving a path forward. Behind her, the others—seven soldiers and an android—fired their weapons in the Moses Formation they had learned at basic, four soldiers firing to the left, four to the right, splitting open the sea of enemies. They shouted as they fired. They wept as they fired. They all saw the horror. They all trembled, hated, feared. They all killed.

"Kill them all!" Addy was shouting, tears on her cheeks. "Those sick fucks! Kill them all!"

Their bullets sang. Scum flew toward them, fell, shattered. The sacks of fluid burst above, the prisoners dying on the ceiling, raining down the honey. More scum kept rising from the walls. They emerged from holes in the ground. Dozens. Hundreds. They buzzed through the chamber, claws lashing. One claw tore into Singh's leg, and the sergeant roared, firing his gun in automatic, limping forward. More scum blocked the door ahead. One slashed Beast's side, and the beefy soldier bellowed, fell, and rose again. Marco suffered a cut to his arm. It sizzled with poison, and he groaned and ran onward, tears of pain in his eyes.

"There are too many!" Elvis shouted.

"Kemi, with me!" Ben-Ari cried. "Plasma forward, carve a way to the tunnel!"

The two plasma guns—one a pistol firing a thin ray, the other a rifle gushing forth a torrent of fury—carved a path through the carnage. The enlisted soldiers ran behind the officer and the cadet, and Sergeant Stumpy followed, barking madly. The soldiers began to race into the tunnel, but the scum were converging, diving toward them. Marco spun around, firing bullets, backing up into the tunnel.

"They're following!" he shouted. "Hurry!"

Elvis and Lailani ran into the tunnel after him, leaving only Beast in the chamber. The giant was limping, fell again, and suffered another gash to his side. He rose and limped onward as scum stabbed at him from all sides.

"Beast, come on!" Marco shouted from the tunnel entrance. He fired a bullet over the Russian's head, hitting a scum.

Beast was bleeding, sweating, barely able to walk, but he managed to trudge toward the tunnel, gun firing in all directions. When he reached the doorway, he froze and looked into Marco's eyes.

"Go, friend," he said. "Run."

"Beast, come on!" Marco said. "Into the tunnel!"

But the giant turned his back toward Marco and the others. He stood in the tunnel opening, blocking it with his massive girth. As the scum in the chamber flew toward him, Beast howled and fired his gun, emptied a magazine, loaded another, and sprayed more bullets. The scum tore into him. His blood splashed.

"Beast!" Elvis cried from behind Marco, standing in the tunnel, eyes wide.

"Beast, come on, damn it, into the tunnel!" Addy cried. "What are you doing?"

"He's blocking the scum," Marco said, tears in his eyes. "He's letting us run."

"Soldiers, come on!" Ben-Ari shouted from farther down the tunnel. "Follow me, now!"

Yet how could Marco run? How could he leave his friend? Beast still stood within the passageway, blasting out bullets, the scum falling before him, cutting him, biting him.

"Run!" Beast cried. "Run, friends!" He roared out in pain, blood spraying. "For Boris! For Russia! For Earth!"

The giant fell to his knees, his legs shattered. His gun fell. He unhooked two grenades from his belt.

"Beast!" Elvis cried.

Marco ran. He grabbed Elvis, pulled him back. Addy was crying out, reaching toward Beast, but she ran with them, and—

The tunnel shook as the grenades exploded. The ceiling cracked and chunks of stone fell. More grenades burst, and the scum screamed as the cavern collapsed above them, blasting out clouds of dust. The soldiers kept running as the mines trembled, as dust stormed over them, as the scum died, until finally the rumbling ceased.

When Marco looked behind him, he saw a pile of stones. The chamber full of scum was gone.

Elvis fell to his knees.

"Beast!" he cried, tugging at boulders, trying to dig a path back. "Beast!"

"He's gone, Elvis," Marco said, voice choked. "He's gone."

Elvis lowered his head, body wracked with sobs. Marco held him. The others stood around them, tears in their eyes.

"Damn this place," Elvis said, voice shaking, eyes red. "Damn this fucking moon. Damn this war. Damn the scum. Damn all of it." He pounded at the boulders, harshly at first, bloodying his fist, then weaker, weaker. "Beast . . . My friend . . ."

"Come, Elvis." Gently, Marco helped him rise. "We have to keep going."

The soldiers walked onward, silent, until they reached a chamber where two scum were mixing sticky ooze in a vat. Panting, Elvis raised his gun and fired in automatic, emptying a magazine within seconds, then loaded another, emptied, another, emptied it, kept firing even with no bullets left, even as the scum lay dead.

"Die!" he shouted. "Die! Die!"

"Private Ray!" Ben-Ari said, stepping toward Elvis. "Private Ray, enough! Look at me. Look at me!"

Elvis turned toward his officer, pale, trembling, and let his gun fall to his side. "I hate them," he said, voice cracking. "I hate them so much. I want to go home. I want to stop losing people.

Why do they all have to die? Why do they always leave me? I want to go home, Lieutenant. I just want to go home."

Marco thought that Ben-Ari would admonish the private, would slap him, shout at him to get a grip. But instead, the officer embraced him, held him close against her. Elvis was only eighteen, and Ben-Ari was only a couple of years older, yet she comforted him like a mother comforting her child.

"I will lead you home," Ben-Ari said. "I promise you." She looked over Elvis's shoulder at the rest of them. "I chose you all for this mission. I led you here. And I promise you. I promise. I will do whatever I can to take you home."

"That's what Beast thought too," Elvis said, head lowered. "That's what Diaz thought. What they all thought. That we'll go home. But there is no home. There is no hope."

"There is always hope," said Ben-Ari. "I learned that from my family, from my country, from my soldiers. So long as we live, there is still hope."

Elvis lowered his head. "He was my friend. He was my best friend."

Marco approached and embraced him. Addy joined the embrace, then Lailani, then the rest of them. They stood together in the chamber, eight lost souls, holding one another. Marco wished they could be stronger. Wished they could be like those warriors in the old action movies, tough, hardened, able to keep fighting without a tear, without emotion, spewing one-liners as they slew the enemy. But Marco wasn't such a warrior, nor were the rest of them, not even Addy, not even Ben-Ari, perhaps none in this army. They were kids, that was all. Kids with families at home. Kids scared in the dark, this war too big for them. Kids pulled from their homes, drafted into an army, tossed into the depths of space where terror lurked.

"We're just kids," Marco said softly. "We shouldn't be here. We're not brave. We're not strong. We're just kids far from our home. But that's what soldiers have always been, in every war. When were warriors ever strong, ever fearless, ever able to kill and lose friends and suffer pain without a flinch? Wars have always been fought by children—children torn away from their homes. It was like that when millions of boys, some as young as thirteen, fought the Second World War. It was like that when boys were shipped off on the Crusades a thousand years before that. It was like that fifty years ago when the scum first landed, when Earth drafted everyone from age fifteen and up and saw them burn. We're lost. We're afraid. We're too young, too weak for this. We are soldiers. That is what soldiers have always been." They were looking at him, cheeks damp, and Marco took a shuddering breath. "But those soldiers all kept going. They trudged through the muck and death, leaving friends behind, because they believed the world could be good again. Maybe not for them, not for those who fought, who lost their souls. But maybe for those who follow. We're light-years away from Earth. We're trapped underground. We don't know if our ship will ever fly again, if we'll even last the night. But I believe that the world, that this cosmos, can be good again. So we'll keep going. For those we lost. For those who still live."

The others nodded. Addy smiled through her tears and took his hand. They walked onward through the mines. Ben-Ari. Singh. Osiris. Lailani. Kemi. Addy. Elvis. Marco. Eight friends, eight soldiers, leaving a friend behind.

CHAPTER NINETEEN

As they walked through the tunnels, Sergeant Stumpy began to sniff.

"Look," Addy said, pointing at the Boston Terrier. "Look at his nose! He smells something."

"He always smells something," Elvis said. "It stinks down here. It's why I have to wear my gas mask."

The tunnels were narrower, darker, and colder down here in the depths. A sign a while back had labeled the tunnel ten kilometers deep—half the length of Manhattan—and the soldiers had only been descending since. At times it was hard to tell if these tunnels were man-made, natural caves, or carved by the scum. The sticky ooze of the creatures coated the walls, and their stench clung to the air. Elvis was right. It stank here, and Sergeant Stumpy was always finding something to sniff at.

"Look at him." Addy watched the Boston Terrier. "He never sniffs like this. He's onto something. Look at his nose go. It looks like it's about to fall off his face." She knelt and patted the dog. "What do you smell, pup?"

Sergeant Stumpy wagged his stump of a tail and ran. They all followed him.

"This isn't the way," Kemi whispered, walking with her blanket wrapped around her shoulders. "We must go deeper to find the heart."

But the dog was racing forward, and Addy was racing after him. Reluctantly, the others followed. Stumpy took them down a tunnel away from the tracks and toward a doorway. There he scratched the door and sniffed underneath it, pawing as if trying to crawl through.

Marco and Elvis raised their guns, ready to fire into the room while Addy kicked open the door. They burst inside . . . and froze.

"My god," Addy whispered. "Oh god. Oh god."

Elvis actually fell to his knees, and his eyes dampened. His voice shook. "Holy shit."

Marco stared, speechless for a long moment. "It's . . . beautiful."

It was a kitchen. A kitchen stocked with food. Real food. Not Spam in cans. Not battle rations. Not gray glop from powder mixed with water. On shelves stood cans of corn, peas, green beans, mushrooms. Jars of preserves stood on another shelf— blueberry, strawberry, apple jam. Freezers held real meat—steaks, ground beef, chicken wings—still frozen and good to eat. There were bags of flour, dry pasta, breadcrumbs, rice. This was Earth food. It looked better than anything Marco had eaten since joining the HDF several months ago.

Marco wanted to keep traveling the mines, to find the heart, to get off this rock, but his belly grumbled. He had eaten nothing but battle rations since delving underground three days ago. All the soldiers turned toward Ben-Ari.

"Ma'am," Addy said, "Stumpy really wants a break."

"I need some corn!" Elvis said, salivating, eying the cans.

"I think I see a box of mac and cheese!" Addy said.

"Crackers with jam!" said Lailani, licking her lips.

Before Lieutenant Ben-Ari could reply, Sergeant Singh marched to the cabinets, spun toward the other troops, and crossed his arms. "Nobody is eating corn from a can, mac and cheese, or crackers with jam." The turbaned warrior scowled.

"But, but—" they all began.

"Enough!" rumbled the bearded sergeant. He gripped the curved knife that hung from his belt, the traditional weapon of Sikh warriors. "You will not eat these things. Because I'm cooking."

They cheered as Lieutenant Ben-Ari sighed.

"All right!" the officer said. "So long as two soldiers are always guarding the door. And Stumpy doesn't count."

Outside that door lurked horrors worthy of hell, a host of alien monsters, twisted, tortured beings, a nightmarish realm of death and evil. Yet here, for a brief hour, the soldiers filled this little nook with comfort. Lailani found candles in a cupboard, and she lit them across the kitchen, letting the soldiers turn off their flashlights. Elvis sat on a chair, legs stretched out, and sang a rockabilly medley, and Addy soon joined him. Singh hummed along as he cooked, boiling water, defrosting chicken, then frying it in breadcrumbs and flour, heating the stove from a gas canister.

The sergeant opened cans of tomatoes, peas, and chickpeas, added spices, tasted, nodded, spiced some more. He boiled rice in a pot, and he even baked dessert, mixing flour with powdered milk, oil, chocolate powder, and sugar, topping his cake with blueberry jam. The scents filled the kitchen, and Stumpy went so wild Singh kept having to toss him snacks.

Finally the feast was prepared. Singh set the table, and they all sat down—dusty, bloody, covered in cuts and bruises, still wearing their helmets and holding their guns, their souls shattered, but all hungry. They hungered for food but more so for normalcy, for companionship, for a respite from the horror and grief and loss.

"It looks wonderful, Commander," Marco said to Singh.

"I helped." Addy beamed.

Singh smiled. The sergeant had removed his helmet, revealing his army green turban. His Khanda amulet, symbol of his faith, shone around his chest. "Before we eat, may I say a prayer?"

"I think we need prayers in a place like this," Ben-Ari said softly.

They all held hands around the table—even Osiris, who sat with them despite needing no sustenance. Singh lowered his head, closed his eyes, and sang softly in a foreign tongue. Marco couldn't understand the words, but he imagined that it was a prayer for peace, for deliverance from evil, for holiness in darkness.

When finally the prayer was over, Ben-Ari said, "Would you mind if I add a prayer of my own?"

The lieutenant pulled an amulet out from her shirt, revealing a Star of David, and she too sang a prayer in a foreign tongue, and Marco could not understand these words either, but they comforted him. There was goodness to these words. There was hope and love. Marco was not religious, and he didn't know if any gods listened, but one thing he believed in—the goodness inside of Singh, inside of Ben-Ari.

"May I?" Lailani said next, and she too prayed, eyes closed, then crossed herself and nodded, and her eyes were damp. She wasn't the only one. Everyone seemed in awe, sensing if not holiness then companionship, a sense of peace even here in Hell.

Addy spoke in a soft voice. "Sergeant Singh prayed a Sikh prayer. Ben-Ari prayed a Jewish one, and Lailani a Catholic one. May I add my own holy words?" Addy stood up and cleared her throat. "Rub a dub dub, thanks for the grub. Yay God!"

They all groaned, and Elvis pelted her with an empty can.

"Show some respect!" Elvis said. "The prayer goes: Good bread, good meat, good God, let's eat!"

This elicited more groans.

"Let's eat," Marco agreed.

They ate.

The meal was delicious, the meat surprisingly savory for something found thawing in a mine freezer, the sauce rich and creamy. Outside—just outside the door a few feet away—spread a realm of horror, and even as they dined, they could hear the scum scuttling and clattering outside. They talked and laughed loud enough to mask the sound. Osiris told bad jokes, and they laughed, only encouraging the android to tell more.

"Sergeant," Marco said, looking at Singh, "where did you learn to cook like this?"

"Back home," Singh replied. "For my wife and daughter."

"Pics or it didn't happen," Elvis said.

Singh pulled a tattered photograph from his wallet. It showed a smiling woman in a sari holding a toddler.

"They're beautiful," Marco said, then frowned. "But Sergeant . . . when did you have time? We're all drafted at eighteen. Were you a teenager when you got married? Is that part of your culture?"

Singh shook his head, smiling. "No, I wasn't a teenager. I got married at twenty-three, only joined the military at twenty-six. I'm thirty now."

"Joined at twenty-six!" Addy gasped. "How the fuck did you avoid this shithole for eight years after turning eighteen?" She whistled. "You must have been damn good at hiding."

Singh's smile grew sad. "If you consider lying in a hospital bed hiding." They all fell silent at this, and Singh continued in a low voice. "I got cancer only a few months before I was to be drafted. I was seventeen and terrified I was going to die. It took two years to beat the disease. Once I was cured, well . . . they let me off the hook. Said I didn't need to join the HDF at all. So I spent a while working in a meat factory, packaging pastramis and hot dogs—and yes, even Spam. Got married. Had a kid. And then when my daughter turned three—this was four years ago—I walked up to the nearest military base and told them I wanted to serve."

"You *what*?" Elvis gasped and looked ready to faint. He began choking on his food, and Addy had to slap him on the back and dislodge a bite.

"I'm inclined to share Elvis's sentiment," Marco said. "If you were off the hook, you could have avoided all this, Sergeant. You could be cooking for your family now."

Singh smiled. "I *am* cooking for my family now."

"Aww, he's a lot sweeter when he's not yelling at us," Addy said.

"I never particularly enjoyed yelling at anyone," Singh said. "It was part of my job at Fort Djemila. To train you. To prepare you for battle. You see, back home, I lost too many friends. I saw too much death. I couldn't bear to watch my daughter grow up in such a world, a world terrorized by the scum. I knew I had to do my part. So I enlisted. I fought. I taught. Now I fight again. With a new family. I've been in the military for four years now, and in one more year I'll go home to my beautiful wife, to my beautiful daughter, and I'll know that I made the world a little safer for them."

"I still think you're mental," Elvis said. "With all due respect, Commander."

Singh nodded. "I probably am, but who isn't in this army?"

Volunteering. Marco could barely wrap his mind around it. He had been drafted. If he had refused to join, he'd have spent years in a prison cell. He hated it here. He hated every moment of it. He could barely imagine what it took to walk up to a military base, to have that medical pass, to toss it aside, to join the fight—with a wife and child, no less.

"Sergeant," Marco said, "forgive my language, but you've got balls."

Addy gasped. "The poet cursed! The poet cursed!"

"Balls isn't cursing," Marco said.

"For you it is!" Addy hopped up and down in her seat. "Oh dear, oh boy, I think we've finally corrupted him."

"I volunteered too," Lailani said quietly.

They all turned to look at her. Elvis pointed his spoon at the little soldier.

"You're mental. You're all mental."

Lailani shook her head. "No I'm not. Well, I am. But not because I joined the army. My life before . . ." She lowered her head. "It wasn't a life. It wasn't much better than these tunnels. I spent some nights sleeping by the train tracks in the slums of Manila, one eye open, watching for thieves and rapists. Some nights I slept behind brothels, waking whenever a man grabbed me. I spent days in alleyways behind fast food restaurants, rummaging in garbage bins for chicken bones, and I'd pick off the little bits of meat still left, fry them up, close my eyes and force them down, often puking it all out later because it was rancid." She looked at her plate of food. "A meal like this? Hell. Even

Spam back at basic was a feast for me." She looked at Singh. "Your daughter is very lucky, Sergeant. My mother was a child prostitute who starved to death when I was ten. I still don't know who my father was, just some story that he was an American soldier, but he could just as well have been a homeless drunkard who paid my mother with drugs. So yes, I'm a bit mental. I love the army. I love it here. I have food. I have shelter. And more importantly, I have a family here." She looked at them all. "I have people who I love."

Marco, who sat beside her, placed a hand on her shoulder. Addy, who sat at Lailani's other side, gave her a hug and kissed her cheek.

"We love you too, Tiny," Addy said.

Marco turned to look at Kemi. She sat at his other side, gazing at him, eyes soft. Marco reached under the table and held her hand. She let him hold it. She leaned her cheek against his shoulder, and her curls brushed his cheek.

Singh sliced the cake and handed out the pieces. They all tucked in, other than Elvis. He lowered his head, staring at the dessert.

"I just wish the others could be here with us," Elvis said. "The rest of our family. Beast. Caveman. Sheriff. Diaz. Hell, I even miss Pinky and the Chihuahua. We lost so many. It feels so empty."

They all paused from eating. Singh rose from his seat, found a bottle of grape juice in a cupboard, and poured the drink into Styrofoam cups.

"To family lost," the sergeant said, raising his cup.

"To Beast!" said Elvis. "To Caveman. To Sheriff. To Diaz. To Captain Petty. To everyone we lost. We will remember them always. We will fight for them always."

They drank, and as the sweet juice slid down Marco's throat, he wondered how many more friends he would lose in this war—and how long he himself would live.

Ben-Ari raised her glass a second time. "To life!" she said.

"To life!" they all repeated. Here in this hive of death. Here, the last survivors of a massacre. Here, in a burning cosmos, humanity rising from devastation—to life!

When their cups were empty, they stared at the door. With the conversation at a lull, they heard the creatures moving through the mine.

"We're close," Kemi said, eyes closed. "I saw it so many times. I feel it. Pulsing. Calling to us. The heart."

Marco walked toward the door. "Then let's go get it."

None of them wanted to leave this sanctuary. They wanted to sleep, to laugh, to remember, to eat another meal, not to return to the nightmare so soon.

Let's be done with this, Marco thought. *Enough of this place of death. To life. To life.*

He opened the door, and they returned into the labyrinth.

CHAPTER TWENTY

The tunnels grew so narrow that they had to walk stooped, then crawl. The burrows sloped downward, twisting, stinking. Kemi crawled at the lead, and Marco followed, his gun strapped to his back, banging against the ceiling. Sometimes the tunnel was so narrow he could barely squeeze through. As they crawled here, eight soldiers, Marco felt as if he were a scum himself, a burrowing insect, traversing the hive. At times the tunnels forked, but Kemi always knew to choose the right path. There were no more rails here, no sign of humanity. No miners had carved these tunnels.

Scum tunnels, Marco thought.

"Kemi, are you sure you know the way?" he asked.

Crawling before him, Kemi looked over her shoulder. "I saw these tunnels. All of them. They are branded in my mind. I traveled these paths ten thousand times in the bodies of ten thousand creatures. I know the way." She resumed crawling.

They headed deeper, the tunnel so steep at times Marco fought to slow himself down, to cling to the walls, to avoid sliding headfirst into Kemi. The stench of the scum was everywhere, their claw marks in the walls. Sometimes they passed burrows that led into chambers full of stinking piles of scum waste, bloated sacks of honey, and even corpses of dead scum slowly being dismembered by living creatures. Each chamber served a purpose—scum latrines, scum larders, scum crematoriums. The scum themselves here in the deep were different than the warriors, smaller, many no larger than dogs, arthropods with long hooks and feelers, some with claws made for digging rather than fighting. Here toiled the workers, the servants, the slaves, carving pathways and chambers, tending to the young, consuming the old.

The soldiers crawled onward, avoiding the arthropods, conserving their ammo. Marco was down to a single magazine—only sixty rounds—and three grenades. A few of his comrades had only thirty or twenty rounds left. Once those were spent, it would be down to bayonets—woefully inadequate against even dead scum propped onto poles, let alone the living beasts. To make things worse, their flashlights were running out of juice. Every hour, the light was dimmer, and Marco's flashlight was soon flickering, and he had to keep tapping it to keep its light on.

"Are we there yet?" Addy asked, crawling behind Marco. She reached up, grabbed the seat of his pants, and tugged. "Are we there yet, are we there yet, are we—"

He kicked her shoulder. "Shut up or no dinner at Chuck E. Cheese's."

Addy grabbed his ankle. "Please, Daddy, please please please—"

A hissing rose from ahead.

Addy released him, and Marco reached for his knife.

"Kemi?" he whispered.

She froze ahead of him. "Scum!" she whispered. "Wait. No. They're smaller. They're here." She flattened herself onto her stomach. "Down!"

In the light of his flashlight, Marco could see them in the tunnel ahead. Elongated, gray creatures sprouting whiskers, more like silverfish than centipedes. They reminded Marco of the catfish he used to catch with his grandfather. He had been crawling on hands and knees, but now Marco flattened himself onto his stomach. The creatures scuttled forward, clinging to the ceiling, their many legs long and feathery, brushing his back. Each creature was as large as him, very flat, their bodies soft and covered in fuzz. A hundred or more passed above, hissing all the while, sounding almost like humans whispering. Marco wasn't sure what their purpose was in the hive, but thankfully, they soon passed by and vanished into the distance.

"Useless buggers," Addy said, twisting her head to watch the last one vanish behind them. "Must be the scrawny nerds of the scum world. Hey, Marco, maybe they're writing novels too!"

"Almost as funny as an Osiris joke," Marco said, then resumed crawling after Kemi.

They kept crawling, deeper and deeper. They passed by one chamber that was protected by a translucent sheet like a window. Through this window, Marco saw a mountain of scum maggots all writhing and bustling in a pile. Older scum—nurses without sharp claws—were rolling balls of dung from a deeper chamber, breaking up the foul spheres, and feeding chunks to the maggots. The little creatures fed with gusto on their parents' waste.

"Ugh, poop-eaters!" Addy gagged, peering through the translucent curtain.

"Like some animals on Earth," Marco said. "It's how naked mole rats feed their young."

"Well, after exterminating the scum, we can exterminate naked mole rats," Addy said.

Marco looked around him and scraped his fingernails against the ceiling. "You know, Addy, there's some binding mortar here, holding these tunnels together. It looks a lot like what the baby scum are eating."

Addy turned green. "I need my gas mask."

"Come on, everyone." Kemi looked over her shoulder at them. "Hurry up and follow. We're close. Very close now. We'll be there in moments."

Marco dared to feel a glimmer of hope. They had found no survivors underground, discounting the wretched hybrids, but they would soon find the azoth heart. They would soon be able to repair the *Miyari*. They would soon blast off this moon and nuke the damn thing from orbit.

As they crawled through the darkness, Marco's flashlight gave a last flicker, then finally died. Kemi's was still working, and Marco followed the soft light. Behind him, Addy's flashlight was giving its last flickers too. When he looked past her, he could see the others—Ben-Ari, Singh, Osiris, beyond them mere shadows, their lights fading. They crawled onward, moving faster now.

Marco didn't know how they'd have enough light and ammo to flee the mines—it had taken days to crawl this far deep—but they would have to cross that bridge once they got to it.

The air grew warmer, then hot, then sweltering. A sickly sweet aroma of honey and blood filled the air, the smell of overripe fruit and rotting meat in a forgotten feast under the sun. An orange glow filled the tunnel, turning yellow and brighter as they crawled onward. The air seemed to pulse, caressing Marco with damp waves, and dust vibrated on the ground. Marco felt like a parasite crawling through the veins of a beast toward its pulsing heart.

After a long time of crawling, the tunnel widened, allowing the soldiers to walk again.

The light shone ahead, and the sweet smell grew, spinning Marco's head. They all put on their gas masks, and sweat drenched them. They walked toward the orange light, like the light of a hearth reflected in amber, and even with his gas mask on, Marco smelled the place, smelled blood, organs, flesh, sex, birth, honey, vinegar, arthropods, humanity, decay, life.

It's a language, he realized. *The smells are a language the scum use.*

A doorway loomed ahead, and beyond he saw the dripping, corrugated walls of a pulsing chamber. No, not a doorway. The opening was organic, fleshy, like a cervix leading into a womb, quivering, whispering of life within. Only a thin crack was visible, like a closed curtain, veined, translucent.

The soldiers paused and stared at one another.

"It's here," Kemi whispered. Her eyes widened, and her fingers trembled. "It's beyond the doors. Evil. Evil guarding the heart." She still wore Addy's old sweatpants and shirt, dirt filled her hair, and her gun trembled in her hand. "She's calling to me. She's afraid. She's so afraid. She's so cruel."

Kemi was shaking. Marco approached her and placed a hand on the small of her back.

"It's all right, Kemi. We're with you. We survived this far. Whatever's in there, we'll face it." He looked at the others. "I'm ready."

They stared back. Lieutenant Ben-Ari, her blond ponytail sticking out from under her helmet, scum blood staining her drab fatigues, her plasma gun in her hands. Addy, taller than the lieutenant, her gun longer, her eyes narrowed, her fists clenched, the hockey player who had beaten up men twice her size, ready to fight—Marco's best friend, always at his side. Elvis, slender, short, the boy who had lost so much—his brother, his fiancée, his friends—the boy who had begun his service singing and dancing, who had grown up in darkness, who had lost his light, his voice. Sergeant Amar Singh, wearing his turban under his helmet, a curved blade hanging from his belt, a pendant gleaming around his neck—the drill instructor who had once terrified Marco, who had become a mentor, a friend, a pillar of strength in the platoon. Osiris, a strange light in her eyes, a strange smile on her lips, suddenly looking hungry, a huntress, venomous, a machine with constant racing, scheming thoughts and the heart of a child.

Finally Marco turned to look at Lailani, and a little of his fear eased. Lailani. His tiny soldier. A woman broken inside. Hurt. Haunted. A woman who had suffered more than anyone he knew, a woman with anger, sadness, desperation inside her. A woman with scars on her wrists, a woman who had joined this army to die in battle, who had survived with him through wars. She looked at him with her dark, almond-shaped eyes, and Marco thought of how he had first met her, how he had mistaken her for a boy, how he had made love to her in their tent, slept with her in his arms. He loved her. She was shattered, she could perhaps never be fully his, but he loved her, and he would always fight to protect her, to heal her, to make her happy—no matter what darkness still lay before them.

"I'm afraid," Kemi whispered.

Marco looked at her, looked at them all. He spoke softly. "I remember Earth. Here in the dark, it's hard to remember sometimes. Hard to imagine that Earth is truly still out there. But I remember candlelight in my library, the rustle of pages, the scrape of my pen against paper, the taste of tea and my father's whiskey. I remember walking by the beach, the wind in the maple trees, the flowers in spring, the snow falling in winter, and the taste of coffee. I miss coffee. I miss my father. But you are my new family—every one of you. Whatever still awaits us in the darkness, I can think of no better people by my side. Let's go find that heart."

Elvis's eyes were red, and Ben-Ari smiled at him and nodded.

Addy mussed his hair. "Silly Poet," she said.

"More poet than warrior," he said.

Addy shook her head. "No. Just as much a warrior. Now come on! Let's go kick ass."

They stepped closer to the fleshy cervix. Marco turned toward Ben-Ari. "Ma'am, may I take the lead?"

The lieutenant nodded. "I'm right behind you, Marco."

He reached toward the entrance and began pulling back the fleshy curtains.

At once, scum burst out.

Marco fell back, hit the ground, and fired his gun.

The creatures swarmed out from the chamber, different from any scum Marco had ever seen. They had the bodies of centipedes but heads like anglerfish, deep-sea predators with teeth like swords, and luminescent lanterns dangled from their heads. Each of the creatures wore a necklace woven from the rotting arms of human babies, lurid trophies from their conquests, and human bones and skulls and strips of dry skin covered their bodies like armor.

"Tool use!" Osiris said. "Fascinating. I did not know that *scolopendra titania* could use tools. I must update the HDF encyclopedic databases!"

But the others were too busy firing their guns to be fascinated. Marco hit one of the creatures, shattering its teeth. The alien leaped toward him, its suit of bones and flesh jangling, and a claw slammed into him, cutting his leg. Marco screamed, slammed his muzzle into the creature's shattered mouth, and fired a bullet.

The head exploded, and the scum fell, scattering its suit of bones and skulls.

The other soldiers fought around him. Singh suffered a gash to his cheek, bellowed, and swung his gun in circles, slamming the barrel into two scum. Lailani pressed her back against the wall, screaming, firing bullet after bullet. Ben-Ari and Kemi stood back to back, and the air crackled with plasma, and scum burned.

More of the scum kept emerging, clad in their clattering suits of bones, biting, screeching. Teeth scraped across Ben-Ari's helmet. More teeth closed around Osiris's arm, yanked back, and exposed her inner circuits. And still the scum emerged from the chamber ahead, towering, a dozen feet tall, all claws and fangs and dripping venom. Osiris fell, followed by Ben-Ari. A blow knocked Singh against the wall.

"For death and glory!" shouted Lailani, firing her gun, and a blow knocked her down too.

"No," Elvis said. "No!" He loaded his last magazine. "No! No more death. No more!"

Shouting, Elvis flipped his rifle to automatic and fired. Bullets sprayed out. Fragments of bone flew. Scum fell.

"No!" Elvis shouted again. He reached into his boot and pulled out another magazine. "No more will die." He fired again and again, tearing the scum down. He ran out of bullets. He snapped on his bayonet, and his eyes burned, and still he screamed. "I lost enough. Enough! Enough!"

He charged toward the scum, lashing his bayonet, tearing into one's skull. His blade flew again, slicing a creature's abdomen. Elvis reached down to Singh, as if to help the sergeant rise, but grabbed his gun instead. He fired, tearing down more scum. And before him, they died. The last creature wobbled, then crashed down, and Elvis slammed his bayonet into its skull.

The aliens all lay dead and smoking.

Elvis spat. "Fucking scum."

Then he began to weep.

"Goddamn," Addy whispered. "Elvis is a savage."

Marco approached the weeping boy and slung an arm around him. "You all right?"

Elvis nodded. "I hate them. I just hate them. For what they did. To Beast. To us. To the world."

Marco rummaged through his pack for his medical kit, and he spent a while tending to their wounds. Everyone had suffered cuts and gashes, and they needed shots of stinging antidotes and heavy bandages. But all could stand. All could still fight. All turned toward the fleshy opening from which the creatures had emerged.

Marco took a deep breath and stepped through the membranes and into the chamber. The others followed.

CHAPTER TWENTY-ONE

Entering the chamber was like entering a womb. The walls were rounded, coated with sticky red membranes. Many coiling white tubes were attached to the ceiling, running down, feeding her. There in the middle of the chamber she lay, pulsing, corpulent, gasping for air. Royal. Holy. Worshiped.

"The scum queen," Marco said.

They all stood and stared.

Here in the depths of the hive, she dwelt, too obese to move. Her body was as large as a whale, ridged and soft and quivering and the color of cream. With every pulse, the queen expelled another egg, a scum larva twitching inside. Ooze dripped onto the floor, stinking, yellow, bubbling. With each egg birthed, one of the smaller, softer scum, those like silverfish, lifted the treasure and carried it away from its mother, vanishing into a hole in the ceiling.

"God, she stinks," Addy said. "I can smell it even through my gas mask." She raised her gun. "Let's roast this bitch."

Marco had objected to killing the larvae before, but faced with this corpulent, quivering creature, he found no pity inside him. This was an alien spawning a scum army—the army that had killed his friends. Armies like those that had destroyed the world, butchering billions, that had killed his mother. Marco nodded and raised his own gun. Standing before the queen, as small as toy soldiers by the corpse of a cat, the others raised their own weapons.

Marco placed his finger on the trigger when he heard a voice.

"Help . . . me . . ."

A woman's voice. Weak. Afraid.

Marco lowered his gun. The voice sounded again.

"Help . . . me . . ."

It came from behind the queen. Marco walked, rifle held before him, frowning. The others followed. They walked around the creamy body of the queen, more eggs expelled with every one of its pulses. Moisture dripped from the queen's body, oozing around their feet.

"Help . . ."

Marco reached the end of the queen's massive abdomen, walked around the last fold in her flesh, and froze.

He couldn't breathe.

Darkness spread around him.

Panic began to rise, drenching Marco with sweat, spinning his head, shaking his fingers.

The scum queen had the upper body, arms, and head of a woman.

The woman stared at them, eyes damp. Below the ribs, her body flared out into the bloated abdomen that filled the room.

"Help me," she whispered. "They hurt my husband. They hurt my children. I think they're dead. Help me. Help me." Tears flowed down her cheeks. "What happened to me?"

Marco saw a name tag still attached to what remained of the woman's shirt. *Kara Lason, Inventory.*

"Sweetness," Ben-Ari whispered, kneeling by the woman and stroking her hair. "It's all right, Kara. It's all right now. We're here. We'll help you."

"My children," Kara whispered. "Have you seen them? I think I killed my daughter. I was holding her, keeping her so silent. The monster was hunting us. I think she suffocated. Have you seen her? Have you seen my daughter?"

Lieutenant Ben-Ari shed a tear. "She's safe now," she whispered, holding Kara's hand. "She's safe. Everyone is safe."

"How long have I been here?" Kara said. "I can't move. Why can't I move?" She looked at the massive, quivering mass that grew from her, filling the room. "What happened to me?"

"She must have been here since the scum first landed," Marco said. He turned toward Osiris. "Osiris, remember when we received the distress signal on the *Miyari*? Communications can only travel through space at the speed of light, and this system is light-years away. How old was the signal?"

"Checking memory banks . . ." The android thought for a moment. "Four Earth years, two months, four days, and seven hours, master."

"She's been here for four years." Marco exhaled slowly. He couldn't even imagine this agony stretched out for so long. "No. No, that's impossible." He shook his head wildly. "Ships would have arrived here within the past four years. Bringing supplies. Picking up azoth. How could this have been going on for years?"

They were all silent for long moments.

Finally it was Ben-Ari who whispered, "They knew."

The soldiers all turned toward her.

"Ma'am?" Marco said.

"They knew," Ben-Ari repeated, face pale. "Chrysopoeia Corp. Maybe even the HDF high command. They knew this was going on. They let it keep happening. This could not have gone unnoticed for four years. We stumbled across something here, something we should never have seen." The lieutenant stared at the queen, then back at her soldiers. "Guys . . . what's going on here?"

Lailani, who was standing farther back, ran up toward them. She grabbed Marco's arm. "Marco!" she said. "Marco, come look." She pulled him a few feet away and pointed to the top of the queen's body. "Do you see?"

Marco looked. Yes. He saw it. A blue glow.

"The color of azoth," he said.

"Let me climb onto your shoulders," Lailani said. He knelt, and she hopped on. When Marco stood up again, hoisting her on his shoulders, Lailani nodded. "I see it, Marco! I see it pulsing through the skin. It has to be it. The azoth heart. The machine that once powered the mines—now here inside the queen, giving her a second heart."

Lailani hopped off Marco's shoulders, grabbed the queen's distended abdomen, and scampered up, slipping, grabbing again, finally making her way to the top. The abdomen quivered beneath her, dripping moisture. Lailani lowered her hand for Marco to grab. As he climbed after her, Marco had the vision of himself as a child in a bouncy castle, and even here, in this chamber of horrors, an army of monsters in the mines around him, Marco found himself laughing—a pained, sick, wonderful laugh, tears in his eyes. What else could a man do when confronted with torture and horror than laugh?

He reached the top with Lailani. To one side, the abdomen stretched out, vaguely segmented, still expelling eggs, and Marco could feel many eggs below them, waiting to be birthed. At their other side, the abdomen sloped down, connecting with Kara's human chest. And here, between him and Lailani, the blue glow—just under the skin. Marco could make out the vague outline of a mechanical heart.

"The azure engine!" he called down to Lieutenant Ben-Ari. "It's here, ma'am. Embedded into her. The scum must have placed it inside her."

"Why would the scum put the heart here?" Lailani said.

"Maybe they believed the azoth could give power and fertility to the queen," Marco said. "Maybe the scum worshiped its glow the way ancient human tribes worshiped gems. I think I can cut it out." He looked down to Ben-Ari. "Ma'am?"

The lieutenant still knelt by Kara, holding the woman's hand. The other soldiers stood around her. Eyes damp, Ben-Ari nodded. "Cut it out." Ben-Ari squeezed Kara's hand. "This might hurt just a bit."

Marco drew his knife. He looked at the heart pulsing beneath the skin, pale blue and black, no larger than a human heart.

This is a dream, he thought. *Just a fever dream. I was hurt in Fort Djemila. I'm asleep. I'm feverish. I'm dreaming.*

He sank the knife into the skin.

Kara screamed.

The distended abdomen trembled. Marco worked quickly, incising, carving an opening, and he reached his hand in. There, resting above the eggs, the heart lay. Mechanical, forged of metal, the azoth crystal inside it shining through lenses. Instead of metal pipes, fleshy cords were attached to the heart's valves. Marco cut through them, then took the heart into his hands and pulled it free.

"I got it!" he said, placing the heart into his pack. "I'll bandage her up."

He opened his first aid kit, knowing that Kara's life was pain but knowing he could not kill her, that her life was not his to take. He was unpacking a bandage when the abdomen convulsed and began to wilt. He swayed. Lailani grabbed him. The queen was deflating. They fell, slid down the side, and hit the floor. Without the heart, the queen's body was shriveling, expelling its last eggs, fading away, detaching from the human body.

Marco walked toward Kara. She lay, holding Ben-Ari's hand, her body now ending with an empty sack. She gazed up at Marco, eyes glazed.

"Thank you," she whispered.

Her eyes closed.

Her breath died.

The soldiers gathered together, bloody, bandaged, weary—but with their prize.

Goodbye, Kara Lason, Marco thought. *I'm sorry we could not save you. I'm sorry.*

"I know a way out," Kemi said, pointing at a tunnel across the room. "Only two kilometers up this tunnel, we'll reach another shaft, another cage lift. We can make our way back to Corpus City, then back to the *Miyari* . . . then far, far away from this cursed place."

Sergeant Singh nodded. "I'll lead the way this time. My flashlight still has some juice, and my gun still has some bullets." He hefted his weapon. "Let's get out of here. Let's go home."

The soldiers walked around the eggs and toward the tunnel.

It's over, Marco thought, following his sergeant. *It's over.*

"Traitors!" rose a shriek.

Sergeant Singh froze at the tunnel's entrance.

Blood bloomed across his back.

"Amar!" Ben-Ari cried.

Claws lifted the sergeant into the air, ripping him apart, tugging out his insides, then tossed him down. The sergeant hit the ground, torn to pieces. He died without even the time to scream.

The remaining soldiers all raised their guns, staring ahead.

At the entrance to the tunnel stood Captain Coleen Petty, their company commander. Her human body now ended below the ribs, sprouting a great centipede body lined with claws. She rose like a cobra about to strike, a dozen feet tall, stitched onto her new lower half.

"You are all traitors!" the creature screeched. "You ruined my ship! You left me to the scum! You made me this creature!"

The hybrid leaped forward, claws lashing.

The soldiers opened fire.

Bullets slammed into Captain Petty—or at least the creature Petty had become. Holes opened in her centipede and human bodies, but still she advanced, claws lashing, screaming through a shattered jaw.

"Traitors! Traitors! Trai—"

Lieutenant Ben-Ari shot her last plasma charge. The inferno blazed across Captain Petty. The creature screamed, burned, melted, curled up. Petty fell to the floor. She gazed up through the flames, and suddenly she seemed so scared, so hurt.

"Help," Petty whispered. "Help me. I don't know what I am. Help me, Ben-Ari. Please . . ."

The flames consumed her, and her bones burned.

From the tunnel behind, the burrows they had crawled through, rose the shrieks of many creatures.

"More scum approaching, masters!" said Osiris.

"Run into the opposite tunnel!" said Ben-Ari. "Kemi, lead the way! *Run!*"

CHAPTER TWENTY-TWO

Kemi ran into the tunnel and the others followed, leaving Singh's ravaged body behind. Last in line, Marco glimpsed scum entering the hall of the queen—hundreds of them. He unhooked a grenade, rolled it backward, and felt the impact against his spine. He hurled another grenade back toward the hall, and the tunnel collapsed behind him. The soldiers ran onward.

"This way!" Kemi shouted. "There's another lift cage only a couple kilometers away!"

They ran, firing their guns, tearing down any creature that approached—scum and hybrids alike. They ran upward through the tunnels, ran through metal mines, ran along the tracks, ran from all the horrors of the cosmos, ran from death, from nightmare, from pain, from visions they knew they would never forget, from trauma they knew would forever haunt them. They were running from Hell, Lailani would say. They ran until they reached another shaft, and there! Marco saw it. Another lift cage!

They ran inside. They rose together, higher and higher, as scum squealed below and leaped up the shaft.

As Addy and Elvis spun the winch, Marco dropped grenades down the shaft. Explosions rocked the mines, rocked the cage, belched up fire. Shrapnel peppered the bottom of the cage lift. The scum below screamed, kept surging upward, a gushing torrent, and Marco dropped more grenades, and fire roared and stones and metal flew.

Marco tossed their last grenade with still a hundred feet of shaft above them.

The scum still shrieked below, scurrying up the shaft walls.

"Anyone have any bullets?" he shouted.

"We're down to two magazines, but we need them for the run to the ship!" Ben-Ari replied.

Addy grumbled, snapping on a bayonet. "Blade time."

Marco attached his own bayonet, as did Lailani and Elvis. Kemi had no bayonet but took a combat knife from Addy.

The scum leaped from below, grabbing the cage bars. The soldiers stabbed, trying to reach between the segments of hard exoskeleton, to cut the flesh within. One centipede tumbled down, stabbed below the head, nearly yanking the rifle from Marco's hand. Another bent the cage bars and made it inside, only for Lailani and Addy to crack it open with their bayonets.

Finally the soldiers reached the top. They raced out of the cage, emerging back into the ruined city. The abandoned towers rose around them, jagged and dark. The red surface of Indrani roiled above, hiding nearly all the sky. The scum were everywhere. They crawled on the walls and roofs, scuttled along the streets, emerged from sewers.

"Run!" Ben-Ari shouted.

The others needed no encouragement. They raced through the city, firing their last few bullets, knocking back scum. The ruins shook. Walls collapsed. A tower cracked and fell, belching out clouds of dust, crushing buildings beneath it. With the queen dead, the thousands of centipedes were emerging from underground, burying the city. Corpus was falling apart.

Falling bricks pelted the soldiers, banging against their helmets, cracking against their shoulders. Lailani cried out and fell, and bricks pelted her, and a scum grabbed her leg. Marco stabbed the creature, then lifted Lailani and slung her across his shoulders. He ran, following the others, whipping from side to side as the buildings crumbled around him. Cracks opened in the streets, exposing more creatures within. Marco leaped over them. He ran onward, clinging to Lailani, not even knowing if she still lived.

By the time they emerged onto the hills, they had fired their last bullet. The scum swarmed behind them, racing across the black soil.

Ahead they saw it—the HDFS *Miyari*.

The engine casing was reattached but still dark and cold. Without the azoth heart, which Marco carried in his backpack, the ship wasn't going anywhere.

The *Miyari*'s back hatch slid open, and a ramp slammed down onto the ground. Major Mwarabu stood at the entrance, holding a grenade launcher. Two of his crew members emerged around him, holding their own RPGs. All three fired. Grenades soared, arched over the running soldiers, and slammed onto the pursuing scum. Explosions rocked the hills. Shards of exoskeleton flew. Marco screamed as hot, sharp pieces cut his back. He nearly fell but kept running, holding Lailani, and behind him rose the screeches of thousands of scum. Sergeant Stumpy ran beside him, a bleeding gash on his side.

"Come on, come on!" Mwarabu shouted, waving them toward him.

Ben-Ari reached the ship first, grabbed a handgun from Mwarabu, and knelt, firing bullets toward the scum. One bullet whistled by Marco's ear, and he screamed, and when he touched his ear, he felt blood. He kept running, reached the ramp, and entered the ship's hangar. He laid Lailani down on the floor. She was still alive, bleeding from several cuts. The other survivors of the mission—Kemi, Addy, Osiris, and Elvis—ran up the ramp too, and Sergeant Stumpy entered last, barking.

The ramp began to rise. A few scum managed to grab its rim and spilled into the hangar as the ramp closed. Mwarabu and his crew fired bullets, killing a few of the creatures. One scum leaped onto Mwarabu and shoved its claws into his chest. The major, commander of the *Miyari*, screamed and fell as the scum tore out his heart. Other scum leaped onto his crew members, cracking them open, and blood splashed the hangar. Marco and the others fired their guns, tearing into the scum in the hangar, and chunks of the creatures flew. The hull dented as scum leaped against it—only a handful at first, then hundreds, then thousands. The *Miyari* rocked.

"Fuck, the scum already got the wounded we left here!" Addy shouted, emerging back into the hangar from a corridor. "They were fighting all the while we were gone."

"We got no pilots!" Marco shouted, looking at the corpses of Mwarabu and his crew.

"I can fly the ship, master," said Osiris. "May I have the azoth heart?"

Marco nodded, pulled the heart out of his pack, but hesitated. For an instant, he wondered if Osiris was the saboteur who had shattered the original heart. He remembered Ben-Ari's words in the hall of the queen.

The high command knew about this place, Marco thought. *They must have if it's been going on for years. They let it happen. This isn't just the work of scum. Does Osiris know more than she reveals?*

But Marco had to trust the android now. What other chance did they have? He handed Osiris the heart.

"Osiris, fix the engine, then get us off this moon," Ben-Ari said. "As fast as you can. The hull won't shield us for much longer. Everyone else, follow me to the gun turrets. We'll hold off the scum while Osiris is working."

They all ran out of the hangar. Lailani was able to limp while leaning against Marco, and Stumpy ran behind them. While Osiris hurried down into the engine room with the heart, Ben-Ari and the other warriors ran upward. As they raced through the ship's dark halls, the *Miyari* kept rocking, and the scum kept screeching outside. The hull dented as the aliens slammed against it.

"Up this ladder, then branch out," Ben-Ari said. "There are six gun turrets atop the *Miyari*, bulging out like six eyes."

Six gun turrets. Six surviving soldiers. They climbed the ladder, emerging into the attic of the ship, where glassy tunnels branched into six paths like a candelabrum. Ben-Ari, Kemi, and Lailani raced to the left. Marco, Elvis, and Addy ran into the three right tunnels.

The *Miyari* began to rumble. The power was coming back on, lights flickering across the tunnels. The engines coughed and growled.

Marco reached a transparent silica dome that bulged out from the hull. A cannon thrust out, attached to a two-pronged handle inside the dome. He grabbed the prongs, pulled hard right, and aimed the cannon at scum that were racing up from below. Through the silica, he could see Addy and Elvis emerging into their own turrets. The scum were everywhere, thousands swarming from the ruined city like rats from a drowning ship.

As the Miyari rattled, Marco fired the cannon.

Bolts of plasma blasted out, slamming into the ground. Scum flew, torn apart, their claws peppering the ship and denting the hull. The cannons boomed across the ship, ripping holes into Corpus, sending creatures flying. But more kept racing forward and climbing the hull. A few scuttled up toward the turret, and their claws slammed into the silica. A hairline crack appeared in front of Marco.

The engine's grumble grew to a growl.

The ship began to rise, belching out dust and smoke and steam.

Fire blazed.

The *Miyari* soared.

Flames roared and dusty air streamed across the turret. The scum tore free and tumbled into the fire. Across the hull, the aliens slid down, claws making last, desperate attempts to cling on, then tore off and fell toward the moon.

The ship rattled as they rose higher through the atmosphere. The hairline crack grew on the turret's cockpit. From up here, the ruins seemed so small, the towers mere needles, the swarm of scum a mere puddle. Finally they emerged from the atmosphere into space. Corpus, a rocky moon, and Indrani, a swirling red gas giant, filled nearly the entire view, but in the distance, Marco could just make out a sliver of stars in the black. He breathed out in relief.

I'm alive. Addy is alive. Lailani is alive. Kemi is alive. He found himself shaking. *Some of us made it out. We survived.*

He was about to leave the turret when Osiris's voice emerged from speakers, booming across the ship.

"We've got trouble, masters!" said the android. "Enemy ships flying in from every side."

Damn.

Marco saw them. Purple, fleshy spheres rising from the planet, built not of metal but of the hard, organic material the scum could spew, design, shape. If humans were masters of synthetics, the *scolopendra titania* were lords of bioengineering, building even their starships from flesh and hardened bone and shell, living vessels, veined and pulsing and wreathed in fire.

Marco pulled the trigger. His cannon roared out plasma. The scum ships ahead scattered. Marco yanked the cannon sideways, raised the muzzle, fired again. The cockpit shook and the handles thrummed in his hands as the plasma spurted, an expanding torrent. A scum ship tried to flee but the flames caught it. It expanded, cracked, and another bolt of plasma shattered it. Centipedes spilled out and floated across space. The *Miyari* banked and spun in the sky, revealing a view of a dozen more scum ships flying toward them. The cannons blasted, shooting streamers of plasma across the sky, hitting enemy vessels. Shards of scum exoskeletons and ships showered through space, pelting the *Miyari*. From across the ship, Marco could hear Addy whooping in triumph.

More scum ships emerged, screaming forth. The cannons blasted. One enemy pod zipped across space, dodging the cannon fire, and slammed into the *Miyari*. The starship shook so madly Marco nearly fell. Scum spilled out of the cracked pod, slamming their claws against the hull. Marco lowered his cannon as far as it would go and sprayed plasma, burning off the creatures. The *Miyari* jolted as another scum ship slammed into it. Smoke and fire filled the *Miyari*. Marco kept firing, blasting incoming pods, and again the ship rattled.

Three more scum ships remained. A blast from Addy's cannon took out one. Two more swarmed forth, zipping around the plasma. The *Miyari* rose higher, dipped, and flipped over. The surface of Corpus now spread above Marco's head, and the red storms of Indrani swirled below. The two scum ships streamed toward him.

He fired. A scum vessel burst, its fragments slamming into the other pod. Streams from three cannons blasted out, and the *Miyari* swerved, and the plasma formed a ring of fire through space. The last scum pod tried to reach them, passed through the plasma, and melted. It hit the hull of the Miyari with a thousand hot pieces.

The *Miyari* floated through space.

The last of the centipedes floated around them, then sank back toward Corpus.

Marco exhaled in relief.

He left the turret, climbed down the ladder, and met his comrades in a white corridor. They looked at him. His friends. Survivors. Bloody, bandaged, covered in filth, their uniforms tattered. Six survivors—seven if you counted Osiris down on the bridge. Marco stepped toward his comrades, and they embraced one another, laughing, crying, holding on for long moments. They were no longer a lieutenant and her soldiers. They were barely soldiers at all. They were humans. They were alive. They had survived where two hundred had fallen.

Ben-Ari inhaled deeply. "We're light-years away from any HDF command center," she said. "As the highest-ranking soldier on board, I'm authorizing the discontinuation of Corpus City's mining operations. In other words, we're nuking the whole damn place. Osiris, do you copy?"

"Yes, ma'am," replied the android through the speakers.

Marco and his friends limped along the corridor until they found a viewport. They stood together, staring out into space, watching as streams of light flared down from the *Miyari* toward the surface of Corpus. Clouds of light spread over the ruins of the city like lightning within clouds, like watercolor stains, almost beautiful from up here. One blast. A second. A third. Ten, one after another, pulsing, lighting the moon before fading. And the city was gone. And the scum were gone. And the pain, the monsters, the evil below—gone.

But not what remains inside us, Marco thought, turning away from the view. *Not the nightmares. Not the memories. Those will always remain.*

He held his friends close again. They stood together in the corridor as the *Miyari* floated above the devastation.

CHAPTER TWENTY-THREE

They lay in the infirmary, six warriors, six survivors—the last of their company. The company medic had died on the surface of Corpus, along with nearly two hundred other soldiers, and so these six survivors tended to themselves, cleaning wounds, bandaging, even stitching the deeper cuts. Six among two hundred. The six who lived.

Lieutenant Ben-Ari, her blond hair stained with blood, her eyes haunted. Private Benny "Elvis" Ray, the song gone from his lips. Cadet Kemi Abasi, still wrapped in a blanket, her body bruised where the scums' tubes had pierced her. Addy "Maple" Linden, once brusque and loud, now silent, her head lowered, her eyes red. Lailani "Tiny" de la Rosa, the girl who had lived through one hell, only to survive another.

And me, Marco thought. *Of all the two hundred, me—the son of a librarian, here among the survivors. Why do I deserve life when so many others fell?*

Bandaged, he looked out the viewport of the infirmary. The HDFS *Miyari* was orbiting the gas giant Indrani, waiting for its hyperdrive engine to warm up. The red storms of Indrani swirled outside, tainted with orange and yellow—a planet twice the size of Jupiter, lacking a solid surface. A red god. So small from here, a mere black marble, the moon Corpus floated languidly across the red spacescape.

This place will always haunt me, Marco thought. *We can never forget what happened here. What we saw here. Who we lost here.*

Osiris's voice emerged from the ship's speakers, breaking the silence in the infirmary. "One hour to hyperspace jump. Estimated length of trip to Nightwall Outpost on the frontier: Eighteen days, three hours."

Elvis sat on an infirmary bed, staring out the viewport. "Well, I for one cannot wait to blast away from this hellhole and never see it again."

"Let's never come back," Addy said.

As Osiris counted down the minutes through the speakers, Kemi rose from her bed. Wrapped in a blanket, she walked toward the viewport, placed her hand against the silica, and stared out at the storming gas giant. The planet painted her red. Slowly, she turned around and faced them, her eyes gazing at a different world.

"We can't leave," Kemi whispered.

"What?" Elvis leaped off the bed. "We can't leave fast enough, you mean."

A tear shone on Kemi's cheek. "Our war here isn't done. He waits." Her voice dropped to a trembling whisper. "He watches."

Marco approached her. She barely seemed to see him.

"Who, Kemi?" he said. "Who watches us?"

She turned back toward the viewport. "He lurks within the storm. On the planet of Indrani. When I was trapped in the dreamworld, connected to the hive, I saw him. I floated through the minds of his children, and he watched over us. He watches us still." She reached out and grabbed Marco, clutching his arms, digging her fingernails into him. "We killed his children, Marco. We killed his bride. He plans his revenge now against the world. If we do not stop him, he will release his evil, release Hell itself into the cosmos."

"Who is he, Kemi?" Marco whispered, a shiver running through him.

A chaotic smile touched her lips. "A scum hive has more than a queen. It also has a king." She pointed at the gas giant outside. "And there he lies in wait, there in the storm he plans his revenge." Her voice cracked, and terror flooded her eyes. "He is evil itself. He is pure malice. We must kill him." Her voice grew stronger. "We cannot leave while he lives. We must kill him, or he will forever hunt us."

They were all silent for long moments, staring at one another. A collective shiver seemed to pass through the infirmary. Even Ben-Ari looked disturbed.

Finally Elvis cleared his throat. "All right! Fine. Fine, no problem. So, we fly a little closer to Indrani, we wait to see the scum king flying around, and we nuke the son of a bitch. Shouldn't take more than an hour, right? And then we can fly on. No more mines or anything, are there?"

Lieutenant Ben-Ari approached the cadet, her uniform in tatters, her limbs bandaged, her plasma gun slung across her back. "Kemi, we came here on a rescue mission. We came because of a distress call. But we were too late. We lost so many. Facing a scum king is not our mission." She stared out the viewport, at Corpus floating across the gas giant, and her voice was haunted. "I should never have brought you here."

"Einav," Kemi said softly, breaking protocol and addressing the lieutenant by her first name. "We have but one mission. To face the scum everywhere. To kill them everywhere." Her fists clenched, and her voice shook. "You, none of you, can ever know how evil they truly are. Their brains fester with it. They breathe it, nurse it as maggots—evil in its purest form, existing for no purpose but to hurt others." Blood dripped from her palms where she dug her fingernails into the skin. "The creature on this planet . . . he is not the emperor, not the supreme leader of the scum empire. But he was the king of the hive we destroyed, and his wrath knows no bounds. Left here, he would spawn a new bride from his own flesh, rebuild his army, and seek vengeance against Earth. But now he is weak. Now we can exterminate him."

"Then we'll come back with more firepower," Ben-Ari said. "With a hundred ships and—"

"It would be too late," Kemi said. "Already he prepares to spawn. We must kill him now. We must. We must." She fell to her knees. "You cannot imagine his cruelty, how he spoke in my mind, mocking, tormenting me. How I can still hear the buzzing." She covered her ears. "We have to make the buzzing stop."

They all stared outside at the red planet, its surface a massive storm many times the size of Earth.

Addy sighed. "Well, fuck it. What's one more bug to crush?"

Lailani placed a hand on her gun. "I'm game."

"You're all crazy," Elvis said. "But fine! One last hunt before the frontier. How do we find this scum king anyway?"

"He flies within the storm," Kemi said. "I'll lead us to him." Her eyes hardened. "And then we'll fire every cannon on this ship and rid the cosmos of him."

* * * * *

They stood on the bridge of the *Miyari*, a semicircular hall with viewports from floor to ceiling, affording a panoramic view of the storms of Indrani. They now flew only a thousand kilometers away from that roiling maelstrom.

"All right, soldiers, listen up," Ben-Ari said. "We emptied our nuclear arsenal on the mines of Corpus, but the *Miyari* has still got her plasma cannons. Osiris is going to fly us through the storm, following Kemi's directions, taking us toward the scum king. The rest of us will man those cannons. Once we see the king, we'll burn him down. Understood?"

"Yes, ma'am!" they cried, and it felt like basic training again, like a real army. It felt normal. It felt in control. And that was comforting to Marco.

"Ma'am?" Elvis said. "Does anyone even know what the scum king looks like? Is he just some giant bug flying through the storm?"

They all turned to look at Kemi. The cadet was wearing Addy's spare uniform. It was the drab fatigues of an enlisted soldier, not the white uniform of a cadet, but it was better than her previous sweatpants and blanket.

"When I was attached to the scum hive, I felt more than saw," Kemi said. "I sensed things through senses that humans don't possess. The scum communicate ideas, concepts, and feelings through pheromones, and they all chatter at once, thousands of them. It's like being in a forest full of smells. But above everything else, I sensed *him*. The king. Watching, controlling, commanding. Indrani is a gas giant. It has no solid surface to stand on, is just swirling clouds all the way through, a massive floating storm in space, that is all. And in that storm, I sensed a great creature, looming, gargantuan, filling the storm, bending it to his will, consciousness in an exoskeleton. So . . . yes, in a sense, a giant bug flying through the storm."

"Great," Elvis said. "And we'll be the windshield that crushes it."

Ben-Ari nodded. "All right, soldiers. We're beginning our descent. It'll get rocky once we enter that storm. To the cannons! We'll have a clear view from your turrets, and we'll keep in touch via our communicators." She grew solemn. "Godspeed, warriors of Earth."

They saluted and stepped off the bridge, leaving Osiris and Kemi to steer the ship. The soldiers marched through the ship, climbed the ladder, and headed back into the six gun turrets that protruded from the *Miyari*. Marco manned the same cannon as last time, staring out through the cockpit at the approaching storms of Indrani. It felt like flying toward lava in the pits of Hell itself. From where Marco stood, he had a view of every direction. In the other cannon turrets, he could see his comrades at the guns. The *Miyari*'s engines glowed pale blue as the ship descended toward the massive planet.

Marco narrowed his eyes, seeking the monster. How could one see anything here? This planet was larger than all the planets back home in the solar system put together. Storms, each of them larger than Earth, swirled and spun, red and yellow and white. Great bands of swirling umber and crimson flowed around the planet like gushing rivers. As they descended closer and hit the first layer of the atmosphere, the *Miyari* began to shake. They had patched up the crack in the cockpit with liquid silica, but Marco was beginning to worry that it would crack again. The ship rattled. The gun's handles threatened to rip out from his hands.

They entered the storm.

Swirls of red and orange flowed around them. The clouds whipped the ship, and the *Miyari* rocked and rattled. Marco could just make out the other cockpits, the soupy atmosphere flowing around them. It felt like flying through a vat of red and yellow paint.

Through his earbud, he heard Kemi's voice.

"He's still far. He's still deep."

"Hang in there, Kemi," Marco said into his helmet's microphone. "We're going to get this son of a bitch."

With a crackle of static, Addy's voice emerged from the earbud next. "The poet cursed again!"

"Quiet, soldiers," Ben-Ari warned.

They kept descending through the storm. A gust of wind slammed into the ship. The *Miyari* was as large as an apartment building, but that gust tossed it through the air, and they spun three times before righting themselves and flying onward. Marco kept scanning the storming atmosphere, seeking the enemy. The gusts of wind swirled and splashed color across the sky. With every gust, Marco thought he saw the scum, but it was always a shadow or drift of dark cloud.

"I can feel him," Kemi whispered, voice strained. "He's watching me. He knows I'm here. Marco . . ."

"I'm here, Kemi," he said, though he was a hundred meters away in his turret. "I'm right here, ready to smoke the bastard. Be strong. I'm here."

"We're all here," said Lailani, and Marco could see her looking at him from another gun turret fifty meters away. "We're all with you, Kemi."

Marco wished he could be with Kemi now, wished he could hold her, comfort her in person, not just through his communicator. But he had a more important task now—roasting that damn king scum. He leaned forward, eyes narrowed, seeking it. He could hear the storm now, even through the thick silica of the cockpit. It grumbled like a living beast, growled, whispered, rumbled. Suddenly Marco had the strange feeling that the planet itself was alive, a vengeful deity, swallowing them, digesting them. They kept diving deeper, and the storm thickened, darkened. The *Miyari* turned on its headlights, and the beams drove through the storming crimson clouds.

"He's here," Kemi said, voice shaking. "Oh, God. Oh, God. He's here. He's here. He knows my name."

Marco stared. He saw nothing.

"Kemi, where—"

His voice died.

A black tail flowed through the storm, then vanished behind crimson clouds.

Marco inhaled sharply. It was impossible to judge size from here, but he could swear—could feel it—that this tail was *large*, large as a bus. The *Miyari* swooped in pursuit, headlights cutting through the rumbling storm, and leveled off. The engines cast their blue glow against the clouds as they drove forth. The creature was gone. The ship kept flying, and red swirls flowed around them, but nothing. Nothing but the storm.

"Is it gone?" Marco said. "Did it flee? Did—"

Hard blackness.

Roaring thunder.

The ship careened, and Marco clung to the gun, nearly falling.

"It hit us!" rose Osiris's voice through the speakers.

"Where is it?" Ben-Ari was shouting. "Osiris, turn toward it!"

The ship was spinning madly. It blasted out blue flame and managed to straighten and fly forth. They made a wide turn, dived down, faced upward, and—

A massive black shape swooped, larger than the starship. It moved so quickly Marco couldn't see anything more than a flash of shimmering black. Again something massive hit the ship, and the hull dented, and they tumbled through the storm and flew like a leaf on the wind. Addy and Lailani were both firing their cannons, but the plasma flew toward nothing but storm.

"Osiris, turn toward it, damn it!" Ben-Ari was shouting in her gun turret.

"I can't, ma'am, it's too fast!" the android replied from the bridge.

"Turn us toward it, you damn piece of junk, or we're toast!" Elvis shouted.

The ship soared higher. When Marco stared down, he saw massive dark fingers tipped with claws emerging from the clouds. His heart sank. Those claws looked large enough to crush the *Miyari*. The ship blasted upward, then spun and faced the creature below.

The alien emerged from the storm.

Marco lost his breath.

"Fuck me," Addy whispered.

The scum king was massive—larger than the *Miyari*. It would have dwarfed the scum queen like a cockroach by an ant. It wasn't a centipede like its spawn. It was like some massive deep-sea creature, black and shimmering, with six legs, each tipped with claws, and a spiked tail that coiled and whipped. Its head was heavy, coated with armored plates, and teeth like the pillars of buildings filled its mouth. It shrieked, a sound so loud Marco cringed and nearly released his cannon to cover his ears.

A soft voice emerged from the ship speakers, barely a whisper, barely human, and Marco didn't recognize it. "Master . . ."

"Fire!" Ben-Ari shouted. "Kill it!"

Marco pulled the cannon's trigger.

His cannon gave a sputter.

No plasma emerged.

The other turrets were cold too.

"There's no plasma!" Addy shouted.

Osiris's voice rose through the speakers. "Our plasma supply has been turned off! Down in deck four—"

Before the android could complete her sentence, one of the scum king's massive hands hit the ship.

It felt as if a mountain struck them.

They tumbled through the storm. Marco was yanked free from the gun, and his head banged against the cockpit. He hit his hip against the floor. The storm spun madly all around them. The scum king rose again. Marco caught sight of the tail whipping through the sky. It slammed into the ship with the fury of a god.

"Deck three is breached!" Osiris said. "Losing air!"

"Osiris, we need plasma!" Ben-Ari shouted.

Marco managed to rise, to grab the cannon, to pull the trigger again. Nothing happened.

"Ma'am, the plasma supply has been cut!" Osiris said. "Somebody turned it off. I'm detecting a figure on deck four, section b. Right in the engine room."

"Emery, Ray, do you hear me?" Ben-Ari said. "Get down there and turn the juice back on!"

"Yes, ma'am!" Marco and Elvis replied. They left their gun turrets, raced down the ladder, and ran along the hall. Another blow hit the ship, and they fell, rose, ran again. Sparks flew. The power went out, and they ran through shadows.

"The ship's falling apart!" Addy cried through their communicators. "We need that plasma back on!"

"Osiris, pull back, get us out of here!" Ben-Ari said.

"I cannot retreat, ma'am," replied the android. "It's got a grip on us!"

Marco and Elvis ran, swaying, falling, racing down staircases and ladders.

"Osiris, what am I looking for?" Marco shouted into his helmet's communicator, running toward the engine room.

The android's voice emerged through his headset. "You'll see two red pipes emerging from a massive tank. My controls show that the valve has been shut off. Spin the valve open to return the plasma supply to the cannons."

"Shut off?" Marco said. "Not damaged in the—"

The ship shook again, and Marco flew against the wall. He could hear him. He could hear the king bellowing outside. The hull dented where claws slammed against the metal, only a few feet away from Marco.

"Scans show tank and pipes still operational, master," Osiris said. "Simply turn on the valve. I suggest hurrying, master."

The valve—shut off. The saboteur.

Marco cursed and ran. Elvis ran close behind.

"Fucking scum on board," Elvis said. "Has to be. Get ready to riddle the bastard with bullets."

They reached the door to the engine room. It was round, forged of blue metal, and taller than them.

"Looks like a door to Bilbo's bunker," Marco said.

"Bill who now?" Elvis said.

"Never mind." Marco grabbed the winch that thrust out from the door. "Help me."

They spun the wheel together, and the heavy blue door swung open. They stepped into the engine room. Here was a vast hall crowded with pipes, silvery engines, pistons larger than men, and spinning wheels that flared out with cables. Control panels were everywhere. The lights flickered off, then came back on, then died again. Backup generators kicked in, and dim lights shone.

"See any red pipes?" Elvis said.

They walked between the machinery. The pistons rose and fell around them, silver and thrumming. Three turbines rose ahead, large as cars, glowing blue. The engine room shook, and the engines died for a second before crackling back to life.

"He's tearing us apart!" Ben-Ari shouted through their communicators. "We need that plasma, soldiers!"

"There!" Elvis pointed. "Red pipes."

They ran between the pistons, paused, then leaped over a canyon full of electricity that crackled between rods. There— Marco saw it in the flashing lights of the engines and electricity. Two red pipes flowing up from a generator toward the ceiling. Marco spotted a valve where the pipes met the tank.

"I see it," Marco said, racing with Elvis toward the plasma generator. "We're turning it back—"

A figure emerged from the shadows, blocking their way. "No."

Marco and Elvis skidded to a halt.

Between them and the plasma generator stood Lailani.

Elvis breathed out in relief. "Damn it, de la Rosa, you scared the shit out of me. Help us turn this fucker back on."

Lailani didn't move. Her voice rumbled out. Low. Deep. Guttural. "No."

"What the fuck is wrong with you?" Elvis said, trying to walk around her.

Lailani smiled.

Her hand thrust forward.

Claws sprouted from her fingertips and tore into Elvis. Her hand burst out from his back, clutching his dripping heart.

Marco stood, frozen, eyes wide.

God, no, God, no, God, no.

Neck creaking, Lailani turned her head toward him. Her smile stretched into a grin. She dropped Elvis's heart, then pulled her hand free. The heart hit the floor with a splatter. Elvis's corpse followed.

"Hello, Marco," Lailani said.

No. No. This has to be a nightmare. This can't be happening. This has to be a dream.

The ship rattled. Ben-Ari was shouting something through the communicator. Blasts dented the hull and one turbine died. Marco fell to his knees and looked down at Elvis. His friend stared up at the ceiling, eyes glassy.

Marco looked back at Lailani. His head spun. He could barely breathe, barely speak.

"Who are you?" he whispered.

Lailani licked the blood off her claws. Each of those claws was as long as a dagger. "You know us." Her voice was impossibly deep, demonic. "You slew us in the desert. You murdered our children and wives in the mine. Now you will worship us. Now you will join us. We are the Masters. We are the Ancients. We are those who rise."

"Scum," Marco whispered, kneeling in the blood, staring up at Lailani. He rose to his feet and grabbed his gun. "Let her go!

Get out of her body!" His shout was hoarse, his eyes damp. "Take me instead. Let Lailani go!"

Lailani laughed. A deep, rumbling laugh, a sound impossible for one so small. "Let her go? Lailani has always been one of us. We were always inside her. It was we who impregnated her whore of a mother. It was we who lurked inside her throughout her childhood, keeping her frail body alive. It was we who broke her soul. It was us she tried to banish by slicing her wrists, we who saved her life again and again, reviving her from death so many times. She died in Fort Djemila, crushed by her burden in the sand, and we gave her new life." The creatures inside of Lailani laughed again. "She has always been our slave. She has always carried the soul of the Masters inside her, waiting for orders . . . waiting to be our soldier. And now this soldier kills."

Marco stared in shock. Grief for Elvis. Grief for what Lailani had become. Pounding, screaming, ringing noise, roaring in his ears like jet engines. His heart slamming against his ribs. He stared as the cosmos shattered.

"It was you," Marco whispered. "The saboteur. It was you who unscrewed the engines and shattered the azoth heart. You who sabotaged the cage lift. You who shut off the plasma."

Lailani reached out and stroked his cheek with her claws. They scraped his stubble like razors. "My sweet, beloved lover." She hissed, and her canines lengthened into fangs, and her eyes shone red. "This human body enjoyed fucking you. Now we will mate as arthropods. Now you will become one of us. Now you will join the hive."

She grabbed Marco's throat, and her foot slammed into his kneecap with incredible strength. He heard the bone shatter. He felt it with the blaze of ten thousand searing suns. He tried to scream, could not with her clutching his throat. She pulled him down to his knees, and white light flared, and tears flowed down his cheeks as his shattered kneecap hit the floor. Lailani stood above him, constricting him, smiling thinly. Blood dripped down his neck where her claws cut him.

"Marco!" Ben-Ari spoke in his communicator. "Marco, what—"

Lailani tore off his helmet and tossed it aside. The voices from the communicator died. With her free hand, Lailani slammed a control panel. Across the engine room, the round blue door slammed shut and its wheel turned, locking it. She looked back at Marco, still gripping his throat.

"I will pass you this gift," Lailani whispered, leaning above him. He could not believe her strength. "The gift of my pheromones. Of my masters. Of my hive. Join us. Join us. We will mate. We will create our own hive."

She leaned closer, mouth opening as if to kiss him, and saliva dripped down her fangs.

Marco turned his head aside, struggling to speak, to wrench off her claws. They cut his fingers when he grabbed them. "Lailani," he whispered hoarsely. "Lailani, this isn't you. Fight it. Fight them."

She sneered and tightened her grip, cutting off his words. Her eyes glared. "This has always been me! You fool. I've always been one of the hive. When you fucked me, you were fucking scum spawn." She laughed. "You pathetic humans. I was always there, always with you, and you suspected nothing, you—"

"No!" Marco managed to pry off one claw, to suck in some air. Blood dripped down his fingers. "If what you say is true, that was a buried part of you. A part you controlled. A part you can still control. You're human, Lailani!" His voice was barely a rasp. "You were human when you fought with me against the scum. You were human when I held you, kissed you. When you loved me. I love you, Lailani. I love you. You're human. You don't have to obey them."

Fists were pounding against the engine room door, and he could hear Ben-Ari shouting for him. The ship rocked madly, and massive claws still slammed at the hull. The second of the three turbines shut down. Marco remained on his knees, Lailani gripping him. Tears flowed down her cheeks.

"I was never human," she whispered, and now her voice sounded like it always had. A high voice. Soft. Afraid. "I was always broken. I never knew. I never knew why I was different. Marco. I can feel them inside me. I . . ." Her voice deepened, and the red glow returned to her eyes. She leaned forward to kiss him again, mouth dripping saliva. "You will be infected now, human. Soon we'll be together forever. Mates in the hive."

His eyes began to roll back. He couldn't breathe. She kissed him. Her saliva entered his mouth, sizzling hot, sickly sweet, filling him with the essence of the hive. That hive opened up before him. He could see them. Millions of them. Networks of tunnels, spreading out, filled with larvae, the great intelligence of the hive, and above them all, him, the master, the emperor, calling to him, welcoming him, and he scuttled through darkness, and—

Marco coughed, spitting out the foul liquid. Lailani recoiled, hissing, enraged. She clutched his chest with her free hand, digging her claws into his skin, ripping into the muscle, and he screamed.

"Lailani," he whispered, feeling consciousness fading. He could barely see her. Shadows spread around him. "I ruv you."

The claws released him. He fell onto his back, gasping for air, every breath like a saw inside his throat. The darkness drew back. He pushed himself onto his elbows, then onto one knee. Lailani stood before him, tears flowing, trembling. The ship rocked around them. Cracks raced across the hull. The scum king laughed outside, a bellowing, grumbling sound like living thunder.

"I'm scared," Lailani said. "Help. Help me, Marco. Help me." She reached out toward him. "I ruv you." She laughed through her tears. "It's hurting me. It's hurting me so badly. I'm so scared."

Marco dragged himself closer to her. He held her hand, even as her claws cut him.

"Lailani, do you remember how we lay together in the tent, how we held each other all night long? That was real. It was real, Lailani. That is the real you."

"I'm diseased," she whispered, tears flowing. "My father wasn't a soldier. I'm a creation of the scum. I'm a monster."

"I don't care," Marco said. "You're Lailani. You're someone I love."

He pulled her into his arms. She struggled against him. She screamed. She tore into his skin. She arched her back, howling, fangs dripping, spraying saliva. She convulsed. She screamed horrible things, screams of breaking him, of shattering humanity, of stitching him into creatures like in the mines. But still he held her. Still he whispered into her ear. I love you. I love you.

Her body grew limp. She trembled against him.

"Help me," she whispered. "Don't let me go."

As he held her, stroking her hair with his bloody fingers, her claws retracted. Her fangs pulled back into her gums. Her eyes closed, and she lost consciousness in his arms.

He laid her down on the floor by Elvis's corpse. She slept, chest rising and falling, her claws gone. Marco dragged himself forward. The ship jolted. He fell, banging his crushed knee again, and fought to cling to consciousness. He crawled. From his helmet several feet away, he could hear Addy shouting, "It's tearing us apart!"

He reached the plasma generator, a towering metal tank. He grabbed it. He pulled himself up, the cuts on his hands dripping. He grabbed the valve, smearing it with blood, and grimaced, turning the handle. Indicators lit up on the generator. The red pipes lit up and thrummed, flames racing through them.

"We're back in business!" Addy's voice rose from the helmet. "Eat fire!"

Flames roared. The generator heated, burning Marco, searing his hands, his uniform. He fell backward. He hit the floor. From outside, he heard the scum king roaring. A viewport, round and distant, peered in the wall like a porthole, and he could see the plasma streaming, swirling like the storm of the planet, washing over a dark form. All was black. All was floating lights. Marco reached out and found Lailani's hand, and he held it. They lay side by side, and his eyes closed, and the ship rocked them, and they were as survivors adrift in a dark sea, the stars spreading endlessly above.

CHAPTER TWENTY-FOUR

He drifted on the sea.

Endlessly he rose and fell, rose and fell on the waves, floating beneath a field of stars.

He washed onto a cold shore, and he ran through snow in the night, fleeing creatures, as comets streamed down from the sky. He reached to his mother as the insects consumed her. He crawled through a labyrinth, seeking a way out, as laughter rolled around him and a thousand eyes stared.

"Lailani," he called in his dreams, seeking her in the tunnels. She cried out to him, in pain. She laughed. She wept. He found her in a glittering hall, and she had swollen to the size of a starship, her naked wet body birthing eggs, and she kissed him.

"I ruv you," she whispered, cutting him, as insects crawled around her. "Look at our children."

Marco's eyes opened.

He stared at a white ceiling. His ears rang, but past the ringing he heard the low hum of engines. Everything hurt, but the pain felt buried, blurred. He struggled to focus his eyes, to turn his head.

He was in the *Miyari*'s infirmary. Monitors, an IV drip, and a small table stood beside him, and a viewport showed the streaming stars of hyperspace.

We're out of Indrani, he thought. *I'm alive. Some of us survived.*

He turned his head, and he saw Osiris standing beside him, smiling thinly. He started and nearly jumped out of the bed.

"Hello, master," the android said.

Marco's heart raced. "Hello, Osiris. I didn't know you were here."

"The ship is on autopilot, master. I've taken over the duty of medic for the duration of our flight, as well as pilot, as well as all other duties." The android tilted her head. "You were wounded. When Lieutenant Ben-Ari found you, your body was lacerated, your knee broken, and did you know that one of your eardrums was pierced and a bone in that ear shattered?"

He wasn't surprised, considering the ringing in his ears. One didn't survive a battle full of exploding grenades and whistling bullets without some hearing damage, it seemed. He looked down at his body and saw it bandaged, and another bandage covered his left ear.

"I have many medical books in my memory banks," Osiris said. "Your kneecap has been replaced with an artificial hardened silica replacement. Your wounds are stitched. I even replaced the broken bone in your ear with a synthetic and stitched up your eardrum using the tiniest of tools. You'll fully heal, but you'll be sore for a long time. I've been administering painkillers regularly while you slept, and—"

"How long have I been asleep?" He sat up in bed. "Where is Lailani? What of the others?"

His belly twisted to remember. Lailani sprouting claws. Stabbing him. Lailani—only half human, implanted into her mother's womb as a scum agent. Lailani—killing Elvis. Marco still reeled.

"Lailani is in the brig, master," Osiris said. "After watching security video footage of the incident, Lieutenant Ben-Ari commanded her imprisoned until we reach our destination in eighteen days. To answer your other questions, you have been sleeping for fifteen hours, and the others are on the bridge." The android's face grew somber. "I have something else to tell you."

That didn't sound good. "What?" he said, belly twisting.

"A horse walked into a bar. The bartender asked him why his face is long. It's funny because horses don't walk into bars. They drink from troughs."

"Osiris." Marco reached out to touch her cold hand. "I'm sorry. When I first met you, I didn't trust you. I could have been nicer to you."

"You were always very courteous, master. I am buggy. I know it. I'm only a few months old, and I still make many mistakes. But I'm learning. I'm improving. Would you like to hear another joke?"

"I'd like to see my friends," Marco said softly. "And I'd like to see Lailani."

He removed his IV drip and stepped off the bed, swaying. He was wearing nothing but boxer shorts, and his uniform was nowhere to be found. He grabbed a blanket, wrapped it around his shoulders, and left the infirmary. He walked the halls of the *Miyari*. The place seemed too silent, and even the shuffling of his bare feet seemed loud. When he had first boarded this vessel, he had shared it with hundreds of soldiers. Now it seemed deserted, bunk after bunk empty, the mess hall vacant, the chapel barren. He made his way to the bridge, a semicircular room at the prow of the ship with viewports showing the panorama of hyperspace.

He found his friends there.

My family.

They stood side by side, staring out into the darkness, the survivors of Corpus. Lieutenant Ben-Ari, still in her old uniform, her plasma gun slung across her back. Beside her, tall and covered in scrapes and bruises, stood Addy. Beside Addy, her black curls cascading down her back, Kemi. The three stood in silence.

The last of us, Marco thought. *The ones who lived.* And the deaths of his friends—of Jackass, Caveman, Sheriff, Singh, Diaz, Beast, Elvis, all the rest of them—felt too great to bear.

Fuck this war, he thought, eyes stinging. *Fuck it. Fuck it. Fuck it.*

He must have made a sound, because the three soldiers ahead of him turned around, saw him, and rushed toward him.

They held him. The four of them stood together, embracing, silent.

"It's over," Kemi whispered. "It's over. It's over."

But no, Marco knew. It wasn't over. That labyrinth underground would remain inside him. His friends would still be gone. The nightmares would still haunt him. He had left Corpus, but Corpus would never leave him, and this battle would rage forever inside him. Inside all of them.

Maybe someday the scars on my body will heal, he thought. *Maybe someday we will defeat the monsters. But the scars and monsters inside me—those cannot be healed or slain.*

"Marco." Lieutenant Ben-Ari touched his cheek, her eyes soft, and her voice was hoarse. "I'm sorry. I'm so sorry. I chose you for this mission. I led you into the mines. I'm so sorry."

Marco shook his head. "Ma'am, I'm proud to have followed you here. To follow you still. You led us bravely. I'm honored to be your soldier, to learn from you, to fight with you."

"We beat them," Addy said. "We beat the damn scum. We lost so many. But we won."

Yet this didn't feel like a victory to Marco. Not without Elvis here. Without Diaz, Singh, Beast, the rest of them. Not with Kemi looking so hurt. Not with Lailani in the brig. Not like this.

Perhaps there is no victory in war, Marco thought. *Perhaps even those who win battles lose their souls. Some return from war in body bags. Others return in victorious parades. But we all come home dead.*

"What now, ma'am?" Marco asked.

Ben-Ari turned toward the viewports that surrounded the bridge. She looked out into hyperspace. "Our war is not yet over. We still haven't reached the frontier. We will continue on our mission. We will travel to the front line, to the very edge of humanity's war with the scum. One battle has ended. One hive was destroyed. One scum leader was slain. But hundreds of hives still spread across the cosmos. And the scum emperor still reigns over them all." The lieutenant turned back toward her soldiers. "This war will not end until the scum homeworld itself falls."

Marco thought about their discovery in Corpus. That it had been overrun for four years. Surely somebody in Chrysopoeia Corp—or the HDF itself—must have known. Must have left Corpus to fester. Must have kept it a secret.

They knew, Ben-Ari had said in the mines.

Marco shuddered. Perhaps, on the frontier, he would find more enemies than the insects.

He looked out into space. The frontier. It still lay many light-years away. Somewhere in that darkness his greatest battle awaited him. Somewhere in that impossible distance awaited the home planet of the enemy. The front line. A war that could burn the cosmos.

"Then we will face them," he said. "We will defeat them. Even if we die trying."

Because I no longer have a life on Earth, he added silently. *Because I'm already dead.*

They stood together. Four soldiers. Staring out into the darkness.

* * * * *

Lieutenant Ben-Ari sat alone on her bed, head lowered. She caressed the shadow box on her lap, gazing at the medals inside.

The medals of her ancestors. Of all the officers in her family, going back for generations, all the way to the horrors of the Second World War two hundred years ago. Her burden to bear. Her pride and her yoke. The expectations that forever haunted her.

"How did you deal with it?" Ben-Ari whispered, and her tears splashed the glass frame. "How did you live on after so much loss, after watching your soldiers—your brothers and sisters in arms—die under your command?"

She wished she could speak to them. To her ancestor who had fought the Nazis, losing his entire family. To his son and grandson who had fought in the hot deserts. To her grandfather who had fought the scum during the Cataclysm when the world burned. She wanted to hear their wisdom, their guidance, for though she was a leader of soldiers, Ben-Ari felt alone, lost, in need of her own mentor. Yet the ghosts of her family did not speak.

I have to remain strong, Ben-Ari thought. *For Marco. For Addy. For Kemi. For Lailani.*

Medals. Medals from a dozen wars. Ben-Ari had not chosen this life. She had been born on a military base, born to a family with no home, no nation. Born to become an officer, to lead warriors in battle. Born to suffer loss. Born to kill. Born to die. And Ben-Ari knew that she would die in this war, knew that she had cheated death too many times. Knew that love of family, of motherhood, of peace—that these would never be hers.

"I hope you're proud of me, my family," she said, staring out the viewport. "Because I find no pride here. I'm scared. I'm so alone. I want to go home, and I don't know where home is, if I have a home other than the battlefield."

She lay on her bed. Her soldiers shared a bunk, shared some companionship in this dented, empty starship. But she was their officer, forever apart from them. She lay here alone in the darkness, gazing up at the ceiling, and she did not sleep.

* * * * *

"Marco," Kemi said, "once we reach Nightwall Outpost, I'm going to find transport back to Earth."

They stood in the *Miyari*'s lounge, the one with the dusty Colonel Coffee machine and the table where they had played poker. The place was small and cluttered, but it seemed so empty now, so full of memories.

"I understand," Marco said. "This was never meant to be for long."

Kemi looked out the viewport at space. She was silent for long moments. When she spoke again, her voice was soft. "I was a fool. I thought this would be an adventure. But I found only horror. There is such evil in the darkness. There is such pain."

Marco embraced her. "Kemi, I'm sorry."

Tears filled her eyes. "And I thought you and I could be as we were. But we're not, Marco. We're different now." She looked back outside. "The people we were, two youths in love . . . those people died on Corpus. Maybe our bodies survived. But the people we were lie dead on that moon."

"I know," he said.

Kemi wiped her eyes and smiled tremulously. "Maybe someday I'll come back into space. Come back to you. But not yet. I need to return to the academy. I need to learn. And I need to heal. From this. From everything that happened. From us."

"I love you, Kemi," Marco said. "I always will. Even if we part ways. Even if we don't end up together. I love you."

She held him closely. They stood together by the viewport as the stars streamed outside.

"I love you too," she whispered. "Goodbye. A real goodbye this time."

"Hey, it'll be seventeen more days until we reach Nightwall, until you leave." He smiled and gave her shoulder a playful punch. "This isn't goodbye yet."

But her tears still flowed. "It is. Because she's waiting for you. Go to her, Marco. She needs you. She will need you for many days ahead. Goodbye." She kissed his lips. "Goodbye."

Kemi left him in the lounge. He remained here for a long time, alone in the small room, thinking of Kemi, thinking of those he had lost. He had never felt so alone, so trapped, so lost in the dark. Finally he left the lounge. He walked through the ship, this shadowy labyrinth. And he went to her.

The brig was a small chamber, even smaller than the lounge. Addy was guarding the locked door, gun in hand. She gazed at Marco, wordlessly nodded, and opened the door to let him in. She closed the door behind him.

Marco stood in the narrow white chamber, gazing down at Lailani.

She lay strapped to her bed, asleep. She seemed so peaceful. So young. So frail. Her stubbly black hair had grown over the past couple of weeks, and Marco stroked it, stroked her cheek, and reached down to hold her hand. She mumbled in her sleep, and her eyes opened to slits. Dark eyes. Eyes Marco used to gaze into for hours in wonder.

"Marco?" she whispered.

"I'm here, Lailani."

"I feel so weak. They stuck a needle in me. I think they sedated me." Lailani blinked and tried to move, could not. Her arms, her legs, her torso—all were strapped onto the bed. "I can't move."

Marco nodded, voice choked. "It will keep you safe."

"Marco . . ." She tugged at the straps. "Marco, help me."

It broke his heart to see her confused, struggling in her bonds, here in this small white chamber. A prisoner.

"Do you remember what happened?" he said.

She looked at him, confusion on her face, then nodded. A tear ran down her cheek. "I remember. I'm scared, Marco. Is it still inside me?"

He nodded, unable to stop his own tears. He held her hand tightly. "We're going to fix this. We're going to heal you. Once we reach the frontier, they have the best doctors in the cosmos. They'll get it out of you, whatever is inside. They'll heal you, Lailani."

She closed her eyes. "I cannot be healed. It's who I am, Marco. I was so stupid. So stupid." She wept. "I'm a monster."

"No." He shook his head and stroked her hair. "No, Lailani."

"I hurt you. I killed Elvis." She trembled. "I'm so ashamed. I'm so scared."

"They made you do it," Marco said. "The scum."

"The scum fathered me," Lailani whispered, and she opened her eyes again, eyes flooding with tears. "Help me, Marco. Help me, please. Take it out of me. I can hear it inside me even now."

There was just enough room for Marco to lie on the bed beside her. He lay on his side, caressing her cheek, gazing into her eyes.

"Do you remember that time Elvis smuggled all those packets of jam out of the mess in basic, and they burst open during our crawl under the barbed wire, and Singh thought Elvis had shredded himself half to death?"

Lailani nodded. "I remember."

"Do you remember how Addy and I found the vending machine, how we feasted that night? My God. Addy must have eaten half the machine, but you only had a few bites."

"I was full," Lailani said. "And too slow."

"But nothing beats that meal the old lady in Greece cooked us. Remember? We sneaked into her yard to pee, during that rescue drill, and instead of kicking us out, she fed us peppers stuffed with rice, tomatoes, and beef."

Finally a faint smile touched Lailani's lips. "That was a good day. That was my best day. The best day in my life."

"Better than Sundays at Fort Djemila, when we just lay in our tent all day, holding each other, naked, while the others played soccer outside?"

And now her smile turned into a grin that showed her teeth. "Okay, those were even better."

Marco slung an arm across her, and he kissed her cheek. "We'll have more good days together. Because that's who we are. Those two people in that tent. Those two people who ate stuffed peppers. That's us. That's who we'll always be."

Let us never know loss again, Marco added silently. *Let us never forget who we are.*

Lailani nodded and leaned her head against him. He lay beside her, holding her, as the stars streamed outside. The *Miyari* flew on through space, leaving their nightmare far behind, heading toward the frontier.

The story continues in

EARTH RISING

EARTHRISE, BOOK III

NOVELS BY DANIEL ARENSON

Earthrise:
Earth Alone
Earth Lost
Earth Rising
Earth Fire
Earth Shadows
Earth Valor
Earth Reborn
Earth Honor
Earth Eternal

Alien Hunters:
Alien Hunters
Alien Sky
Alien Shadows

The Moth Saga:
Moth
Empires of Moth
Secrets of Moth
Daughter of Moth
Shadows of Moth
Legacy of Moth

KEEP IN TOUCH

www.DanielArenson.com
Daniel@DanielArenson.com
Facebook.com/DanielArenson
Twitter.com/DanielArenson